THE RETURN OF THE FALLEN

By
John Buhr

Trade paperback ISBN 978-1-7349148-2-5
Ebook ISBN 978-1-7349148-3-2
Hardcover ISBN 978-1-7349148-4-9

Prologue

Santorini, 1578 BC

The ground split with a deafening crack. Buildings shuddered. Statues toppled. From the heart of the city, fire rose like a living being.

"Anthansia!" Eros shouted, his voice swallowed by the chaos. "You must stop—before you destroy everything!"

She didn't turn. Didn't flinch.

Power radiated from her like heat from the sun, bending the air around her, warping reality itself. Her eyes— once warm, once human—were now oceans of light and fury.

She couldn't hear him.

She wouldn't.

Eros stepped forward, shielding his face from the scorching wind. The sky had darkened to a sickly red. Ash fell like snow. The once-beautiful city—their city—was unraveling before his eyes.

"Please!" he cried again. "You're going too far!"

She heard nothing.

A temple collapsed behind her in a roar of stone and flame. The gods had gifted her power beyond reckoning, they had turned her into one of them, one of their own—and now that same power, that gift, was consuming everything.

Including her.

Eros stood frozen, helpless, as the woman he loved unleashed devastation on a scale mortals could never comprehend. Not for vengeance. Not for justice. Just raw, unrelenting rage.

Tears blurred his vision—not for the city or the people, but for her. He knew what came next. The others would feel this. They would sense it. And they would come.

Not to reason.

Not to forgive.

To punish.

Even he wouldn't be able to stop them.

The mountain groaned—a low, ancient warning—then exploded in a pillar of fire and ash that split the heavens.

The city was gone.

And in the distance... thunder. Not from a storm. From something older. Greater. Something angry.

They were coming.

Eros turned slowly, eyes fixed on the scorched ruins of the city before him.

"Anthansia..." he whispered. "What have you done?"

Chapter 1

Los Angeles, CA

9:15 AM

"What can I get started for you?" the barista asked with a smile.

"I'll have a latte," the man replied, "with an extra shot of espresso, please."

"No problem. Name?"

"Alek," he said, his voice laced with a sophisticated yet unplaceable accent.

The barista smiled, clearly charmed. "Alek. I like that name. I'll call it out when it's ready." She winked—flirtatiously, almost involuntarily—then turned away, cheeks-tinged pink, to make his drink.

Alek waited patiently, his hands clasped behind his back, taking in the familiar bustle of Fast Awakening—a quirky café tucked on the edge of downtown. It had quickly become his favorite since arriving in Los Angeles. He'd lived all over the world, but there was something about the West Coast—the energy, the contradictions, the careless ambition—that appealed to him.

Los Angeles was known for its glamor, its film industry, its endless obsession with reinvention. But beneath the glitz, the city was a crossroads of history and culture. History, especially, was something Alek knew well.

Intimately, in fact.

And just a few blocks away stood one of his favorite places in the entire city: the Los Angeles Museum of World History. A new exhibit had opened recently—Gods of the Nile: Power, Myth, and Legacy. It was impressive. And deeply familiar.

"Latte, extra shot for Alek!" the barista called.

He stepped forward and accepted the drink with a charming smile. "Thank you." He tossed a generous tip into the jar.

"Anytime," she said, blushing as their hands briefly touched.

Alek grinned—a sultry, effortless thing—and turned to go.

He was used to attention. Admiration followed him like a shadow, and not without reason. With his striking grey eyes, flawless olive skin, and jet-black hair that seemed to fall perfectly into place, Alek was, quite simply, beautiful. Tall, athletic, and exuding a quiet confidence, he moved through the world with the ease of someone who had always belonged—everywhere and nowhere at once.

As he navigated the crowded café, he noted the unusual bustle for a Tuesday morning. Outside, the sidewalks were alive with the usual chaos: distracted pedestrians, barking dogs, endless traffic. Alek weaved through the crowd, sipping his drink, eyes scanning out of habit rather than need.

And that's when it happened.

A woman barreled straight into him—her head buried in her phone, a large messenger bag slung over one shoulder. Coffee exploded between them, soaking the front of both of their shirts.

"Watch out!" he exclaimed, startled.

"Watch where you're going!" she snapped, stumbling back, eyes widening at the mess. "Are you kidding me? Look at this! Fuck! I'm already late and now I have to find new clothes. Perfect, just fucking perfect."

Without so much as a second glance, she pushed past him and stormed toward the café.

"I... I'm sorry," Alek called after her.

"Piss off!" she shouted over her shoulder.

Alek stood frozen, drenched in coffee, half amused, half stunned and completely captivated.

She was breathtaking. Even in her disheveled state—or maybe because of it—she was unlike anyone he'd ever seen. Her thick brown hair was pulled into a messy bun, strands falling out to frame her sharp features. Her eyes—dark and blazing—had flashed behind square, black-framed glasses. There was a fire in them.

Who was she?

Rude. Glorious. A walking catastrophe wrapped in chaotic beauty. And somehow, in the instant their eyes met, Alek felt something unfamiliar stir inside him.

It had been a long time since anyone had made him feel... anything.

It wasn't just her looks—though she was stunning. It was her energy. Unapologetic. Fearless. She didn't just command attention—she demanded it, without even trying.

He should've let it go. He had a meeting to get to, after all. But something pulled at him—something deeper than curiosity.

Fate? Perhaps.

He approached the waiting Rolls Royce parked at the curb. Martin, his driver, stepped forward and opened the door, noticing the mess that the coffee had made of his clothing.

"Is everything alright, sir?" he asked.

Alek hesitated. Glanced back toward the café.

"Martin, hold this for me," he said, handing over the half-empty cup. "There's something I need to do."

"Very good, sir."

Alek turned and hurried back toward the coffee shop, dodging distracted pedestrians with ease. He pushed through the glass door and scanned the crowd. His eyes searched frantically.

But she wasn't there.

Where is she? he wondered. He looked again, then again, but there was no sign of her.

"Did you forget something, Alek?" the barista asked sweetly, catching his eye from behind the counter.

He blinked. "Ah... no," he stammered. "I thought I saw a friend come in. I guess I was mistaken."

The barista's smile widened, her cheeks flushing crimson again.

Alek offered a polite nod and stepped back outside. His eyes swept the sidewalk, but she was gone.

How did I miss her? I watched her walk in...

Martin handed him back the coffee as he reached the car.

"Are we ready now, sir?"

"Yes," Alek said softly, slipping into the back seat. "Let's go."

But as the car pulled away from the curb, his mind stayed behind—on the woman who had collided with him, shouted at him, and then vanished.

Who was she?

And why did it feel like this morning was more than a coincidence?

Chapter 2

9:03 AM

Cleo rolled over, still half asleep, and squinted at the time on her phone, which teetered precariously on a haphazard pile of books on her nightstand. "Shit, I overslept! Why didn't my alarm go off?!" she shouted, jolting out of bed in a panic.

Half-awake, she rushed to the bathroom, haphazardly throwing her hair into a messy bun while scrambling for her toothbrush and deodorant. "Shit! Shit! Shit!" she repeated, realizing she had no time for a shower or makeup—not that she wore much anyway. She made a mad dash out of the bathroom, yanked her glasses from the nightstand, and in the process, sent the teetering tower of books crashing to the floor.

"How did I forget to set my fucking alarm?!" she groaned, tearing through piles of what she hoped was clean laundry on the floor. After digging through two heaps, she found a pair of gray dress slacks and a matching blazer. A white silk blouse emerged from another pile. She threw on the clothes, snatched her messenger bag, and slipped on her four-inch black heels. The apartment looked like it had been ransacked—not that it didn't always look that way.

She dashed down the street, glancing again at the time: 9:14 AM.

"Shit! I need coffee! Do I have time for coffee? Fuck it, I'm already late. I'm going to need it today."

As she power-walked toward Fast-Awakening Coffee, her phone chimed. Digging through her bag while dodging pedestrians, she finally retrieved it. The screen lit up with texts and missed calls—all from Jasper Carrera, her boss and close friend, who also happened to be the director of the Los Angeles Museum of World History.

Jasper:

"Where are you? You were supposed to be here 30 minutes ago!"

"We need you here now! The donor is coming in this morning. I need help getting everything ready."

"This could be huge for the museum. He's talking about a massive donation."

"CLEO!!!!"

She grimaced. She couldn't exactly tell Jasper she forgot to set her alarm and overslept like a teenager on what could be one of the most important day of the year for the museum. They had been preparing for this donor visit for over a week, and she was supposed to give him a private tour of the new exhibit, A Tribute to the Ancient Gods.

She typed a quick reply: Sorry, I had some trouble at my apartment this morning. I'm on my way!

As she hit send on the message, a voice yelled, "Watch out!"

Too late.

A man's coffee spilled all over her blouse as she crashed into him.

"Watch where you're going!" she snapped, stepping back to survey the damage.

"I'm so sorry," the man replied.

"Look at what you've done! FUCK! I'm already late, and now I have to find something else to wear!" she growled, pushing past him into the coffee shop. "Piss off!"

She made a beeline for the restroom, cursing under her breath. She dabbed the coffee with a paper towel. "Ugh! I hope I still have that extra shirt in my office." She buttoned her blazer to cover the worst of the stain.

After freshening up, she joined the growing line. When she finally reached the counter, the barista gave her a once-over followed by a disapproving expression.

"What can I get for you?"

"Iced mocha, two extra shots of espresso."

"Name?"

"Cleo."

After a wait that felt eternal, she finally heard her name. She grabbed the drink and took a long, satisfying sip.

Finally, something was going right.

It was a ten-minute walk to the museum on a normal day. Today wasn't normal. Looking at her phone and seeing that it was now 10:12 AM, Cleo realized just how late she was and broke into a near sprint in her heels. Good thing I ran track in college, she thought, arriving breathless at the museum steps.

"Good morning, Dr. Tenner," said Gary, the security guard as she sprinted by.

"Morning, Gary—in a hurry," she called back.

The donor was scheduled for a 10:15 appointment. She prayed he was late—they usually were. In her experience, the ultra-wealthy ran on their own time.

Still, the stakes were high. Donor funding had been drying up over the past few years, and this one could support operations for years to come. But she loathed pandering to rich people. It always felt like groveling before royalty for coins, and most of them didn't give a damn about history— just publicity and tax breaks.

As she turned down the hall toward her office, she spotted Jasper approaching—and beside him, a man. Of course, he'd be early today.

She tried to duck into her office, but Jasper saw her. "Cleo!"

She froze, forced a smile, and turned around.

"Good, you're here," Jasper said. "I'd like you to meet our guest of honor, Mr. Aleksander Cooper."

Her eyes widened.

It was the man she'd told to piss off earlier after quite literally running into him.

Her face turned red as she glanced down at the coffee stain on her blouse, then back up at Alek. She bit her bottom lip, momentarily speechless.

"Cleo?" Jasper prompted.

"Yes, I—I'm sorry, Mr. Cooper. I'm Dr. Cleo Tenner, assistant director here and curator of our newest exhibit. It's nice to meet you."

"A pleasure to meet you. Again," Alek said with a smirk, his gray eyes locked on hers. "Dr. Tenner and I had the great fortune of meeting this morning. I fear I may be responsible for the state of her blouse. I did try to follow her into the shop to apologize, but she vanished. I would've searched longer, but I didn't want to miss this appointment."

"Don't worry about it," Cleo said, flustered. "I should be the one apologizing." She glanced at his spotless clothes. "How are you not covered in coffee?"

"Luck, I suppose," he replied.

"If you don't mind, I'd like a few minutes to change into a clean blouse. I think I have a spare in my office."

"Take your time," Alek said. "I'm sure Jasper can entertain me."

His piercing gray eyes met hers again. She found herself smiling and, to her annoyance, blushing.

Inside her office, she rummaged through desk drawers until—

"Got it!"

She pulled out a wrinkled but clean blouse. At least it's wearable, she thought. She changed quickly, threw her soiled shirt onto the desk, grabbed her clipboard, and paused.

Something about Alek didn't sit right. He was handsome—annoyingly so. But more than that, there was a quality she couldn't pin down. Arrogant, yes, but masked with charm. Unlike other donors, he didn't immediately trigger her disdain.

That bothered her most of all.

She hated that he made her blush. Even just slightly. Although she was unsure if it was out of embarrassment or from the fact that she found herself unnaturally attracted to the man.

Taking a deep breath, she opened the door and stepped out to lead the tour.

Chapter 3

Cleo entered the museum's atrium where Alek and Jasper were waiting. Well, at least Alek looked patient. Jasper, on the other hand, radiated thinly veiled annoyance. Cleo could read it all over his rigid posture and tight expression.

I am going to be in so much trouble later.

As she approached, a wave of anxiety returned. Why is this guy making me nervous? Just get through this without any more embarrassment. Think of the museum. She straightened her blazer and steadied her breath.

Jasper and Alek were admiring one of the new pieces near the exhibit entrance. Jasper was pointing to the hieroglyphic inscriptions on a massive stone tablet recently loaned from their partner museum in Cairo. The figure carved into the stone depicted a man with a hawk's head wearing a headdress adorned with a golden disk.

"You see this piece here, Mr. Cooper," Jasper explained, "this was found at the entrance of a newly discovered temple in Heliopolis. The figure is the Egyptian god Ra. The inscription beneath translates to: 'We honor you, Ra, god of all things.'"

"Creator," Alek corrected smoothly.

"What was that, Mr. Cooper?"

"It translates to 'creator of all things,' not 'god of all things.'" Alek then read the full inscription aloud in Egyptian. "A small distinction, but an important one."

Jasper blinked, taken aback. He leaned in for a second look. "Yes... yes, you're correct. My apologies."

The embarrassment and shock on Jasper's face was clear. Cleo could practically see the calculations behind his eyes as he reassessed his opinion of Alek.

"I didn't know you were fluent in Egyptian and hieroglyphics," Jasper said, trying to recover.

"History is a bit of a passion," Alek said, smiling. "That's why I'm here—and why I'm considering making a donation."

Jasper, eager to escape the moment, cleared his throat. "Well, on that note, Mr. Cooper, I have some administrative duties to attend to. I'll leave you in the very capable hands of Dr. Tenner. She'll guide you through the exhibits, and we'll regroup afterward to discuss your donation if you so choose."

Cleo gave Jasper a tight-lipped smile as he left. She turned to Alek.

"Alright, Mr. Cooper, shall we begin? And again, I want to apologize for this morning, outside the coffee shop."

"Don't think twice about it," he said warmly.

"Still, I was completely out of line. That's not how I usually behave."

"Ms. Tenner, everyone has bad days. Accidents happen."

He motioned for her to lead the way.

"Thank you. This way."

They entered the first exhibit. Cleo launched into her well-rehearsed presentation but quickly found herself upstaged. Alek seemed to know as much—if not more—about every piece.

He didn't just recite facts. He spoke with a familiarity that unsettled her, as if he had seen these artifacts in their prime. His words painted living images of the past.

"If you don't mind me asking, where did you study?" she asked.

"All over, really. Oxford, Yale. And I travel a lot. I've seen many of the original sites of these artifacts."

She was forced to admit it: she may had misjudged him.

Her initial nerves faded, replaced by a curious warmth. With each new display, they traded glances and quiet smiles. She caught herself watching him too closely, and each time she tried to refocus, the growing infatuation she was developing for him crept back in stronger.

It wasn't one-sided. Alek's flirtation became steadily more obvious.

"Ms. Tenner, could you tell me more about this piece?"

They stood before a sarcophagus, the final display.

"This was found in an unmarked tomb near the Valley of the Kings. We believe the remains are of a pharaoh, but scholars are still working on confirmation."

Alek examined the sarcophagus. He knew exactly who it belonged to. He had asked only to prolong their time together.

They're wrong, he almost said aloud. It's the favored son of a forgotten pharaoh.

Instead, he simply said, "Fascinating."

Cleo wrapped up the tour. "And that piece, Mr. Cooper, concludes our exhibit."

"Please, call me Alek."

She smiled. "Of course."

"You know, Cleo," he said, clearly enjoying the sound of her name, "I have a collection of antiquities of my own. All acquired legally, I assure you" he added with a grin, hands raised. "I think a few of the pieces would make great additions to your exhibit. If you're interested, I could lend them to the museum."

"Yes! Absolutely. That would be incredibly generous, I would love to take a look at them."

"Great. Would tonight around seven work? I could show you the collection."

"Yes," she said too quickly, surprising even herself. "That works."

"Perfect. I'll leave my address with Jasper. Speaking of which, looks like he's ready to talk numbers."

Cleo glanced over to see Jasper wringing his hands in anticipation.

"Yes, I think he is," she said with a laugh.

Alek extended his hand. She took it, expecting a shake, but he bent and kissed the back of it.

Her cheeks flushed as their eyes met. His were a striking gray, and for a moment, she thought she saw something flicker—like a flash of lightning within them.

Startled, she broke the gaze.

"I look forward to seeing your—your collection tonight, Alek."

"As do I," he said, then turned and walked toward Jasper.

Cleo stood motionless for a moment, then sighed.

What are you doing, Cleo?

Chapter 4

"Judging by how quickly your Mr. Cooper wrote that check, the tour must have gone well," Jasper said inquisitively.

"Yes, I believe it did," Cleo replied, not looking up from behind the mountain of papers on her desk as Jasper leaned against the frame of her open office door.

"What's with the "your Mr. Cooper?"" she chided.

"Oh, nothing," Jasper said, raising his hands in mock surrender. "I just couldn't help but notice the way you two were looking at each other. And he did seem quite interested to learn more about you during our discussion after your tour."

"Oh please, Jasper, give me some credit. Do I find him interesting and attractive? Yes. But I'm hardly a teenage girl swooning over the captain of the football team. Besides, you and I both know he was just here for the publicity—and the tax write-off."

Jasper rolled his eyes. "Tax write-off, maybe. But he did request that his donation be anonymous."

"Anonymous? Really? How big was the check?"

"Seven figures."

Cleo looked up, stunned, nearly falling off her chair. "He wrote a seven-figure check anonymously?"

Jasper nodded. "Cleo, I know you, I saw how you were with him, just be careful with that one. Mr. Cooper is... a mysterious individual."

"What do you mean 'be careful'? And mysterious how?" Cleo asked.

"I'm just saying—I could tell by the way you two interacted, your body language... there's more than just professional intrigue there. I don't want you to get hurt."

"Thank you, Jasper. But you don't have to worry about me. I'm a big girl. Now, what do you mean by mysterious?"

"It's just... nobody really knows anything about him. I've been asking around—both in the antiquities community and around L.A.—and it's like he appeared out of nowhere. And in my experience, whenever someone with that kind of money and that much knowledge of antiquities shows up out of the blue, it's never a good thing."

"You think he's some kind of black market antiquities dealer?" Cleo joked.

Jasper didn't laugh.

"There has to be some sort of non-nefarious explanation for where he gets his money. Maybe he owns a business or a hedge fund or something."

"Nothing that I could find. And no one I spoke to has even heard of him."

"Maybe it's family money? European nobility, some obscure country? I couldn't quite place his accent, so it's not that much of a stretch."

"Maybe. Maybe I'm wrong. Maybe there's nothing nefarious about your Mr. Cooper. I just—like I said—be careful."

"I appreciate your concern, Jasper. You're a good friend. But like I said, I can take care of myself. By the way, did he mention anything to you about possibly donating antiquities to the museum?"

"Not a thing. Why?"

"He told me he had some rare artifacts he was considering donating. He wants me to stop by his place tonight and take a look."

Jasper straightened. "Well now it makes more sense as to why he asked me to give you his address. Tell me you're not seriously considering going alone. Did he mention what kind of antiquities?"

"I think I am going. He seemed sincere enough. He didn't say much about them—just that they were rare and relevant to our new exhibit."

Although, if Cleo was being honest, she wasn't just going for the antiquities. But she wasn't going to tell Jasper that.

"Cleo, please—if you're going, be cautious. Call me at the first sign of anything strange. Something just feels off about that guy. I can't explain it."

"You're just still upset that he corrected your mistranslation of those hieroglyphics," she teased.

"I'm serious, Cleo."

"Fine. If anything seems off, I'll call you straight away. Scout's honor." She held up her hand in a mock Girl Scout salute.

"We both know you are not, nor have you ever been, even remotely close to a Girl Scout."

***

As the museum closed and the final visitors filtered out into the evening, Cleo gathered her things and locked up her office. The late-afternoon sun cast a golden hue across the atrium's polished floors, and for a moment, she paused to take in the stillness. The chaotic energy of the day had finally settled. She checked her watch—just after six.

With one last glance at the exhibit floor, Cleo made her way out the front door and headed to retriever her car from her apartments parking garage. Her heels echoed through the quiet space as she approached her car. She opened the door, tossed her bag onto the passenger seat, and slid behind the wheel. The engine sputtered before turning over, and she let out a breath.

"Alright, Tenner," she muttered to herself. "Let's see what secrets Mr. Mysterious is hiding."

She pulled out of the garage, the city lights flickering to life around her as she headed west.

She couldn't shake a growing tension in her chest. Something about Alek didn't quite add up. The timing of his donation, his perfect knowledge of the artifacts, the effortless charm—it all felt too polished. And those artifacts he claimed to possess... If they were as rare as he suggested, how did he get them? Provenance was everything in the world of antiquities. Without a paper trail, even the most stunning object could be a forgery—or worse, stolen.

Jasper's words echoed in her mind: Whenever someone with that kind of money and that much knowledge of antiquities shows up out of the blue, it's never a good thing.

No one that wealthy and connected should be so... invisible.

As she made the final turn and pulled up to the estate gates, Cleo took a deep breath and muttered, "Alright, Mr. Cooper. Let's see what you're really hiding."

Chapter 5

7:00 PM — Aleksander Cooper's Estate

Cleo's battered hatchback rolled to a halt before a grand, wrought-iron gate flanked by ivy-wrapped stone pillars. Atop the gate, curved iron spikes gleamed beneath the dying light. A brass intercom box blinked with a single red dot. She pressed the button.

A beat of silence.

Then a voice crackled through, crisp and composed, tinged with an Eastern European accent.

"This is Mr. Cooper's estate. Please state your name."

"Cleo Tenner," she replied, leaning toward the speaker. "I have an appointment."

Another pause.

"Good evening, Miss Tenner. Mr. Cooper is expecting you."

With a soft hum, the gates parted, gliding open with machine-smooth silence. Cleo exhaled and nudged the car forward.

The driveway unfurled before her in sweeping curves, lined with sculpted olive trees whose silvery leaves shimmered in the warm dusk. Lanterns on wrought-iron posts bathed the path in amber light, throwing long, shifting shadows across the gravel.

She rounded the final bend into a wide cobblestone turnaround, centered by a tiered fountain of pale stone. Winged lions bore the top basin, water pouring from their mouths in graceful arcs. The soft, constant splash echoed in the golden air.

The mansion loomed beyond—elegant and commanding. Cream stucco walls met sandstone trim and curved wrought-iron balconies. Massive arched windows reflected the dusky sky, while soft light glowed behind sheer drapes. Modern lines met Mediterranean charm in a design that felt both ancient and impossibly new.

Landscaped gardens sprawled in all directions—hedges sculpted with almost mathematical precision, marble statues half-veiled in blooming trees, winding paths of pale stone threading through citrus groves. A wisteria-draped pergola framed a courtyard where another fountain flickered under hidden lighting.

The front entrance emerged at the top of a broad staircase flanked by twin lion statues. Tall oak doors stood inlaid with abstract ironwork, and the air carried a delicate perfume of jasmine, sea salt, and something faintly resinous—incense, maybe.

As Cleo pulled to a stop, she noticed two attendants, dressed identically standing near the front doors. They descended the stairs—one opening her door while the other extended a gloved hand for her.

"Miss Tenner," the first said with a professional nod. "Welcome."

The car door shut behind her with a quiet finality, she was then lead up the front steps and before she could fully catch her breath, the grand doors opened.

She stepped inside.

The foyer was a stage set for awe—an atrium of marble, brass, and hush. Cream-colored floors gleamed under inlays of darker stone. Above, a skylight crowned a soaring dome, catching the last rays of sun and scattering them through a chandelier of crystal and brushed gold.

Twin staircases swept upward, their polished marble steps hugged by iron railings that curled like vines. Pale walls bore large oil paintings and modern art: portraits whose eyes watched, landscapes blurred with motion, abstract works in moody hues. Carved alcoves held gleaming busts, each piece curated with deliberate care.

The house thrummed with quiet efficiency. Maids glided past. A steward reviewed notes on a tablet. A doorman adjusted a tall side window's seal. Far ahead, a corridor flickered with firelight from a distant hearth.

Despite the grandeur, warmth bled into every detail. The scent of sandalwood mixed with fresh flowers. A silk runner muted her footsteps as she moved deeper inside.

To her left, a sunken parlor opened into a nest of leather and velvet, lined with bookshelves stuffed with everything from illuminated manuscripts to glossy art tomes. A glass-roofed conservatory spilled orchids and ferns into the space, its waterfall whispering into a koi basin.

To the right, a modern drawing room housed minimalist furniture around a black-marble hearth. Through an archway, a gallery stretched into visual contradiction—suits of armor beside surrealist canvases, antique mirrors beside kinetic sculpture.

She passed a music room, where a grand piano sat in reverent stillness beneath tall windows. Through French doors, she glimpsed a garden lit from below—stone steps descending into a maze of hedges and glowing trees.

Each room revealed itself like a secret.

And yet the library pulled her.

Heavy double doors marked with constellations opened onto a vaulted space of reverent calm. Bookshelves stretched two stories high, ladders riding along brass rails. The ceiling overhead was a night sky—deep blue, scattered with gold leaf stars. A fire crackled gently in a marble hearth. Low lighting encouraged silence.

She drifted in, inhaling parchment, ink, and cedar. Her fingers grazed leather spines. She passed alcoves filled with scrolls and ancient manuscripts, the air still and weighty with thought.

Then—she stopped.

A pedestal. A glass case. Beneath it, a stack of yellowed paper bound by ribbon. One word handwritten on the top page.

She leaned in, whispering, "Does that say Macbeth? Like... by Shakespeare?"

"It does," said a voice behind her.

Cleo jumped, spinning.

Alek stood in the doorway, firelight gilding the edges of his frame. His shirt was unbuttoned at the collar, sleeves rolled to his forearms. Damp hair suggested a recent shower. He watched her, unreadable.

"Did I scare you?" he asked, amused.

"I didn't mean to snoop," she said, recovering.

"You weren't," he replied easily. "And yes—it's an original manuscript. Most of the books here are first editions or one-of-a-kind."

Cleo crossed her arms, but her gaze lingered on the room. "As impressive as this room is, I don't think you invited me here just for story time."

He smiled. "No. I've had a few items brought up from my private collection—artifacts I'm considering donating or lending to the museum."

He turned, and she followed.

At a table near the window, artifacts lay in quiet reverence: carved figures, stone tablets, and a pair of cotton gloves resting like a challenge.

She slipped the gloves on, reverent.

"These are incredible," she breathed. "Ra... Hathor... These are Egyptian deities—hand-carved. Alek, these are in incredible condition, some look like they were made last week."

"Some are over four thousand years old," he said softly. "That Ra figure—Early Dynastic Period. Saqqara, if my source is right."

She laughed, breathless. "It's perfect. Where did you get these?"

Alek gave a slow smile. "Would you believe... Istanbul?"

She arched a brow. "Not unless you wrestled them from a dealer in an alley."

"Nothing quite so dramatic. But let's just say, the seller was... motivated."

"Desperate, you mean. These are priceless. Some curators would kill for these to be in their museum."

"That's why I keep them private," he said, voice lowering. "Very private."

Her excitement warred with caution. "This could be an ethical nightmare. Or a breakthrough."

"Maybe both," he replied. "That's why I need your opinion. Do they belong in your museum?"

"If they're real—and I think they are—they belong in every museum."

Alek tilted his head. "Would you like to see more?"

"There's more?"

"Oh, much more."

He moved to a bookshelf and pressed something unseen. With a quiet click, the shelf swung open.

A hidden staircase spiraled down.

Cleo blinked. "A secret passage? Behind a bookshelf? If I disappear tonight, I hope someone checks the wine cellar."

He grinned. "The wine's excellent. But what I'm about to show you—far more intoxicating."

The staircase descended farther than Cleo expected—far beyond a simple cellar. The air cooled with every step, stone walls darkening in hue and grain. Modern sconces gave way to soft, recessed lighting embedded in the stone, casting an amber glow that felt both ancient and surgical.

At the bottom, a steel door waited beneath a granite archway—clean lines, industrial heft. Alek withdrew a small key from his jacket and slid it into a nearly invisible slot. A soft mechanical click echoed in the stairwell.

The door whispered open.

Cleo stepped through—and stopped breathing.

The room beyond wasn't a room. It was a vault, a sanctum. The floor was obsidian, polished to a mirror-sheen and threaded with veins of gold inlaid in the shape of ancient constellations. Overhead, the ceiling curved into a gentle dome lit by panels that cast a warm, diffuse light. It was like stepping inside a memory, held still by reverence.

The walls were lined with glass-fronted niches, each artifact lit as if on stage. Not sterile. Not museum-cold. This was curated intimacy—preservation with a soul.

A Roman legionary's helmet gleamed beside an Incan quipu. A Babylonian cylinder seal rotated slowly on a hidden mount. A series of jade masks from Mesoamerica sat behind UV-protected glass, each one glowing like forest ghosts. A Zoroastrian fire urn. An obsidian-carved lingam. Each object seemed to vibrate, not with sound, but significance.

In the center stood a cluster of elevated glass cases, spotlighted from above. One held a Phoenician fertility idol, another a Celtic torque wound in gold so fresh it looked molten. A Hattusan lion, chiseled in sandstone, snarled from beneath glass. A carved ebony staff topped with a Yoruba deity's face gleamed like it had been polished that morning.

Cleo moved as if underwater—slow, reverent, stunned.

Then she saw the statues.

A near-life-sized alabaster figure of Inanna, delicate and cold, stared from a far alcove. A limestone bust of an Egyptian priestess held court beside it, her face worn but unmistakably serene. A Sumerian relief of Chang'e, the Chinese moon goddess, gleamed in ivory. Figurines from

Hittite, Olmec, and Nubian cultures filled smaller pedestals, each whispering across centuries.

And in one corner, nearly lost in the soft dark, stood a basalt giant—eight feet tall, the shape of an unnamed god. The eyes, inlaid with lapis lazuli, followed her.

On a central table lay smaller wonders: Mesopotamian guardian figures with ringlets carved in dizzying detail. Mycenaean drinking cups. An Akkadian lyre ornament shaped like a bull. Cycladic idols, so pristine they looked like modern sculpture. A scroll, bound in gold thread, pulsed under the glass like something alive.

Cleo exhaled, finally. "How... how is this not a museum?"

Alek's voice came quietly from behind her. "It is. A museum for one."

She turned to him, stunned.

"You built this?"

"For preservation," he said. "And for protection. Not all history is ready for the public."

Her eyes narrowed. "That sounds noble. Or incredibly secretive."

He gave a faint smile. "Why not both?"

She moved toward a glass case housing a scroll inscribed with Sumerian cuneiform..

"This text, it must be thousands of years old. It's a creation myth."

"I know," Alek said, stepping beside her. "That piece alone passed through fourteen hands before it reached me. I acquired it two years ago."

She looked up at him, one eyebrow raised. "Acquired. A cozy euphemism."

"I paid well," he said, unbothered.

She folded her arms. "You're telling me every piece here has a receipt and a customs declaration?"

He grinned. "Not exactly. But none of them are stolen. Let's just say... the channels I use are private. Not illegal. Just inaccessible to most."

"That sounds extremely shady."

"I'd be disappointed if it didn't," he said with a glance.

"Still..." She shook her head, unable to hide the awe. "If even half of this is real, some of it looks like it could rewrite what we know about history."

"That's why I wanted you here."

She turned to him.

"I need someone who can tell truth from legend. Someone who sees what these really are—and what they mean."

Her gaze hardened slightly. "And what exactly do you think they mean, Alek?"

He smiled again, slower this time. "I think history is far more alive than we've been taught, the ancient mythical gods and creatures not mythical at all, just forgotten or hidden from the current world."

She eyed him, skeptical. "Mythology is just that myth and nothing more. The stories of gods and monsters are just metaphors."

"Are they?" he asked. "Thunder gods. Sun gods. Underworld rulers. Civilizations across the world that never spoke, never met—yet they made the same or similar divine beings and creatures. Over and over."

"It's called pattern recognition," Cleo said. "Humans invented these myths to explain what they did not understand. It's not proof."

"No," he agreed. "But it is a pattern. And patterns, Dr. Tenner, beg to be studied and do you not believe that there is even a little bit of truth in every myth."

Before she could reply, a voice echoed faintly from the stairwell above.

"Mr. Cooper," said a butler. "You have a guest in the drawing room."

Alek frowned. "I wasn't expecting anyone."

"He insisted, sir."

A shadow passed behind his eyes—quick, alert. "Thank you, Martin. Tell him I'll be there shortly."

He turned to Cleo with regret etched into the corners of his mouth. "I'm afraid we'll have to pause here. But I'll have the library artifacts delivered to the museum first thing tomorrow."

"Thank you," she said, disappointed. "I'll examine them properly—if they're prove to be genuine and you can provide providence for them; I will let you know which ones, if not all, we would like to feature in the museum."

"They are and I will," he said. "Take your time examining them. May I walk you out?"

She nodded, caught off guard by the sudden shift. They climbed the stairs in silence.

On the way out, Cleo caught a glimpse through an open doorway—just a flicker, a passing image.

A man sat alone in the drawing room, posture casual, but radiating something sharper—an alertness that bristled beneath the stillness. His features mirrored Alek's: sharp cheekbones, pale eyes, that same confident smirk. But where Alek was warm shadow, this man was steel.

He looked up—and smiled directly at her.

There was no kindness in it.

Something inside her shifted.

As they reached the doors, a footman stepped forward with her coat. Alek helped her into it with surprising care.

"Miss Tenner," he said, voice lowered, "I meant what I said—I enjoyed tonight. I hope we can continue this conversation soon."

She gave him a tight smile. "I'm always happy to educate the curious and misinformed."

"How about tomorrow?"

She blinked, surprised. "Tomorrow?"

"The museum closes at six," he said. "I'll send a car at seven."

He took her hand and pressed a kiss to it—old world, disarming.

Before she could respond, Thomas appeared.

"Thomas," Alek said, eyes still on Cleo, "please see Miss Tenner to her car."

"Of course, sir."

Cleo followed the attendant into the night. The evening air felt heavier now. Charged. Unfinished.

She glanced back once before the doors shut behind her.

Something had changed tonight.

And she wasn't sure if it was the thrill of discovery...

Or the warning of danger.

Chapter 6

Alek paused at the doorway to the drawing room, jaw clenched. He heard the ice clink in the glass—his guest had made himself comfortable.

Pol.

Of all the people to show up unannounced.

He stepped in. "Did no one ever teach you to call first?"

Pol looked up from the armchair, legs crossed, drink in hand. "And miss the look on your face? Never."

He stood with a smirk, arms wide like a showman taking a bow. The years hadn't touched him, not that they would: same dark curls, same crooked grin, same predator's grace in a tailored coat. He could've been mistaken for Alek's twin if not for the glint of trouble in his eyes.

Alek didn't move. "You're centuries late."

Pol tsked. "Don't be like that. I've missed you. Truly."

Alek narrowed his gaze. "What are you doing here?"

"Passing through." He wandered to the window, peered out at the citrus groves in the distance. "Thought I'd visit my favorite brother. Stretch my legs. Stir the pot."

Alek poured himself a drink, ignoring the chair across from him.

"Who was that?" Pol asked suddenly. "The girl I heard leaving."

Alek's jaw tightened. "Not your concern."

"Oh, don't be coy. I caught a glimpse—mortal, yes?" Pol turned, eyes bright. "You've always had a type."

"She's a museum liaison."

Pol raised a brow. "Is that what we're calling it now?"

Alek said nothing.

Pol grinned wider. "Oh, Alek. Always trying so hard to be human. I can't believe that they buy you're act, that they actually think you're one of them, human."

Alek stared into his glass. "Why now, Pol? After all this time?"

Pol's voice dropped. "Because I'm bored. The Celestial Realm is a mausoleum. The same faces, the same politics, the same endless banquets with food that never runs out and joy that never feels real."

He turned back to Alek, serious now.

"I want to return. For good."

A beat of silence passed.

Then Alek laughed, cold and sharp. "And do what? Start a religion? Burn down another century?"

Pol spread his hands. "You say that like it's a bad thing."

"You're not allowed here, not for long. You know that. After the war—"

"Yes, yes. I sparked a global catastrophe. We've all made mistakes."

"You manipulated governments. Do you even remember how many died?"

Pol's tone turned mocking. "Still brooding over mortals like they're porcelain dolls."

"I live among them. I've seen what they build. What they endure."

"And what they destroy." Pol leaned in. "They've forgotten us, Alek. You feel it too. That ache. That hollowness. We were worshipped. Feared. Now we're bedtime stories, myths and legends. Don't you want to be remembered?"

"No." Alek's voice cut the air. "I want peace."

Pol tilted his head, amused. "Still clinging to that noble image of yourself. You always did like playing the martyr."

He paced, slowly. "Do you remember what they called me in Scandinavia? Loki. Trickster, shapeshifter. God of chaos. They feared me because they knew me."

"And yet," Alek said, rising to his feet, "you were silent when the council voted. When they decided we should take a step back from humanity, I didn't agree with the council at the time brother, you know I didn't want to take a step back from humanity, I wanted to guide them, lead them to their true potential. If you wanted me on your side you should have said something to me back then."

Pol's smile faltered.

"I was outvoted," he said.

"You were afraid."

Pol's eyes flashed. "We couldn't fight them all, not even together."

"You didn't even try."

The silence between them crackled.

Pol broke it first, brushing lint from his sleeve like shaking off guilt. "Maybe now's the time to try again. A second act. We rally a few of the old ones. Show the world who we are."

Alek stared at him. "You will start a war."

"I want to wake them up. No more hiding. No more pretending."

"I won't help you."

Pol sighed dramatically. "You're such a buzzkill."

He moved to the door, then paused.

"One more thing."

Alek didn't respond.

Pol turned, expression shifting—mockery gone, something darker surfacing.

"Be careful with the girl."

Alek met his gaze. "She's not—"

"Don't lie to me." Pol's tone was razor-thin. "I saw the way you looked at her. You remember what happened the last time one of us fell in love with a mortal, you know relationships are no longer allowed."

A memory surged—unwelcome, sharp, buried.

Pol stepped closer. "She'll be your ruin, Alek. Just like Anthansia was his."

Alek's hands curled into fists. "Get out."

Pol smiled again—wide and wolfish. "Of course. But don't worry. I'm not done trying."

And then, with a shimmer of light and the scent of ozone, he vanished.

Alek stood alone in the room, heart pounding.

Outside, a storm was gathering.

Chapter 7

"How did last night go? I see we have a few new pieces in the examination room—very impressive," Jasper said as he and Cleo stepped through the museum's grand front doors, the heavy glass easing shut behind them with a hushed, reverent thud.

Cleo laughed, brushing a stray curl from her face. "I take it you were snooping around again?"

"Snooping? Never. Just taking a healthy professional interest in museum acquisitions," he said with a grin. "Though I might've hovered long enough to spot that bronze ceremonial dagger. Nineteenth Dynasty Egyptian, right?"

"Very good. You must be learning something from all my ramblings."

"Only the useful parts. Like how to tell if a dagger is ceremonial... or deadly."

She chuckled, then glanced at him sideways. "You seem extra curious today."

"I am. I've been dying to ask how last night went, but I was buried in meetings and department inventory all day. Haven't had a second to breathe until now."

Cleo smiled, the memory already flickering to life behind her eyes. "It was... a great night. You wouldn't believe the collection of antiquities he has in his house."

"I'm sure. Judging by what he's donating, I can only imagine. But that's not what I'm asking." Jasper gave her a pointed look. "How did it go with him?"

Her cheeks pinked. "Fine. We didn't get to spend too much time together. Someone showed up just as we were getting into a debate on ancient religion, and he had to leave."

"Probably his black-market antiquities broker," Jasper quipped.

"I don't think so. I caught a quick glimpse—it almost looked like they were related. And Alek didn't exactly seem thrilled to see him."

"Or maybe he was just annoyed that your date got interrupted."

"It wasn't a date," she shot back, more flustered than she intended.

"Mm-hmm." Jasper's gaze flicked past her. "Who's that?"

Cleo turned. A sleek black Rolls-Royce Phantom waited at the curb, paint gleaming under the late sunlight like obsidian. The engine purred with quiet authority.

She hesitated. "I think... that's for me."

Jasper blinked. "What?"

"Last night, as I was leaving, Alek asked if I'd like to continue our discussion tonight—finish our debate since we didn't get to last night."

"So not a date, huh? Sure looks like one to me. You're being picked up in a luxury car like royalty."

She gave him a look, already walking backward toward the curb. "I'll tell you all about it tomorrow."

"You better!" Jasper called, but his playful grin faltered, softening into something more cautious.

The chauffeur, dressed in an immaculate black suit, stepped forward and opened the door with the precision of a seasoned butler. "Good evening, Ms. Tenner."

Cleo slipped into the car, the whisper of leather welcoming her as the door shut with a quiet click. The interior was cool and dimly lit, fragrant with leather and a hint of jasmine.

I could get used to this.

"Where are we meeting Mr. Cooper? He never said," she asked as the city began to drift by outside her window.

"Mr. Cooper will meet you at the Rose Gardens, ma'am. I believe he intends to take you to dinner downtown afterward."

Cleo nodded, a flutter of anticipation stirring in her chest. The quiet hum of the engine, the luxury wrapped around her—it was all so surreal. But a whisper of doubt crept in.

Does he do this for every woman? Is this just a polished act?

"Does Mr. Cooper do this a lot?" she asked cautiously.

The chauffeur met her gaze in the rearview mirror. "Do what, ma'am?"

"Have you pick up... guests. For meetings. Or dates."

His eyes didn't waver. "No, ma'am. He does not."

Cleo exhaled. The answer settled warm in her chest.

Her phone buzzed in her lap. A message from Jasper lit up the screen:

[Jasper]: Just be careful, okay? Something about all this feels a little... too polished. Trust your gut.

She stared at the message, her fingers curling around the phone. Her smile returned, faint but real.

Thanks, Jasper.

Outside the window, the city stretched past like a river of light and shadow—skyscrapers catching the last glow of twilight, neon signs flickering to life, people drifting through the streets like scenes from a silent film. The night was alive. And whatever this was—this strange pull toward Alek—it was already changing her.

She leaned back against the seat, her heart thudding softly in her chest.

Whatever Alek had planned tonight, she was ready for it.

Ready, even if she wasn't sure what it meant.

Chapter 8

The Rolls-Royce Phantom glided along the private road like a shadow through twilight, its polished frame reflecting the gold and crimson streaks of the setting sun. As it approached the entrance of the Rose Garden, the gate eased open with silent deference. Cleo spotted Alek waiting just beyond the entrance arch, flanked by tall rose-covered trellises glowing faintly in the evening light.

He stood in the last blush of day like a portrait come to life—his tailored charcoal jacket hugging the breadth of his shoulders, the white button-down beneath it clinging to the contours of a chest clearly sculpted by more than wealth alone. His silhouette was statuesque, illuminated from behind by the amber garden lights, making the shadows on his face more striking, more mythic.

Cleo's breath caught. Every time she saw him, she felt disarmed, as if the rules of her carefully ordered life no longer applied. Her skin prickled under her blazer, and not from the cool air. Pull yourself together, she told herself, willing her heartbeat to calm.

She wasn't sure what startled her more—his impossible beauty or the magnetic mystery that clung to him like a second skin. How could someone she'd only met twice make her feel like this?

The car came to a gentle stop, and before the chauffeur could even move, Alek was at her door. He opened it with an old-world flourish, extending his hand.

"Good evening," he said, his voice rich and velvety with just a trace of an accent she still couldn't place.

"Good evening," she replied, slipping her hand into his. A jolt of electricity buzzed up her arm at the contact. Her cheeks flushed despite herself.

"I hope you don't have anything too extravagant planned," she said lightly, stepping onto the stone path. "I didn't have time to change after work."

"Of course not," he said, his gaze raking over her appreciatively. "You look breathtaking. Shall we?"

He offered his arm, and she took it. The moment her fingers looped through the crook of his elbow, she felt grounded—and yet somehow weightless. Together, they walked beneath the arched entryway and into the garden.

The air was heavy with the scent of roses—damask, wild, climbing—their perfume swirling around them in soft waves. Lamps shaped like lanterns lined the garden paths, casting pools of warm gold across the cobblestones. The fountain at the center gurgled quietly, and soft classical music drifted from hidden speakers, giving the illusion that the garden itself was humming a lullaby.

But beneath the serene exterior, Alek's mind was anything but calm.

Being near Cleo awakened something in him—something wild, something ancient. Emotions that had lain dormant for centuries surged to the surface. Desire. Longing. A need to protect so fierce it was nearly violent. And with those feelings came danger.

He knew this was a mistake. He should have cancelled tonight, especially after his brother's warning. But he couldn't. The pull toward her was too strong. He was breaking every rule by seeing her again. But if this was the last time, he wanted to savor it.

"Shall we return to yesterday's debate?" Cleo asked at last, breaking the silence as they strolled down a path framed by pale yellow roses.

Alek smirked. "You mean our spirited intellectual engagement? I assumed you thought this was a date."

She laughed, the sound light and musical. "Is it?"

He glanced at her, trying to read the answer in her eyes. "Do you want it to be?"

Cleo hesitated, then smiled. "I'll let you know at the end."

He nodded, feeling a flicker of both relief and dread.

"Well then," he said, steering them around a curve lined with deep crimson blooms. "Back to the question at hand. Do you really believe that all ancient civilizations independently created their own pantheons of gods? Without any influence from one another?"

"As opposed to what?" she asked, amused.

Alek slowed, watching her closely. "Which seems more plausible? That cultures scattered across the world, many with no contact at all, coincidentally created mythologies with gods that share eerily similar powers, stories, and hierarchies? Or... that they were all remembering the same beings—gods who once walked among them—but by different names?"

She gave him a look, intrigued but skeptical. "The Greeks and Romans shared gods because they were neighbors. There was trade, war, migration, shared ancestry. That's why Zeus became Jupiter, Ares became Mars."

"Granted," Alek replied. "But what about the Norse gods? Or the Egyptian ones? Similar structures. Similar archetypes. Warriors, tricksters, rulers of the underworld. And these civilizations were oceans apart. No trade routes. No shared languages. Yet they created the same pantheon in different forms."

"Archetypes are psychological," she said. "Scholars would argue those gods represent universal aspects of human consciousness. The warrior, the mother, the trickster, the shadow. That's why we see them everywhere."

Alek nodded thoughtfully. "And what if the scholars are right... but only halfway? What if those archetypes were shaped because of actual encounters with divine beings— gods who inspired fear, worship, and imitation? Gods who became imprinted on the collective mind because they were once real enough to leave a scar."

Cleo stopped walking, turning to face him fully beneath an arch of climbing roses. "You're saying... all the gods were real?"

"I'm saying," he said, voice low and serious, "what if the myths were memories? Faded, distorted over time. But based on truth."

She tilted her head, a smile tugging at the corner of her lips. "So where are they now, these gods of yours?"

Alek looked away, eyes scanning the night sky. "Maybe they're still out there. Hiding in plain sight. Maybe they walked away to protect humanity from themselves. Or maybe they're waiting... to be needed again."

"Or maybe," Cleo countered, "people made them up to explain things they couldn't understand. Thunder, death, the stars. Humans crave order. They want a face to put on chaos."

"Maybe," Alek said with a smile. "Or maybe those faces were real, and the chaos had a name."

He reached for a blooming rose from a nearby bush, plucked it with care, and offered it to her. Cleo took it, brushing it under her nose and inhaling its fragrance.

She looked at him through her lashes. "You're not going to convince me. But I admire your conviction. Most people who talk like that come off as lunatics. You... just seem like you know something I don't."

Alek smiled faintly, concealing the storm behind his eyes. "Maybe I do."

Their gazes held for a beat too long. Cleo looked away first.

It was insane, she knew that. But she liked how passionate he was—how alive he became when he talked about history, about belief. Even if she disagreed with him, there was something thrilling about how unshakable he was.

She felt herself falling for him a little more with each step, each sentence. The way his eyes crinkled when he smiled. The careful, courtly way he offered his arm. The elegance of someone who didn't just study the past, but seemed to carry it with him.

"Are you hungry?" he asked, breaking the moment.

"Starving," she said with a grin. "Didn't have time for lunch."

"There's a little Italian place I know just a short walk from here. Family-owned. Quiet. Amazing food."

"Perfect."

They turned back toward the garden entrance, walking past the fountain at its center. The sound of water echoed softly, blending with the music and the rustle of wind in the leaves.

At the sidewalk, Alek offered his arm again. She slipped hers through it with a smirk. "So chivalrous," she teased.

"Would you expect anything less?" he replied, eyes twinkling.

He laughed with her, but his chest ached. He had been alone for so long, watching the world from a distance, keeping himself apart. But Cleo made him feel... human. Made him want to participate again. To live again.

He knew he wasn't supposed to be doing this. Not with her. But he couldn't walk away. Not yet. Maybe not ever.

She was worth breaking the rules for.

Chapter 9

The city had settled into twilight by the time Alek and Cleo stepped onto the sidewalk outside the Rose Garden. A breeze rolled in from the west, carrying the scent of eucalyptus and warm concrete. The last glow of sunlight clung to the tops of palm trees, and the sky shimmered with a dusky violet.

They walked arm in arm down the boulevard, their silhouettes casting long shadows under the vintage streetlamps. Cars hissed by on the wet asphalt, their lights glinting like fireflies. The evening was cool, just enough to make Cleo lean closer into Alek's warmth.

"What made you want to work in a museum?" he asked, his voice cutting through the quiet with a low, curious cadence.

Cleo glanced up at him, the amber light catching in her eyes. "Honestly? I've always been fascinated by the past. Learning about civilizations, their beliefs, their systems... It's like peeking into a world completely alien and yet eerily familiar."

She tripped over a raised seam in the pavement. Alek caught her with reflexive grace, one hand firm at her waist.

"Careful," he murmured with a smile.

"Thanks," she said, a little breathless. "I'm not the most graceful person—especially not in heels."

"I've noticed," he teased.

She smacked his arm lightly. "Rude."

His grin widened. "I like that about you."

They passed a small park, its iron gates latched for the night, and Cleo continued, "What draws me in is that each culture is like a story. It's not just facts or dates. It's people—what they believed in, what they feared. There's so much meaning buried in the artifacts they left behind."

"I like that," Alek said, though his gaze shifted, scanning rooftops and reflections in the restaurant windows ahead. The fine hairs on the back of his neck bristled. A familiar tension pulled at his chest—an awareness that someone was watching.

The restaurant entrance glowed ahead, warm and inviting behind tall windows. Cleo spoke again, unaware of the shift in him. "Alright, enough about me. You've been quiet. We've spent hours together and I still know almost nothing about you."

Alek opened the door for her, slipping back into charm with practiced ease. "My story is... complicated."

Inside, the restaurant wrapped around them like a scene from another era—low ceilings, red-and-white checkered cloths, candles flickering inside smoky glass holders. The scent of basil and garlic lingered in the air, mingling with soft music from a violin somewhere in the back.

"Just the two of you tonight?" the hostess asked.

"Yes," Alek said.

"Right this way."

They were led to a table near the back, tucked into a corner where shadows pooled like ink. Good. Far from the windows. From sight.

Their server arrived with a smile. "Good evening. I'm April, I'll be your server tonight. Here are your menus and wine list. I'll bring water and bread in a moment."

"Thank you," Cleo said, scanning the wine menu as if it were written in code. "I don't know anything about wine," she admitted, glancing at Alek.

"May I?" he asked, taking the list.

"Please."

"We'll have the Château Lafite Rothschild," he said to the server.

April blinked. "Sir, just to confirm, we only sell that by the bottle."

"That's fine," he said, without hesitation.

She leaned in slightly. "It's $1,800 a bottle."

Cleo coughed into her water. "I'm sorry—what?"

Alek didn't flinch. "That's fine."

April nodded and disappeared.

"Eighteen hundred dollars? For grapes?" Cleo whispered.

"You'll love it," Alek said calmly. "And it's my treat."

"That's my rent," she muttered.

Soon, April returned with the wine, poured it with ceremonial precision, and vanished again.

"You should try the chicken parmesan," Alek said. "It's my favorite."

"I'm more of a champagne chicken girl," she replied, scanning the menu.

"Back to you," she said, looking over her glass. "What's so complicated about your story?"

Alek swirled the wine in his glass. "Where to start? You already know I'm not from here. And clearly money isn't a concern. But the rest? That might take time."

"Do you have a name? A job? An origin story? Or are you going to keep answering in riddles?"

He grinned. "Independently wealthy. Let's say I come from old money."

"Still vague," she said, leaning in.

April returned to take their order.

"I'll have the champagne chicken," Cleo said.

"And the chicken parmesan for me," Alek added.

"Excellent choice," April said. "I'll get that started."

She walked away, Cleo smirked.

She tilted her head. "So, what's the real story?"

He paused. The candlelight flickered in his eyes. "Have you ever heard of the Hyperboreans?"

Cleo blinked. "Ancient Greek myths, right? A land far to the north where the sun never sets?"

Alek nodded slowly. "They were said to live for centuries. Some believed they served Apollo directly. Others say they were descendants of something older. Something not entirely human."

"And what, you're telling me you're one of them?" she asked, amused.

"I'm saying," he replied softly, "that time doesn't work the same for everyone. That some of us carry memories that don't belong to this age."

She leaned in, fascinated despite herself. "You sound like a priest or a madman."

"Or a god," he said, voice barely above a whisper. "You study gods, don't you? Their symbols, their stories? Don't you ever wonder if those myths came from something real?"

Cleo paused, her eyes narrowing. "At the museum... We're studying a set of tablets that reference a 'Watcher from the North,' a being who came before Olympus. You're saying those myths are history?"

"History wrapped in metaphor. And fear," Alek said. "Names change. I've had many."

She stared at him, trying to read his expression. "This is either the best story I've ever heard... or you're insane."

"Maybe both," he said with a smile.

Their food arrived, and they ate between sips of wine and bursts of laughter. As the bottle emptied, the conversation became lighter, but the undercurrent of something deeper pulsed just beneath the surface.

By the time they stepped outside, the city was cloaked in velvet night. The streets shimmered with the glow of passing cars. Alek looked around again, but the sensation had faded. Whoever had been watching was gone—or waiting.

Cleo looked up at him. "It's a beautiful night. I'd rather walk."

"Then I'll walk you home," he said.

They strolled through the quiet streets, the silence between them now companionable. When they reached her apartment, she paused.

"I had a great time tonight."

"I did too," he said.

"Let's do it again," she said. "I'll text you?"

"I'd like that," he replied.

He leaned in to kiss her cheek, but she caught the lapel of his coat and kissed him, soft but sure.

When she pulled back, he looked startled—and then smiled.

"Goodnight, Mr. Mysterious," she said, disappearing into the building.

He stood there a moment longer, staring at the door.

Then he turned, the night closing around him like a second skin.

Chapter 10

Pol stood gazing from a second-story window across the street from Cleo's apartment, motionless but electric with intent. The flicker of a desk lamp behind him outlined the edge of his coat, but his face remained in shadow. He had been watching all night, ever since he'd followed them from the restaurant—careful to stay just out of sight.

His eyes, sharp as broken obsidian, tracked every motion as Cleo and Alek said their goodbyes on the front steps. He leaned slightly forward when she grabbed Alek and kissed him—soft yet purposeful, unhesitating.

Pol's lip curled. "Oh, Alek," he murmured, voice like gravel. "You know better than that."

The black Rolls-Royce pulled away moments later, its red taillights melting into the dark like embers consumed by ash.

Pol stepped back from the window. The dim light caught faint scars on his knuckles, half-hidden by black gloves. He exhaled slowly, and the air around him seemed to stir.

The shadows behind him rippled like smoke, stretching unnaturally across the walls and ceiling. They twisted and recoiled, responding to his thoughts.

Then, without a sound, a flare of silver light erupted—sharp and cold like a blade drawn from ice.

Pol vanished into it, swallowed whole.

Chapter 11

"Good morning, Cleo," Jasper said, standing in his usual post, leaning against the frame of Cleo's office door.

"Good morning," she replied, barely looking up from her screen.

"Soooooo, how did it go?" Jasper asked excitedly.

"How did what go?" Cleo asked, feigning ignorance as a sly grin crept across her face.

"Don't play coy with me, Dr. Tenner. You know exactly what I'm talking about. How did it go last night with Mr. Cooper?"

"Honestly, it went well. I had a really good time. He's easy to talk to—charming, thoughtful, a great listener."

"Did you get any details on where he comes from, where he gets his money?" Jasper asked, sitting on the edge of her desk.

"That's where it gets a little strange," Cleo admitted. "When I asked him about his past, he said, 'It's complicated,' like he didn't want to talk about it. He told me he's not from the U.S., comes from old money, and is independently wealthy. But that was about it. He promised I'd learn more in time—whatever that means."

"So… we still don't really know anything about him."
Jasper crossed his arms. "Are you going to see him again?"

"I think I am," she said, her voice softer than before. "I
told him I'd text him. I actually really like him."

Jasper frowned, brows furrowing. "I don't want to
rain on your parade, but… don't you think it's weird? We
don't even know where he's really from. He drops a treasure
trove of artifacts on the museum, says almost nothing about
himself, and now he's showering you with gifts? It's like he
appeared out of nowhere."

"Maybe he had a rough childhood, or maybe
something happened that he doesn't like to talk about," Cleo
offered. "It's strange, sure, but not necessarily a red flag. I
don't get the sense he's hiding anything malicious."

"Maybe not. But people who say 'you'll learn in time'
usually have something big they're sitting on. I'm just saying,
Cleo, there's something about him that doesn't add up. He's
too… polished. Like he's playing a role."

Before Cleo could respond, Gary the security guard
peeked around the doorframe. "Good morning, Dr. Tenner."

"Morning, Gary," she replied.

"A messenger dropped these off for you this
morning," he said, stepping in with a small vase of roses.
"Where would you like them?"

"I'll take them," she said, rising from her chair. She
inhaled deeply as she set the vase on the credenza near her
desk.

"I wonder who those are from," Jasper said
sarcastically.

"There's a package too, ma'am," Gary added, handing
her a small box wrapped in brown paper.

"Thank you, Gary."

"No problem at all, Dr. Tenner," he said as he exited.

"What do we have here, Cleo? A gift from one Mr. Aleksander Cooper, perhaps?" Jasper said, practically bouncing with anticipation.

"I don't know. I hope it's nothing too expensive," she said, tearing open the paper.

She gasped.

"What is it?" Jasper asked.

"It's... it's Macbeth."

"What?" Jasper looked confused.

Cleo pulled a handwritten note from the box and read it aloud:

I hope this makes you smile. Maybe we can see it performed together sometime. ~Alek

She carefully lifted the contents of the box. It was a weathered, handwritten script.

"Wait—by Macbeth, do you mean the play? Like Shakespeare?" Jasper's jaw dropped. "Holy shit, is that what I think it is?"

"If you think it's an original handwritten copy of William Shakespeare's Macbeth, then yes, Jasper. You'd be very correct."

"I was admiring it in his library when I visited his estate. I told him it was one of my favorites. I can't believe he remembered."

"Wow. This guy must have it bad for you," Jasper said, moving closer to examine it. "Cleo, that has to be worth a fortune."

"I can't accept this. It's too much," she said, visibly overwhelmed.

"Are you going to try to give it back to him?" Jasper asked.

"I mean, I have to, don't I? This thing is priceless."

"From what you've told me about his estate and the museum donation, do you really think he cares about money?"

"Still," Cleo said, gripping her phone, "this is a lot. I love it, but it's a lot."

Jasper watched her carefully. "You ever think he might be too good to be true? A private estate full of rare artifacts, he knows obscure languages, and now he gives you a handwritten Shakespeare? He doesn't just have money—he has history. Deep history. The kind that doesn't come with a paper trail."

Cleo looked at him, the hint of doubt finally surfacing. "You think it's fake?"

"No, I think it's real. That's what scares me."

She frowned, then returned her gaze to the phone and typed:

Cleo: I just received your gift. I appreciate it, but it's too much. I can't accept it.

She bounced the phone nervously in her hand, waiting for the three dots to appear.

Alek: Don't worry about it, and don't even think of trying to return it. It's my gift to you.

Cleo: Seriously, Alek. I love it, but this belongs in a museum. Not on my shelf.

Alek: You love it. That's all that matters. I have my reasons.

Cleo: You can't just give something like this away.

Alek: I didn't give it away. I gave it to you.

Cleo: Then I'll give it back. Tonight. Bring an empty box.

Alek: If you try to return it, I'll pretend I don't know what you're talking about.

Cleo: Alek.

Alek: Cleo.

Cleo: You're impossible.

Alek: Only sometimes. Are you free tonight?

Cleo: How's the theatre? We can get tickets to a show. Your treat, of course.

Alek: I wouldn't have it any other way. I'll pick you up this evening.

Cleo: Fine. But I'm bringing the manuscript. You can decide what to do with it then.

Alek: You can bring it. But you'll still be taking it home.

Jasper raised an eyebrow. "So... first priceless artifact, then a romantic theatre date?"

"I guess I'm going all in," Cleo said, trying to sound light, but her eyes lingered on the manuscript.

Jasper studied her a moment. "Just... be careful, okay? I know you're smart. I know you can handle yourself. But this guy... he's an unknown. And the more I hear about him, the more I wonder if we're dealing with someone who's not just rich, but ancient in ways we don't yet understand."

Cleo nodded slowly, still staring at the inked script. "I will."

Chapter 12

Alek stood alone on the balcony of his estate, the moonlight casting long shadows across the stone floor. The wind carried with it the whisper of clouds, soft and unsettling. Behind him, the air shimmered, then snapped with the sudden presence of another.

"Still enjoying your little charade down here, brother?" came Pol's voice, smooth and mocking.

Alek didn't turn. "What do you want, Pol?"

"To talk. To reason with you. One last time."

"Reason?" Alek turned now, facing him. "I already told you no. My answer hasn't changed."

Pol shrugged. "I've had a change of perspective. You're wasting your power pretending to be something you're not. We are gods, Alek. We should rule as gods. We should reclaim the world that forgot us."

Alek narrowed his eyes. "We already have power. We were never meant to rule, only to guide. You want dominion. I want balance."

"Balance?" Pol laughed bitterly. "There is no balance left. Look around you—humans destroy everything they touch. They forgot us, mocked us, replaced us with their own hollow creations. We can change that. Together, we can restore reverence. Order. You have their love, Alek. I want their respect. Their fear. We were worshipped once—we can be again. You and I, brother. Imagine it."

"You want fear," Alek said. "You want worship without worthiness. I won't be part of it."

Pol stepped closer. "You think hiding behind your estate, playing the generous benefactor, falling in love with a mortal—yes, I've seen her—makes you better? Stronger?"

Alek's voice turned cold. "That was you I felt the other night, wasn't it?"

Pol smirked. "She's lovely. Brilliant. A rare spark among the dim. I can see why you'd be tempted."

Alek clenched his fists. "If you so much as lay a finger on her—"

"Relax, brother," Pol said, holding up his hands. "I've done nothing... yet. But you know how delicate mortals can be. So easily lost, so easily manipulated. It would be a shame if anything happened to her because of your stubbornness."

Alek stepped forward, his voice a low growl. "You will not touch her."

"I don't have to," Pol said. "But think carefully. Every choice has consequences. Join me, and I promise she stays untouched, unaware, protected. Refuse again, and I can't guarantee her safety. Or yours."

He leaned in, his voice dropping into a whisper. "She walks alone at night sometimes, doesn't she? Leaves the museum after dark. Trusting. Unafraid. How long do you think that will last? Or maybe it's not a threat to her body you fear—but what happens if she learns what you are? What you've done? How long do you think her love will last then?"

Alek's eyes burned. Power stirred beneath his skin, a deep and ancient fury igniting in his chest. It took everything in him not to strike Pol down where he stood. He could feel the weight of centuries in his veins, a god's wrath threatening to break free. But not yet. Not here. His thoughts raced—not just of Pol's threat, but of Cleo's warmth, her laugh, her trust. The way she looked at him like he was just a man.

She had no idea what danger had been watching her.

Alek's voice shook with restrained rage. "I won't join you."

Pol's expression shifted—amusement giving way to quiet menace. "Then you'll regret it. One way or another, I'll make sure of that."

He took a step back, darkness curling at the edges of his form. "But I'll be generous. I'll give you time to think about your next move. Join me, or don't. Either way... we're far from finished."

With a ripple of wind and light, Pol vanished, leaving Alek staring out over the silent hills, jaw clenched, every muscle taut with fury and fear.

He turned and looked toward the city. Toward Cleo.

"I'm sorry," he whispered. "I should have known this wouldn't stay hidden forever."

Chapter 13

Pol stood in a great hall. The walls and floor were a blinding, seamless white, the surfaces smooth like polished marble but impossibly luminous, as if the light emanated from within them. Colossal columns lined the corridor, stretching skyward with no visible end, vanishing into a ceiling of drifting silver clouds. A radiant light poured from above, bathing the space in a brilliance that allowed no shadows, as if the very concept of darkness had been exiled from this realm.

This was the Celestial Realm—the dwelling place of the old gods. The home of the gods. The great hall lay within a palace of divine architecture, its white towers spiraling higher than any mortal mountain, disappearing into an eternal sky. The palace was the heart of a city that shimmered like starlight, floating above the clouds. Vast plazas of crystalline stone connected spires and domes, while golden bridges arched over waterways of glowing liquid light. Mythical beasts—winged lions, feathered serpents, and luminous phoenixes—circled the skies, their movements graceful and ancient. From every tower and parapet, banners of celestial fabric waved in an unseen wind.

The city beyond the palace was no less breathtaking. White streets wound like silver veins through districts of alabaster and gold, temples and amphitheaters gleaming beneath a sky streaked with otherworldly auroras. Ethereal trees lined the boulevards, their translucent leaves rustling in a wind scented with memory and starfire. Around the floating isles of the city, flocks of winged creatures—griffins, storm crows, and even the occasional dragon of light—glided in languid circles, casting fleeting shadows across domes and towers.

The entire city rested atop a cloud-borne continent, its waterfalls spilling from the heavens into the infinite space below, where no mortal eye could see. The light here held no warmth, only divinity. The air was thick with memory and power.

Despite the grandeur and the bustle of dozens of gods and divine beings gathered in conversation, laughter, and deliberation, the hall held a deep, reverent stillness. The air vibrated with quiet purpose, with timeless power. Pol found it suffocating.

He moved through the crowd, weaving between clusters of immortals engaged in quiet conversation. His sharp gaze scanned until it landed on Theo, who stood near a fountain of floating starlight, speaking with their sister Helena.

"Theo, how have you been, brother?" Pol said smoothly.

"What do you want, Pol?" Theo responded without turning, his voice already edged with irritation.

"Don't worry, I'm doing just fine, thanks for asking," Helena added, her tone cool and dry as she rolled her eyes at

Pol with evident disdain. She crossed her arms, her golden robes shimmering with starlight, and arched a brow.

"So hurtful, both of you," Pol replied with mock offense, pressing a hand to his chest in exaggerated pain.

"Get on with it, Pol," Theo said, clearly unwilling to entertain his brother's antics.

Pol, never beloved among the gods—thanks to a long legacy of meddling, mischief, and unrest—smirked and stepped closer.

"I made a little trip to Earth recently. Went to visit our dear brother Anu—well, I guess he goes by Alek these days—and I was shocked at what I found. I mean, I couldn't believe it."

"You went to bother Alek again?" Theo said, skepticism tightening his brow. "Last time you visited him, we nearly had a celestial incident."

"It was a cordial visit," Pol said, clearly lying. "Just checking in."

"Right," Theo muttered. "Go on, then. Shock us."

"He's with a human," Pol said, savoring the revelation.

"With a human? He lives on Earth, Pol. He's bound to cross paths with them now and then," Theo replied sarcastically. Helena chuckled beside him.

"No," Pol said, his tone sharpening, "I mean he's involved with a human. Intimately."

Theo's amusement faded. "That's a rather large accusation, Pol. Not one to be made lightly—especially not about Alek."

"I know what I saw," Pol insisted. "I saw the woman at his estate. They were very... friendly. When I confronted him about it, he brushed me off—told me she was none of my concern. Naturally, I didn't believe him, so I watched. From a distance. The next night, I saw them together again. And this time... let's just say it wasn't exactly subtle."

Theo crossed his arms. "You're saying Alek—the oldest of us, protector of mankind—is romantically involved with a mortal? After what happened with Eros? Alek, who was among those who ruled that gods were no longer to fraternize with humans in that way?"

"Yes, brother," Pol said simply. "That's exactly what I'm telling you."

Helena tilted her head, brow furrowing. "He wouldn't risk that. Not Alek. He's too devoted to the mortals."

"Devoted to the mortals—exactly. Maybe too devoted," Pol said with a smirk.

Helena's eyes narrowed. "Are you suggesting he's lost his judgment?"

"I'm not suggesting anything. Just presenting the facts," Pol said innocently.

"There's nothing innocent about you," Helena shot back. "And your facts tend to be as flexible as your morals."

Pol gave her a mock bow. "Thank you, sister."

Theo stepped forward, his voice low. "You're never just the messenger. You twist every truth you touch."

"Such harshness. I'm hurt," Pol said, unbothered.

Pol narrowed his eyes. "And what do you plan to do about this, hmm? If what I've said is true—if Alek has broken our most sacred law—what happens next?"

"For now—nothing," Theo said firmly. "Keep watching them. I'll bring this to the others, but no one will take your word alone. They'll want proof. They'll want to see it for themselves."

"I'd be more than happy to 'keep an eye' on our dear big brother," Pol said, his smile dripping with false innocence.

"You're enjoying this far too much," Theo said. "Be careful. If Alek catches you watching, he won't let it slide. You know what he's capable of."

"Oh, I hope he tries something," Pol said at the very beginning, his grin curling like smoke around the words. "I dare him to. Alek may be powerful, but he's far too sentimental. All that time among mortals has made him soft—his heart weighs him down more than he knows. If he lashes out, it means he still has some fire left in him. And if he comes for me? Even better. I've been dying to test just how far he's fallen. It would be... enlightening to remind him what real power looks like. And who still holds it."

Helena smirked, a glint of something sharp in her gaze. "One can hope," she said, her tone light but laced with something darker. "If Alek catches him snooping, we both know he won't just scold him. He might decide Pol needs a reminder of his place. And honestly, it's been a long time coming."

Pol's expression froze for a fraction of a second, the confident grin faltering as her words hung in the air. His eyes narrowed slightly, though the smirk returned just as quickly, now thinner and more calculated. "Tsk, Helena," he said, voice laced with faux amusement, "such violent hopes from such a graceful sister. Are you encouraging Alek to hurt me? I must say, it's nice to know where I stand. Truly warms the heart."

"Report back with anything else you find suspicious," Theo said. "I'll let you know what's decided—if there's anything to decide at all. Now go, brother."

Pol vanished in a flash of light, the echo of mischief clinging to the air like smoke.

Helena watched the space where he had stood. "I really do hate him."

Theo nodded, exhaling. "Don't we all. Still, if he's right..."

Helena's face grew serious. "Then Alek is in more danger than he realizes. And so is the girl."

Theo turned to her. "You believe him?"

"I believe he believes what he saw. And if he's lying, he's playing a long game for reasons we haven't yet seen. Either way, it's dangerous."

She paced a step, then turned back. "If the others find out... if they see it for themselves... they won't debate. They'll punish him. And her."

Theo's jaw clenched. "Then we'd better find the truth first."

Helena nodded. "Because if we don't, Pol won't stop until he's turned all of this into a spectacle—and Alek into a villain."

They stood in silence, the weight of divine consequences settling over them like a gathering storm.

Chapter 14

Alek sat in the back seat of his Rolls Royce, parked just outside the grand steps of the museum, a pair of sleek black tickets nestled in his gloved hand. The gold-embossed words glimmered faintly in the city's fading light: Wicked – Orchestra Center. Evening buzzed around him—horns in the distance, the low hum of streetlights flickering to life, and the occasional rustle of leaves in the soft, early-summer breeze.

He adjusted the cuff of his tailored coat, glancing toward the museum's entrance. His nerves fluttered—an unfamiliar sensation. After all, he was a god. Yet the thought of seeing Cleo again stirred something in him that mortal men might call butterflies.

Then he saw her.

Cleo stepped out of the museum, her silhouette framed by the warm interior lights behind her. She wore a deep emerald dress that hugged her curves with effortless elegance, her hair swept up into a soft, deliberate twist that exposed the graceful line of her neck. She looked radiant, timeless.

Alek exited the car, his breath catching for the briefest moment. He rounded the vehicle with a practiced ease and opened the rear door.

"Good evening, Ms. Tenner," he said, his voice smooth but reverent.

Cleo smiled, her cheeks flushed from the rush of the evening. "Good evening, Mr. Cooper."

He leaned in and kissed her cheek—brief, warm, electric—then offered his hand. She took it, and he helped her into the car before circling around to slide in beside her.

As the driver pulled away, Cleo turned slightly. "Before I forget," she said, brushing a loose strand of hair behind her ear, "I have a huge meeting first thing tomorrow morning. Jasper and I are presenting the museum's annual budget to the board. I'll probably be up all night worrying about it."

Alek nodded, filing the detail away with care. "Then I'll make sure tonight is a perfect distraction."

His eyes met hers, lingering for a moment. "You look stunning tonight, by the way. That dress is... dangerous."

Cleo smirked. "You approve?"

"I'm trying not to let it go to my head. Or anywhere else."

She laughed, her hand brushing lightly against his thigh. "You're not exactly subtle in that suit yourself."

Alek leaned slightly closer, his voice low. "If I told you what I'm thinking right now, we'd never make it to the theater."

Her breath caught as she turned toward the window, trying and failing to suppress her smile. The tension between them simmered, thick as velvet.

"What show are we seeing tonight?"

Alek smiled, eyes twinkling with mischief. "It's a surprise. You'll just have to be patient.""

The city blurred past in streams of gold and shadow. Towering palms lined the boulevard, and neon signs blinked overhead. Cleo leaned back into the plush leather seat, a smile tugging at the corners of her lips.

When the Rolls Royce pulled up outside the ornate Pantages Theatre, Cleo's eyes lit up. The marquee blazed in brilliant lights: Wicked – Tonight Only.

"We're seeing Wicked?" she gasped, turning to him with wide eyes. "I've wanted to see this forever. The tickets are insane—thank you so much."

"I hoped you'd like it," he said, visibly pleased.

"You're spoiling me, Mr. Cooper," she teased as the chauffeur opened her door.

"Not nearly enough," Alek replied.

They walked arm in arm past velvet ropes and awestruck patrons. The theater's gilded interior glowed like something from a bygone era—red velvet drapes, crystal chandeliers, the scent of old paper and perfume. Ushered to the front row, center stage, Cleo took in the opulence around her.

As the orchestra swelled and the curtain rose, Cleo leaned forward, utterly absorbed. Alek, however, barely glanced at the stage. He watched her instead—the way her eyes widened with wonder, the subtle movements of her lips as she mouthed lyrics, the tears she wiped away in the dark.

He was captivated, not by the magic on stage, but by the woman beside him.

When the final curtain fell and thunderous applause erupted, Cleo leapt to her feet, clapping wildly.

"That was amazing," she said breathlessly, turning to him. "Thank you, Alek. That was perfect."

"It was my pleasure. I'd do anything to see you smile like that."

Cleo looked down, cheeks glowing. "Shall we grab a nightcap?"

Alek hesitated. "I'd love to, but you have that meeting tomorrow, don't you? With Jasper?"

She groaned. "Right. Museum budget presentation. Ugh. You're right. I should get home."

"Then let's get you home so you're rested for that big meeting tomorrow."

Their laughter echoed under the marquee lights as the Rolls Royce returned. Alek helped her in, and they rode in silence, fingers entwined in the warm hush of the night.

When they reached her apartment, Cleo lingered. The air smelled of rain on concrete and blooming jasmine from the building's nearby garden.

Alek escorted her to the door, the soft click of her heels syncing with his steps.

"Good night, Ms. Tenner," he said, his voice low.

"Good night, Mr. Cooper," she replied, her voice equally soft.

He kissed her cheek again, lingering just a breath longer than before. "Text me tomorrow?"

"Without question," she said, unlocking the door.

She paused, holding it half-open.

"Alek?"

He turned. "Yes?"

Her eyes sparkled in the dim light. "Do you still want that nightcap?"

Alek smiled, something feral and tender flickering behind his eyes. "Absolutely."

They ascended the stairs quickly, fingers brushing, then gripping. Her door clicked open under the pressure of her back as he pushed her gently against it, their mouths locked in a deep, greedy kiss. Cleo moaned softly as Alek's hands traced the curve of her waist, then lower. Her fingers tangled in his hair, pulling him closer. The door gave way behind them and they stumbled inside, lips never parting.

She kicked it shut with a bang, their bodies already undressing each other in a frenzy of tugged zippers and sliding straps. He peeled her dress down with aching slowness, trailing kisses along every inch of newly exposed skin. Her hands roamed under his shirt, pushing it up to reveal the chiseled planes of his chest—smooth, bronzed, and impossibly sculpted. His abs were like carved marble, defined ridges that flexed beneath her fingers. She dragged her palms down over the taut muscles, savoring the heat of his skin, the inhuman perfection of his body. He looked like something out of legend—flawless, powerful, male in its most divine form. They bumped into the hallway table, a vase crashing to the floor and shattering—but neither of them noticed.

Alek swept her into his arms, carried her into the bedroom, and laid her on the bed like an offering. He knelt between her thighs, his mouth tracing fire along her inner thigh, teasing until she writhed beneath him. When he finally entered her, she gasped his name like a prayer. Their bodies moved in rhythm, a rising tide of passion that built and broke and built again. Her nails scored his back; his mouth found her neck, her collarbone, her lips.

They devoured each other with abandon—tangled limbs, gasps of pleasure, moans that filled the room like music. When she came undone, clenching around him, he followed with a groan, burying his face in her shoulder, whispering her name.

They collapsed together, breathless, trembling. She clung to him as if afraid he might vanish.

Alek lifted her effortlessly, her legs locking around him as if by instinct. He pinned her beneath him again, both of them already hungry for more. Their kisses grew rougher, deeper, hands roaming with a desperation that bordered on worship. He flipped her over with practiced ease, Cleo arched into him as he kissed down her spine, his hands spreading her thighs apart with aching care. He slid into her from behind, and her moan echoed off the walls—low, needy, real. Their bodies moved together in a rhythm ancient and primal, each thrust sending jolts of pleasure that stole her breath.

"More," she gasped, clutching the sheets as he gripped her hips and drove into her harder, deeper, until the bed groaned beneath them.

He turned her over, his mouth claiming her breasts, his teeth grazing sensitive skin, leaving trails of heat. She pulled him into her again, their sweat-slicked skin sliding together as their rhythm built—harder now, faster. Her cries filled the room as another wave hit her, her entire body tensing, shaking around him.

Alek followed seconds later, growling her name into her neck as he came, pouring himself into her with a force that felt like a storm breaking. He collapsed beside her, chest heaving, their bodies tangled in sweat and breathless laughter.

She reached for him again, pulling him close. "I think I may be falling for you," Cleo whispered, her voice hoarse with emotion and exhaustion.

He looked at her, everything in his expression raw. "Then fall," he whispered back, his lips brushing hers as the words passed between them.

They made love again, slower this time—intimate and reverent, more a prayer than an act of pleasure. It wasn't just passion. It was surrender. It was truth.

They spent the remainder of the night talking, mostly about her, places she wanted to travel to art, everything. Alek continuing do avoid topics about himself every time Cleo tried to steer the conversation that way. He answered only with vague responses, turning the conversation back to her as soon as he could. As morning approached, wrapped in sheets and each other, they watched the first light slip through the blinds, painting golden stripes across the bed.

"I have to get up," Cleo murmured, checking her phone. "Jasper will kill me if I miss this meeting."

"Stay," Alek said, brushing her hair behind her ear.

She smiled. "Not all of us are independently wealthy."

"Fine," he grumbled, throwing a pillow at her. "But I want to see you again tonight. My chef can prepare anything you want."

She stood, a sheet wrapped around her like a toga. "Forget dinner. I think I'd rather skip to dessert."

He grinned. "You naughty little minx."

Cleo winked, walking toward the bathroom. "Seven o'clock?"

"I'll be counting the minutes."

She disappeared behind the door, and Alek lay back, arms folded behind his head, a rare smile on his lips.

He had once believed gods couldn't fall in love.

But Cleo Tenner was beginning to prove him wrong.

Chapter 15

Pol watched as Cleo and Alek walked out of Cleo's building, their arms interlocked, Alek still wearing the same clothes from the night before. Alek helped Cleo into the back seat of the Rolls Royce. As soon as Alek closed the door for Cleo, his facial expression changed, becoming more serious, alert. He scanned the surrounding area, his gaze sharp. Pol knew Alek could sense his presence—or at least the presence of another god.

Pol stood in the second-story window of the building across the street, his familiar perch, hidden behind sheer lace curtains. The room around him was cold and dim, filled with the quiet hum of fluorescent lights and the faint scent of dust. He had managed to stay out of sight, cloaked just enough to remain undetected. For now.

There was no doubt in his mind that Alek's involvement with this woman had crossed a dangerous line. Pol knew his brother—knew that Alek was not one for meaningless affairs or one-night stands. He was too careful, too devoted to humanity to indulge lightly. If it had been any of their other siblings, Pol might have laughed it off. The gods had always entertained themselves with mortals. It was tradition.

But Alek was different.

He had always been the protector, the idealist, the one who believed that gods could and should care for their mortal creations. After the Eros incident, it was Alek who had stood before the pantheon, fierce and unwavering, arguing that their role should be one of guardianship—not abandonment. He had implored the others to remember their purpose, to see humanity not as a failed experiment but as something fragile and beautiful, something worth protecting. Alek had spoken of the divine responsibility they carried, the balance they were meant to uphold. He believed the gods should walk among mortals not as tyrants or distant myths, but as protectors, guides—beacons in the darkness. He had pleaded for compassion, for patience, for the grace to lift humanity rather than forsake it. Pol had agreed with him at the time—though for very different reasons.

Ultimately, Alek had abided by the majority's decision to step back from humanity. Pol, less inclined to obey, had not. And it had cost him.

Alek had turned him in. It was Alek who had stood before the others and revealed Pol's manipulations during the 1930s and 40s—manipulations that had helped ignite a global war. Pol had whispered into the ears of leaders, stoked fear, pride, and ambition like embers into flame. He had orchestrated the beginnings of war not for the sake of destruction alone, but with purpose: to drive mortals back into awe. He believed that only through fire and suffering would humanity remember the gods. Every bomb that fell, every siren that screamed through the night was a desperate invocation, a dark prayer. He had hoped they would cry out—not just to survive, but to something greater. To them.

He wanted to show the world that the gods were real. That they were still here, still watching, still capable of bending the world to their will. He wanted belief. And through belief, power. His plan had been carefully constructed—manipulate the rise of conflict, then reveal himself in a moment of global despair. He would end the war in a dazzling display of divine intervention, a spectacle so undeniable that the world would have no choice but to remember. Mortals would fall to their knees, not in fear, but in recognition. Their gods had returned.

He hadn't done it out of cruelty, not exactly. He had done it to remind the world of their place, to reignite reverence through awe and fear. When the gods abandoned humanity, humanity had stopped believing. That belief—the adoration, the offerings, the stories—had once made them powerful.

Pol remembered the golden age, when temples bore his name, when kings feared his judgment, when every flicker of fire and stroke of lightning was a hymn to his presence. He had walked among mortals then, and they had bowed.

But Alek, his noble brother, had stripped that from him. His betrayal had sentenced Pol to isolation, to obscurity. Before Pol could execute the final stage of his plan—before he could reveal himself to the world—Alek had intervened. He had gone to the others and exposed everything. In a single, calculated act, Alek had stripped Pol of his moment, his purpose, and cast him back into the shadows. The decades of punishment had erased him from mortal memory. He was nothing now but a whisper in old books—if that.

And now, Alek, the great enforcer, was breaking the very law he had used to condemn him.

Pol's fingers tightened around the curtain.

This wasn't just about revenge anymore.

He needed Alek—not just to suffer, but to understand. To see what they had lost. To remember what it meant to be worshipped, to be feared, to be needed.

If he could turn Alek to his side, convince him to help take back their rightful place among mortals, then everything could change. The gods could rise again—not as hidden shepherds, but as rulers. As gods.

He just had to show Alek what was at stake.

And Cleo Tenner—she might be the key.

And now, watching Alek defy the very laws he once upheld? It was almost poetic.

Pol's lips curled into a smirk.

Alek, the most powerful of them all, was putting his precious humanity in danger. For what? Love? Lust? It didn't matter. This wasn't about humanity anymore. Not for Pol.

This was about retribution. And it was about reclamation. Taking back what they once had—fear, worship, power, reverence. Restoring the order that had been lost. Reawakening the old ways.

Alek had betrayed him. That could not go unpunished.

Chapter 16

The double doors of the boardroom swung open as Cleo and Jasper stepped into the corridor, the hum of museum staff chatter filling the space beyond. Cleo carried a leather folio under one arm, her expression bright with the satisfaction of a successful presentation. Jasper, still smoothing the sleeves of his blazer, raised an eyebrow and glanced over at her.

"Well," he said, "that could've gone worse."

"That's your takeaway? I thought it went great."

"It did," Jasper admitted. "You crushed the numbers, and the board didn't push back half as much as I expected."

"I told you the donor exhibit strategy would work."

"You were right," he said, holding the office door open for her. "Now let's hope your charming new patron keeps opening his checkbook."

Cleo rolled her eyes but smiled. "He's more than just a checkbook, Jasper."

Jasper held up his hands. "I know, I know. I'm just saying—if he's got connections or influence, now's the time to use it."

They stepped into her office together, still riding the high of the meeting. Cleo set her folio on her desk and took a satisfied sip from her iced latte, a pleased hum escaping her lips. Jasper leaned against the doorframe, eyeing her with that knowing, mischievous smirk of his.

"You've been floating on air all morning," he said, arching a brow. "Even before the meeting started, I could tell. Should I assume last night was the reason?"

"Last night went very well—and so did this morning." She smirked at him as he followed her into her office.

"Good for you. Give me details."

"Well, it started off fairly normal—dinner and Wicked, which was fantastic, by the way. He dropped me off at my apartment like a perfect gentleman, walked me to the door and then, well... you know. But afterward, we just talked. For hours. We never even went to sleep."

"What did you talk about? Did you find out anything new about his past?" Jasper's expression sharpened with interest.

"We talked about everything—well, mostly about me. History, art, places I want to visit... And Jasper, I told him I was falling in love with him." Her face turned red even as she smiled.

"Wait—what? Cleo, from the sounds of it you still don't know anything concrete about his past, and now you're telling me you're in love with him? Are you sure you're not confusing love with lust—or desire? You two have had, what, three or four dates? Sometimes that kind of passion feels like love, especially when everything's new and exciting."

"I know it sounds crazy. But it's true. I can't help it. So what if he's a little closed off? He'll tell me in his own time."

She crossed her arms, leaning back slightly as if bracing herself. Her tone softened but stayed firm, as though she were trying to convince both of them.

"I've never felt this way before, Jasper. It's not just desire—it's deeper than that. I know the difference."

"Maybe... But you literally just said you talked all night, and he told you nothing about himself? You don't think he's hiding something?"

"I think he's more of a listener than a talker. Is that such a bad thing?"

Jasper stepped further into the office, his usual smirk replaced by something more serious.

"Alright. But Cleo, you can't say I didn't warn you. There's something about this guy... I don't know. He's charming, sure. Thoughtful. But it all feels a little too polished, you know? Like he's saying exactly what you want to hear. Like he's rehearsed."

He gave her a steady look.

"Just... don't let passion cloud your instincts. You're sharp, Cleo. Trust your gut. If something feels off—don't brush it aside."

He let that hang for a beat before softening his tone.

"What did he say when you told him how you felt?"

"He said he felt the same."

"That's fantastic, Cleo. Despite my concerns, I'm happy for you—I really am. I just worry. You've only seen him a few times, and this is moving fast. Promise me that if anything feels off, you'll tell me. And maybe... just slow down a little. Learn more about him first."

"I promise. I appreciate your concern, really, I do. Maybe you're right. I'll try to slow things down—at least until I know more about his past."

"Thank you. Now, for business—we have a gentleman coming this afternoon who requested a private tour of the new exhibits. I don't know if he's considering becoming a recurring donor, but he made a small donation and asked specifically for a private showing. Naturally, I offered your services."

"Jasper! You know how much I hate that."

"It worked out for you the last time," he winked. "And he'll be here in thirty minutes, so I hope you're ready."

She threw a pen at him as he darted out of her office, the pen bouncing off the wall near his head.

***

Thirty minutes later...

Cleo was pulled from her work by the ring of her desk phone. "Miss Tenner, we have a gentleman at the front desk asking for you. He says he's here for the tour."

"Thank you. I'll be there in a moment."

She stood, mumbling as she headed to the front. "I hate you, Jasper."

As she approached the reception desk, her eyes widened in surprise. The man waiting there was unmistakable—the same one she'd seen in Alek's drawing room the night he showed her the artifacts.

"Good morning, sir. I'm Dr. Cleo Tenner, assistant director here and your tour guide for the day."

"Good morning. My name is Pol. It's a pleasure to make your acquaintance."

That accent. Just like Alek's—distinct, refined, but from nowhere Cleo could place.

"Shall we?" she offered, gesturing toward the exhibits.

As they walked through the first gallery, curiosity gnawed at her. This might be her chance.

"I hope you don't mind me asking," she said, "but do you happen to know an Alek Cooper?"

"I do. In fact, he's my older brother."

She masked her shock. "Really? I didn't know he had siblings."

"You wouldn't. Alek rarely mentions us."

"Us? There are more of you?"

"We're a large family," he said simply.

"I had no idea."

"How is it that you know my dear brother?"

"Well... we've been seeing each other."

"Really? He never mentioned it."

"It's a recent development. Maybe that's why."

"I'm sure that's it," Pol said, watching her closely. "Alek rarely shares details about his flings. No offense."

Flings? "Does he go through a lot of women?"

"It's not my place to say. Alek is very private. Honestly, I wouldn't know. I didn't mean to cast doubt—if there are real feelings between you two then that's wonderful."

"No, don't worry. It's just... he is so private. I guess I don't really know much about him."

"If there's anything else you're desperate to know, you could always ask me, I may have some answers for you at least. How long have you two been together?"

"Just a short time. But it's been... intense."

Pol nodded slowly, his expression unreadable. "That does sound like him. He has a tendency to draw people in— quickly, deeply. Some would say dangerously."

Cleo tilted her head, studying him. "What do you mean?"

"Oh, nothing alarming," he said with a gentle wave of his hand. "Just... Alek has always been a mystery. Even to us. He's a man of many compartments. He keeps his life in sealed boxes, and rarely opens more than one at a time."

Cleo frowned. "He's mentioned very little about his past."

"I'm not surprised. He doesn't like looking back. And when he does... it tends to cost him more than he lets on."

"What kind of past are we talking about?"

Pol smiled faintly. "Let's just say he's lived many lives. Sometimes I wonder if even he remembers them all."

"But I am glad to hear that your relationship is going so well. He could use someone to shake him out of his seriousness. He's been alone far too long. At least, as far as I know. Though to be fair, with Alek, what anyone truly knows is often just the surface. He's a master at keeping the deeper waters hidden."

"Yes, I think it's becoming serious," Cleo admitted. Then, quickly changing the subject: "But enough about that— shall we continue the tour?"

"Let's."

Everything had unfolded exactly as Pol intended. Each word he offered was deliberate, designed to stir questions rather than provide answers. He hadn't needed to lie—only to plant doubt. A small suggestion here, a pointed phrase there. He watched her closely, noting every flicker of uncertainty in her eyes. She was already beginning to question Alek. Why hadn't he told her about his family? Why the secrecy? Why the deflections?

Pol didn't need to press further—her own imagination would do the rest. Doubt was insidious; it didn't rush. It crept. It rewrote memories. It made her look backward and ask, What else don't I know? That was the beauty of it.

And Alek? He'd never confess. He wouldn't risk telling her the truth—not when it would sound like madness. And when the lies began to pile up—as they would—Cleo would feel it. She would start to pull away.

Pol didn't want to destroy Alek. Not yet.

He wanted to watch him unravel.

Pol continued the tour with feigned interest. Cleo, now uncertain and full of questions, guided him from one piece to the next.

"Well, that's everything. I hope the museum can count on your continued support."

"I'm sure that won't be a problem, Dr. Tenner—or should I call you Cleo? We are almost family now."

"Cleo is fine."

"Then thank you, Cleo. And do say hello to my brother for me."

"I will. Maybe we'll run into each other again soon."

"Oh, I'm sure of it."

Pol flashed a devious smile as he stepped through the front doors, leaving Cleo staring after him, uneasy and intrigued.

She lingered near the entrance a moment longer, arms crossed, her gaze fixed on the space where Pol had just stood. A creeping chill prickled down her spine, the kind that came not from cold but from instinct. She didn't believe in coincidences—not in her line of work. Not when a man with the same rare accent as Alek, who just so happened to be his brother, walked in off the street like something out of a dream—or a trap.

Turning on her heel, she walked briskly back to her office, the sound of her heels sharp and rapid. She sat at her desk but didn't return to her computer. Instead, she stared blankly at the screen, mind buzzing.

A brother. A big family. A string of flings? The words replayed in her head, each one scraping against the image of Alek she had constructed. She thought of the night before— the way he had looked at her, touched her, the things he'd said. He had seemed so sincere. But then again, sincerity could be rehearsed.

And he had never mentioned a brother. Or a family. Or anything, really.

Her fingers tapped restlessly on the edge of her desk. She didn't want to jump to conclusions, but the doubt was there now, burrowed deep. Why had he kept it all from her? What else wasn't he saying?

She reached for her phone, then stopped. No. Not yet.

She needed to see him. Look him in the eyes. Ask him—directly.

But what if she didn't like the answers? What if Jasper had been right? What if this connection she felt—the intensity, the comfort, the desire—was nothing more than a well-executed illusion?

Her stomach twisted at the thought. She didn't want to believe it. Part of her clung to the feeling she had when she was with him, to the way his presence seemed to quiet everything else in the world. But now that Pol had planted the seed, she couldn't help but wonder: how much of Alek was real, and how much was performance?

She didn't want to lose him. But she didn't want to lose herself either.

She hated this—being unsure, being vulnerable. Love wasn't supposed to come with this much shadow, was it?

Still, she had to know.

And she needed to be ready in case she didn't like what she saw.

Chapter 17

"How did the tour go?" Jasper asked.

Cleo looked up from her computer screen, brow furrowed. "Enlightening, you could say."

"What do you mean?"

"Well, it turns out our Mr. Pol is actually Mr. Pol Cooper."

"As in Alek Cooper?"

"Yep. His brother."

"Shut up! You're kidding."

"Nope. I didn't even know he had a brother—let alone multiple siblings."

"How many are we talking? Two or three?"

"I don't know. I didn't ask. Pol just said they had multiple brothers and sisters."

"Huh. I mean, it's definitely strange he hasn't mentioned coming from a big family, but to be fair, you two have only been seeing each other a short time. Maybe it just hasn't come up yet."

"I'm sure you're right, but he keeps changing the subject every time I bring up anything about his past or his family."

"Maybe I'm overreacting," she added, then glanced up. "But you're the one who told me I should be careful."

Jasper nodded, his expression darkening slightly. "Yeah, I did. And I meant it. There's just something about him... I can't put my finger on it. Too perfect, maybe. Too polished." He gave her a sympathetic look. "For your sake, I hope I'm wrong."

"When do you plan on seeing him next?" Jasper asked.

"Tonight. He invited me over for dinner. Staying in."

"Well then, that's your chance. Ask him tonight while you're eating. Maybe there's a reason he avoids talking about them. Could be something personal—like a falling out."

"Maybe," Cleo said softly. But as she stared down at her desk, her thoughts began to spiral.

Why won't he talk about them? Why won't he talk about anything? Her heart told her one story—how safe she felt with Alek, how drawn she was to him—but her mind was now writing a different one. A cautious one.

She tried to rationalize it. Maybe he's just private. Maybe he's been hurt. Maybe he doesn't want to scare me off. But every time she asked about his past, he steered them into another topic, one that left her more enchanted but no closer to understanding who he truly was.

And now this brother—Pol—had appeared, and with him came more questions than answers.

Cleo folded her arms tightly. She didn't want to feel like she was chasing shadows. But it was beginning to feel like Alek had built their connection on a carefully curated version of himself. One that didn't include where he came from, or who he really was.

"I guess I'll find out," she said again, but this time the words were less certain.

Jasper stood and grabbed his bag. "Well, I'm heading home. Hope it goes well tonight."

I'll follow you out," Cleo replied, grabbing her coat and briefcase.

Outside, the now-familiar sight of Alek's sleek black Rolls Royce waited at the curb.

"You have to admit," Jasper said with a grin, "he really does know how to treat a lady—even if he's got his secrets."

"You're not wrong," Cleo said with a half-smile. "Good night, Jasper."

"See you tomorrow."

"Good evening, Ms. Tenner," the chauffeur greeted as he opened the door for her.

"Good evening. How are you tonight?"

"Quite well, ma'am. Thank you for asking."

Cleo paused before getting in. Out of the corner of her eye, she thought she saw someone—tall, motionless—standing across the street. Her breath caught.

She blinked, and the figure was gone.

"Excuse me," she asked, turning to the chauffeur. "Did you see a man standing over there?"

He followed her gaze. "I'm sorry, ma'am, I must have missed him."

"Never mind," she murmured, climbing into the car. "Must've been my imagination."

As the door shut and the Rolls Royce glided away from the museum, Cleo scanned the sidewalk, the storefronts, the alleys.

Nothing.

As they turned the corner, she finally leaned back into the seat, exhaling slowly.

But unease still lingered at the edge of her thoughts, a shadow that hadn't quite vanished.

Chapter 18

Pol stood in the great hall, his boots echoing against the ancient stone like a storm approaching. The chamber was vast and cold, its ceiling lost in shadow, the flicker of celestial flame casting solemn patterns across the marble floor. He spotted Theo and Helena near the twin pillars—monuments older than any mortal civilization—locked in quiet conversation. He moved toward them with urgency.

"Theo," he said, his voice echoing in the vast space, "I've confirmed it. Anu is involved with a human. It's not speculation anymore. I've been watching them. Days, nights—more than chance meetings. He's definitely gone too far with her. I saw him leave her apartment the morning after a long evening, wearing the same clothes as the night before. That alone says enough."

Theo crossed his arms. "You followed him?"

"Yes," Pol replied without hesitation. "Because someone has to. He's not just dabbling—he's invested with this mortal. I confronted the woman. She said it herself—they're in a serious relationship. That's not casual. That's not curiosity. That's a violation."

"You confronted her? we told you to keep an eye on them, keep a distance, not confront anyone." Helena asked, alarm lacing her tone.

Pol shrugged. "She was harmless. Polite, even. She doesn't know who—or what—he really is. She thinks she's in love."

"And what does she think he feels?" Theo asked sharply.

"She said he feels the same."

Theo raised a skeptical brow, but before he could respond, Pol pushed forward.

"I spoke with the woman. She told me herself—they're in a serious relationship. If that's not a violation of one of our most sacred laws, I don't know what is."

"Pol," Theo interrupted, his voice edged with irritation. "Seeing Anu leave someone's apartment doesn't prove anything. We've all spent nights among humans. That doesn't mean we fall in love with them. Even if she believes it's serious, it doesn't mean he does."

Helena folded her arms, her voice calm and measured, yet laced with an ancient weight. "I find it difficult to believe Anu would tread the path Eros once did. Of all our kin, he has ever been the most tempered in heart and judgment. He walks among mortals not to indulge, but to guard. He remembers the price of folly better than most. He knows the cost—not only for himself, but for the entire realm of man and god alike."

Pol's voice sharpened, his frustration slipping into something colder. "That's what should terrify us. Anu has always walked the line between reverence and isolation. If this woman is changing that—if she's making him feel human—then we're past reason. If he bonds with her emotionally, spiritually... he won't just ignore our laws. He'll rewrite them. And then what? Who stops a god who believes love justifies anything?"

He stepped closer to Theo, the energy around him starting to crackle. "You know what happened to Eros. You know what could happen if he takes this relationship too far. And Anu? He's stronger than any of us. If he falls for this mortal and choses the same path as Eros and this mortal can't handle it, if she is consumed by power like Anesthesia, then the world won't be able to recover. Everything we have built could be destroyed."

Helena's voice cut through like steel. "Enough, Pol. You speak of him like he's a weapon pointed at the world. He's done more to protect humanity than any of us. Don't mistake devotion for danger.""

"That's precisely the point," Theo said firmly. "He is the most powerful. He's also the one who's done the most to protect the humans, even when the rest of us stepped away. I'm not starting a war over what might be nothing more than a distraction."

Pol's frustration flared, his tone rising. "So that's it, then? Eighty years ago, you took his word without hesitation to condemn me. But now that I bring you concern—real concern—you treat it like a petty rivalry?"

Theo's jaw clenched, and his voice dropped with a solemn gravity that echoed the weight of ages. "Because you have earned our doubt, Loki. You sowed discord in the hearts of mortals not out of necessity, but out of pride. You turned their faith into fire, their reverence into terror. You do not guide— you manipulate. You twist belief into chains and wield it like a blade."

Pol's temper broke. "Fine! If you won't act, then I will. You want proof? I'll get you proof."

With a flash of light and fury, he vanished.

Helena turned to Theo, her expression carved in unease, her voice like wind brushing stone. "We must speak to him. Not with accusation, but with forewarning. The storm that stirs in Pol's wake is not one we can ignore."

Theo's jaw was tight. "I'm not accusing him of breaking our laws."

"Not for that," Helena said. "To warn him about Pol. Because if Pol really means to bring this to the others... we may be closer to a second fall than we realize."

Chapter 19

She stared through the window of the Rolls Royce as it wound up the long driveway, and Alek's estate came into view. No matter how many times she saw it, the sight of the palatial home always stunned Cleo. Towering columns, trimmed hedges, and warm golden lights framed the estate like something out of a dream. She could already see staff lined up at the grand entrance—and to her surprise, Alek stood among them. He looked... nervous. Like a teenage boy waiting on a doorstep for his first date.

Cleo smiled at the thought.

The car came to a gentle stop. Alek opened the rear door himself, offering his hand. "Good evening, Ms. Tenner."

"Good evening, Alek."

Their smiles met like magnets. Cleo glowed with anticipation; Alek's smile was more reserved, like he was trying to keep something beneath the surface.

"What's on the agenda tonight?" Cleo asked as they stepped inside.

"I thought we'd begin with champagne by the pool, then dinner—lamb, I hope you're a fan—and we can end with a dessert cocktail in the drawing room... or a soak in the hot tub."

"I didn't bring a bathing suit," she teased.

"That won't be a problem," Alek said, smirking.

Cleo followed him through the house and out to the back. At first, she expected a tasteful pool and a handful of chaise lounges—perhaps a fountain or a well-placed sculpture. What greeted her, however, was an Eden carved from luxury and myth.

The air grew warmer as they stepped onto the flagstone patio. To the left, a massive waterfall cascaded over natural rock into a glistening turquoise pool. The water shimmered in the fading sun, reflecting the flicker of strategically placed lanterns and hidden lights beneath the surface. On either side of the pool's entrance, cherubs carved from white marble poured steady streams of water from ornate vessels, their stone eyes blank but somehow eternal.

In the center of the pool sat a concrete island, accessible by a narrow, arched bridge. On the island rose a towering four-tiered fountain, each level a masterwork of craftsmanship: Hercules locked in combat with the Nemean lion, Zeus casting a lightning bolt in mid-scream, Apollo in his chariot, eternal in pursuit of the dawn. The fountain hissed and sang, water trickling and rushing all at once, a harmony of movement and myth.

Beyond the pool stretched an expanse of manicured lawn and sculpted gardens, each segment dedicated to a different culture or mythos. Flowering vines curled over stone benches. Columns supported pergolas wrapped in wisteria. Bronze and marble gods stood in silent witness to it all, their shadows stretching long over the clipped grass.

Beyond the pool stretched acres of manicured lawn, dotted with classical sculptures and flowerbeds that seemed to go on forever.

"Wow," Cleo said, breath catching. "This isn't a pool. It's a private resort."

Alek chuckled. "There's a pool—right there."

"Yes, but it's the size of Lake Michigan, with a Greek monument in the middle."

"Do you think it's too much?"

"Well," she smiled, "everything about your life is too much. But it's beautiful."

"As far as I'm concerned, you are the most beautiful thing out here."

She blushed, leaning into the kiss he offered.

"Shall we sit?" Alek asked. "Poolside or by the fireplace and bar?"

"Fireplace," she said. "I'm not exactly dressed for a pool party."

They crossed the patio to the large, covered seating area. Alek waved one of his staff over. "Two glasses of champagne, please."

"Anything specific, sir?"

"Surprise us."

As the attendant disappeared, Alek turned to Cleo. "So, how was the thrilling world of museum curation today?"

"Oh, edge-of-your-seat excitement," she replied, smiling. "I had a donor come in for a private tour."

"Not my competition, I hope."

"Hardly," she said, laughing. "But... he did say he knows you. He claimed to be your brother."

Alek's face tightened. "Pol?"

"Yes. He made a small donation and asked for a private tour. I didn't realize he was your brother at first. But then I noticed the accent. When I saw his last name was Cooper, I asked. He confirmed it."

Alek didn't respond right away.

"I had a very enlightening conversation with him," Cleo continued, her tone growing more cautious, more thoughtful. "He talked about you a lot. About your distance from your family, how you always kept everyone—even them—at arm's length."

She paused. "I don't know, Alek. He was... charming. But something about him put me on edge. Like everything he said was carefully chosen, as if he wanted to plant ideas without saying anything outright."

"I speak to them as needed," Alek said, voice taut. "The only one I'm distant with is Pol."

"What else did my dear brother share?"

"Not much. He asked how I knew you. I said we were seeing each other. I didn't think it was a secret."

"It's not," Alek said quickly. Then, softer, "I just didn't think he would care to know."

A cloud passed over his face. Cleo saw it clearly—concern, not for himself, but for her.

"What's going on?" she asked.

Alek hesitated. "Pol isn't... a good person."

"What do you mean?"

"Just promise me, if he comes around again, call me. Stay away from him."

Cleo blinked. She had never seen Alek this serious. His voice was calm, but his body was tense.

"Should I be worried?" she asked. "Is there something you're not telling me? Is this some mafia situation? Or something worse?"

Alek managed a small smile. "I'm not in the mafia. And neither is my family. Pol just—he thrives on manipulation. He causes chaos for sport. If he seeks you out again, I need to know."

She studied his face. There was something in his eyes—fear? Not of Pol. Of what Pol might do to her.

"Okay," she said softly, but doubt lingered behind her eyes. A part of her trusted Alek—trusted the warmth in his touch, the sincerity in his gaze—but Pol's words echoed louder now. He'd known just how to needle her, just how to leave room for suspicion.

She wasn't afraid of Pol. Not yet. But the sense of unease he stirred in her hadn't dissipated—it had burrowed deeper, seeded itself in the back of her mind like a splinter she couldn't reach. His charm had felt effortless, too polished. Every compliment, every observation had felt loaded, like a carefully placed stone in a path he was laying for her to follow.

And now, seeing how rattled Alek was, she couldn't help but wonder—what did Pol know that she didn't? What if Alek wasn't just guarded, but hiding something bigger, something older than anything she could imagine? She'd spent her life uncovering truths buried in the dirt, in history, in myth. But what if the real mystery was the man beside her?

Was she falling for someone who only showed her half of himself? And if so... which half was real?

Alek nodded, but inside, his mind churned.

Pol had crossed a line. Not just by seeking Cleo out, but by engaging her—by trying to manipulate her. Pol didn't do anything without motive. And if he'd gone to Cleo, it meant he was trying to undermine trust, to poison the roots of what Alek had begun to build with her.

The weight of centuries pressed against his chest. He had spent lifetimes guarding the boundary between their world and this one. Now, in a heartbeat, Pol had breached it.

He couldn't lose Cleo. Not to doubt. Not to fear. Not to his brother.

He masked his thoughts with a smile, gentle but measured.

"That's enough family talk for one evening."

He gestured to a staff member. "Let's enjoy the night."

A moment later, as the champagne arrived, Alek leaned toward Cleo, his tone shifting to something playful.

"Before dinner," he said, "what do you say we go for a swim?"

Cleo tilted her head. "I told you—I didn't bring a bathing suit."

"That's fine," Alek said, standing and reaching for the buttons on his shirt. "I didn't plan on using one."

Cleo blinked in surprise as he slowly removed his shirt, revealing a torso carved from myth—every muscle defined in perfect symmetry, from his broad shoulders to the ridged lines of his abdomen. His chest was smooth and sculpted, tapering to a lean waist and powerful hips. The lantern light caught the contours of him, casting shadows that accentuated the deep cuts of his obliques and the narrow line of muscle that disappeared below his pelvis.

When he dropped his pants, Cleo's breath caught. He stood confidently in the firelight, unabashed and radiant— his naked body statuesque, virile, and unguarded. Every part of him felt unreal, like a living sculpture from a forgotten temple brought to life.

She watched, speechless, as he walked confidently toward the pool, the muscles in his back rippling with each step, his glutes tight and graceful. The glow of the lanterns shimmered across his skin like oil on marble. He dove in with elegant ease, his body cutting through the water like a god returning to his element.

Cleo exhaled slowly, biting her lip. "Fuck it," she whispered to herself. With a glance toward the pool, she stood and began to undress, her pulse racing as her clothes joined the soft night air.

She slipped into the water, the warmth embracing her, and swam to where Alek waited for her beneath the surface.

What followed was quiet at first—soft kisses, light touches beneath the water. Then passion bloomed like heat from beneath the surface, urgent and undeniable. Arms wrapped around torsos, hands slid over skin slick with water, and gasps replaced words as desire overtook restraint.

They drifted together in the center of the water, their bodies glowing under the soft shimmer of the lanterns. Alek brushed a wet strand of hair from Cleo's cheek.

"You look like you belong to this world," he murmured. "Like some sea goddess sent to torment me."

Cleo grinned, looping her arms around his neck. "And you? You strut out of your clothes like a man who knows exactly what he's doing."

"I do," he whispered against her skin, "but I like when you remind me."

They kissed, slow at first—hungry with tension. Then it deepened, lips parting, hands slipping beneath the surface. Alek pressed her back against the smooth curve of the pool wall, her legs wrapping instinctively around him. Her gasp echoed off the water as his mouth trailed down her throat.

The warmth of the water, the crash of the distant waterfall, and the glow of the night melted everything else away. They moved together with mounting urgency—skin on skin, breathless whispers between kisses, water lapping around them like a rhythm. Her fingers tangled in his hair, his hands gripping her hips as he drove deeper into her, each thrust a tether binding them tighter.

Cleo clung to him, overwhelmed by sensation. Her moans spilled into his mouth as he swallowed them in another kiss—possessive, reverent. Their pleasure crested in waves, crashing and building again until they both shattered in each other's arms, trembling and breathless.

When they finally drifted apart, bodies weightless and hearts pounding, Cleo rested her head on his shoulder, her breath still uneven.

"I think I'm in trouble," she whispered.

Alek brushed his lips to her temple. "So am I."

Chapter 20

Cleo woke to the sound of velvet drapes being flung open by one of Alek's maids. Morning light spilled into the room like liquid gold, igniting the silk sheets and gilded moldings. Startled and confused, she sat up, clutching the duvet over her bare chest.

"What's going on?" she asked, blinking.

Alek rolled over and let out a lazy, amused groan. "Relax. I asked them to wake us so you wouldn't be late for work."

Cleo blinked again, trying to absorb the surreal luxury around her. "I'm just... not used to this sort of thing."

"What sort of thing?" Alek mumbled, still half-asleep.

"The having-staff-open-your-curtains kind of thing."

She slid out of bed and gathered her clothes from the floor. "Aren't you worried they might see something?"

Alek smiled, stretching. "Not in the least."

By the time she stepped out of the en suite bathroom, fully dressed and composed, Alek was tying a robe loosely around himself—though it did little to hide his chiseled, golden-toned torso. Cleo eyed him with mock regret.

"Mmm. I wish I didn't have to go."

"So do I," Alek said, leaning in to kiss her. "Breakfast is ready in the dining room."

The table was set with a buffet fit for royalty: eggs, bacon, fresh-cut fruit, croissants, pastries, and a tower of gleaming muffins. Cleo filled a plate and sat down beside Alek, who joined her a moment later, robe still slightly parted.

"I could get used to this," Cleo said, raising a brow.

"The food?"

"That too."

Alek smirked and pulled his robe tighter. "Ms. Tenner, I'll have you know I'm not just a pretty face."

"That's what you think," she replied, biting into a piece of bacon. She glanced at her phone and groaned. "Ugh—I'm going to be late. Again."

She jumped up, kissed him goodbye, and snatched a muffin from the table. "I'll text you later."

"I'll be waiting," Alek said, watching her disappear down the corridor.

Moments later, standing alone by the window, Alek watched her car pull away. Behind him, a voice cleared its throat.

"Sir. You have two guests waiting in the drawing room."

He turned. One of his staff stood at attention.

"Thank you," Alek said. He had sensed another god's presence the moment they'd arrived. Now he knew who.

As he walked toward the drawing room, his robe shifted, reweaving itself into a tailored obsidian suit.

The doors opened.

Theo and Helena stood in the center of the room, their expressions tight with purpose.

"To what do I owe this pleasure?" Alek asked, stepping in.

"Hello, brother," Helena greeted softly.

"We come bearing grave tidings," Theo intoned, his voice resonant with the solemn weight of centuries. "Pol stirs once more, and the winds carry his discord across the realms."

Alek's jaw flexed. "He visited me a few days ago. I've felt his presence lingering ever since."

"You should know," Theo began carefully, "he's accusing you of violating the Eros Accord. He told us you're getting too involved with a human."

Alek didn't blink. "He saw me with her. That much is true. But she's a mortal companion, nothing more."

"We stood in your defense," Helena said, her voice like the rustle of parchment in an ancient temple. "But he is as a shadow that clings to the past. His hatred festers, nourished by the memory of betrayal. He holds fast to the wound you dealt him eighty mortal years ago."

"Of course he does," Alek muttered. "Pol was punished because he used humans like toys and threw kingdoms into ruin. I simply told the truth. But I don't believe retribution is his only aim."

"He doesn't see it that way," Theo said. "To him, your testimony was betrayal. And he has not forgotten."

Alek shook his head. "I've been waiting for him to act again. But I hoped—"

"That he'd grow up?" Helena offered with a sad smile.

"That he'd learn. But no," Alek continued, his voice tightening. "He's still the same chaos in a polished frame. And now, I believe he's plotting something greater. He wants more than revenge—he wants to pull me into a game of his making. Subtle provocations, whispered accusations—he's baiting me to make a move. And if I do, if I cross the line even once, he'll twist it, use it to validate his schemes. This isn't about the past anymore. This is a trap dressed as justice."

"Tread with care, Alek," Helena warned, her words weaving through the silence like sacred hymn. "What to us was just reprisal, to him was sacrilege. He would burn the firmament itself to reclaim what he believes was wrongfully taken. His vengeance will not be swift—it will be cunning, cruel, and carved with the precision of a dagger honed by centuries."

"Thank you for the warning," Alek said, his voice lowering. "If he makes another move—if he dares come near her—I will not show restraint."

Theo stepped closer, his expression grave.

"You remember the law etched in flame and thunder, Alek," Theo said, his tone steeped in the echoes of divine oath. "If your bond with the mortal defies the Accord, the judgment shall not fall upon you alone. She will suffer the fire meant for gods, and none among us may halt its course once it begins."

Alek met his gaze. "I know."

Theo nodded, then vanished in a soft flash of light. Helena gave Alek a lingering look.

"Come visit us. Before it's too late."

And then she, too, disappeared.

Left alone, Alek clenched his fists. The energy within him surged, divine and volatile. With a roar that shook the house, he unleashed it—windows shattered, crystal decanters burst, the chandelier above cracked and crashed to the marble floor.

He breathed hard, chest heaving. Glass rained down around him like a storm of broken stars.

Pol wanted war.

Alek was ready to give it to him.

But beneath the fury that roared through him like wildfire was something deeper—hotter. Not just anger. Not just defiance. It was the searing realization that Pol had dragged Cleo into this for no other reason than to get to him. She was innocent in all this, a woman who had only opened her heart to someone she thought she could trust.

And now she was a pawn.

Alek's jaw tightened. The shards of crystal crunching beneath his boots seemed insignificant next to the storm building in his chest. He could tolerate Pol's games. He could endure the petty slander and poisonous whispers. But this?

This was unforgivable.

He stared out through the shattered windows, the morning sun streaking across the floor in fractured bands of gold and fire. "You want to break me, brother? You want me to fall?" he growled. "Then come for me directly. Not through her. Never through her."

Because if Pol wanted to test the limits of his wrath— if he truly believed Alek could be manipulated into crumbling—he was about to learn what it meant to provoke a god who had something, someone, to protect.

And Alek would burn down eternity before he let Cleo suffer for Pol's vengeance.

He closed his eyes, drawing in a slow, shuddering breath. Power stirred within him—quiet, controlled, deliberate. The chaos he had just unleashed paused, suspended in the stillness of his command. Tiny shards of glass began to rise from the floor, shimmering as they lifted into the air.

The room glowed faintly, as if time itself had slowed in reverence. Pieces of the chandelier, the shattered decanters, and fractured crystal drifted like stars caught in orbit, gradually returning to their original shapes.

Bit by bit, what had been broken became whole again.

When Alek finally opened his eyes, the drawing room was as it had been before. Pristine. Immaculate. Silent.

But the fury behind his gaze had only just begun to burn.

Chapter 21

The shrill ring of Cleo's desk phone sliced through the quiet hum of her office, making her jump. She snatched it up.

"Ms. Tenner, there is a gentleman here to see you," the receptionist said.

"Who is it?"

"He says his name is Pol Cooper, ma'am."

Cleo froze, her expression shifting instantly. "Tell him I'll be right there."

She hung up the phone and sat back for a beat, her mind racing. She hadn't seen or heard from Pol since the unnerving tour he'd taken three months ago. He'd made a modest donation afterward—forgettable compared to Alek's. So why now? And what did he want?

Her heels clicked sharply on the polished museum floor as she made her way down the corridor, each step echoing like a countdown. She spotted him immediately— impeccably dressed, his smile gleaming like a blade under soft light.

"Good afternoon, Ms. Tenner," Pol said smoothly, his tone honeyed and too casual for Cleo's liking.

She met his gaze with one of her own—cool, composed. "Good afternoon, Mr. Cooper. How may I assist you today?"

"Please, call me Pol. We're practically family now, wouldn't you say?"

"Nearly," she said with a polite, practiced laugh. But something in her chest had coiled tight, the same instinct that warned her when someone tried to get too close too fast. Why did he always talk like they shared a secret she hadn't agreed to?

Pol stepped closer, his voice lowering. "I heard rumors—about a new exhibit. First Dynasty Egypt. True?"

Cleo hesitated, then nodded. "It's a concept that's been floated internally. Nothing official. No budget. No timeline."

"And yet," he said, eyes gleaming, "the winds carry word. I have my sources. Egyptian history is something of a passion of mine."

Cleo narrowed her eyes slightly. "That's interesting. Because only a handful of people in this building even know that exhibit's on the table. Did one of them happen to be your source?"

Pol smiled. "Like I said, I keep my ear to the ground."

"And the part about me leading the project? That's not public knowledge either. How did you know about that?"

He gave a casual shrug. "Just intuition, I suppose. Who else could possibly be more qualified than you?"

Cleo felt a chill work down her spine. The way he answered—so effortlessly deflecting while still managing to flatter—made her stomach twist.

He's being evasive, she thought. And way too smooth. This isn't just about interest in an exhibit. This is about control.

She raised an eyebrow, guarded. "Well, for now, the exhibit is just an idea."

"That's why I'm here." Pol leaned in, his eyes never leaving hers. "I want to fund it."

Cleo stiffened slightly. "That's... unexpected."

She straightened. "A donation?"

"No. I mean everything. The full cost. Front to back."

Cleo blinked. "That's incredibly generous."

"There are a few conditions, of course."

Of course there are, Cleo thought. There always are with people like you.

"Naturally," she said, her voice a degree cooler. "What are they?"

"I want you at the helm. Every detail, every decision—yours."

She nodded slowly. "That's something Jasper would have to approve, but I imagine it's workable."

"And," Pol said, a smile playing at the corner of his mouth, "I'd like to be part of it. Shadow you. Offer insight. Nothing invasive. Just... collaborative."

There it is, Cleo thought. The catch.

"I'll need to run it by Jasper," she said evenly. "And it will likely need board approval."

Pol tilted his head slightly, eyes narrowing. "Of course. I wouldn't expect anything less."

Cleo held his gaze. "Just so we're clear, if you're using this to stir things up with Alek, I'm not interested in being caught in the middle."

He chuckled softly. "Stir things up? Cleo, you wound me. This is about history—passion, legacy."

She kept her tone measured. "I'm just saying, if there's another motive, I'd rather you be honest."

Inside, her thoughts were churning. He was too slick, too polished. He didn't blink at confrontation—which only deepened her unease. Why go to such lengths? Why now? And why her?

"I'm in no rush. You know where to find me."

"I do."

He bowed his head slightly. "Until next time, Cleo."

She watched him leave, his tailored silhouette slipping into the sunlight beyond the museum's grand doors.

Her unease spiked. She turned back toward the front desk. "Is Jasper in his office?"

"I believe so, ma'am."

"Thanks."

Without knocking, she swung open Jasper's door. The familiar scent of coffee and old paper greeted her as she stepped inside. His office, a cozy chaos of books, architectural models, and framed historical prints, felt more like a curator's den than an administrator's workspace. A tall shelf brimming with museum catalogs leaned slightly to one side, while a globe-shaped bar cart sat beneath the window, untouched since the last board mixer. The light filtering through the Venetian blinds cut the room into soft gold and shadow. "You are not going to believe what just happened."

He looked up, blinking. "By all means, make yourself at home."

She closed the door behind her. "Pol just offered to fund the entire First Dynasty exhibit."

Jasper straightened. "What? How?"

"He said he has sources. Knew about the project before we even finalized anything."

"And?"

"He has conditions. He wants me to lead it. And he wants to work alongside me. Closely."

Jasper leaned back, running a hand through his hair. "That's... either a godsend or a grenade. Maybe both."

"My thoughts exactly. I'm going to talk to Alek tonight. There's something off about this whole thing, and it's more than just sibling rivalry. Pol knew too much—about the exhibit, about our internal planning timeline, even about my role in it. That's not coincidence. It felt orchestrated, like he was pushing specific buttons to get a reaction. And the way he kept trying to be familiar with me, smiling like he knew something I didn't... it just creeped me out. If he's playing some kind of game—and I'm almost sure he is—Alek needs to know before it escalates."

"Let me know what Alek says. I won't bring it to the board until I hear from you."

"Thanks, Jasper."

She left his office, her fingers tightening around the strap of her bag. The museum lights gleamed overhead like watchful eyes as she moved down the corridor, her thoughts spinning. Pol didn't just make an offer.

He made a move.

Chapter 22

The doorman welcomed Cleo to the five-star French restaurant where she was meeting Alek. As she stepped into the softly lit lobby, the rich scent of truffle oil and fresh bread enveloped her. The maître d' greeted her with a gracious nod.

"Good evening, madam. Do you have a reservation?"

"I'm meeting a Mr. Cooper. Is he here yet?"

"Of course, madam. Right this way."

Cleo followed him across the elegant dining room, where crystal chandeliers cast shimmering reflections against white linens and glassware. Alek was waiting at a table tucked into a secluded corner, his usual preference. He rose to greet her, the flickering candlelight catching the sharp angles of his face. As she sat, the maître d' helped with her chair.

"Thank you," Cleo said.

"Not a problem, madam. Your server will be with you momentarily."

"Thank you," she echoed.

"How was your day? I missed you," Alek said, his voice low and smooth.

Cleo laughed softly. "You saw me this morning."

"Not the same."

"It was... interesting," she said.

"How so?"

Cleo glanced around the dining room before leaning in slightly. "A donor came in today—out of nowhere—and offered to fund the entire Egyptian exhibit Jasper and I have been working on. The whole thing, no questions asked. It threw me."

The server arrived. "Can I get you anything to drink?"

"Another glass of wine, please," Alek said. "And the filet mignon."

"Excellent, sir. And you, ma'am?"

"Wine for me as well. And I'll have the boeuf bourguignon."

"Very good. The sommelier will bring your wine shortly."

As the server disappeared, Alek leaned forward. "So, who offered to fund your exhibit?"

Cleo hesitated, then said, "Pol."

A flicker of emotion passed through Alek's eyes—rage, perhaps, or something more primal. He masked it quickly.

"Really?"

"Yes. He just showed up this afternoon. Said he wanted to fund the whole thing. On the condition that I lead it... and that he work closely with me."

Alek's jaw tensed, but he forced a calm expression. "And what did you say?"

"That I'd talk to Jasper and the board. I haven't agreed to anything. But the whole thing feels strange. How would he even know about a project that isn't public?"

"He has his ways," Alek said darkly.

"That's what he told me. Exactly that."

Cleo tilted her head. "Do you think he's trying to provoke you? Or is this something else?"

Alek looked away for a long moment. Inside, his thoughts swirled like a gathering storm. This wasn't random—this was calculated. Pol was setting the first stone in whatever elaborate scheme he had been quietly building for months. The museum, the exhibit, Cleo—it was all part of a larger play, one Alek feared he was only beginning to see.

"I think this is the beginning of something he's been planning for a while. But I don't want you in the middle of it. If this happens, I need you to be careful. Don't let him get into your head. And if he tries anything—anything at all—you call me."

"Without hesitation," she said. "After what you've told me about him, I don't trust him either."

She paused, stirring her wine with an absent hand. "Maybe I should just tell him the board turned down his offer. I mean, it's probably what he deserves. But... it's such a great opportunity—for me, for the museum. It's hard to walk away from something that could do so much good just because I don't trust the man. And besides, he hasn't really done anything—he just likes to try and cause drama. I think he's a bit of a narcissist, to be honest with you."

Alek gave her a wan smile, though worry clouded his eyes. "Talking to him won't change anything anyway. Once Pol sets his mind to something, he doesn't let go."

Cleo leaned back, her appetite diminished by the weight of their conversation.

Alek cleared his throat. "On a happier note, there was something I wanted to discuss."

Her brows rose. "Oh?"

"You've been spending a lot of time at my estate these past few months. Practically every night. I thought... maybe it would make sense if you moved in."

Cleo blinked. "Are you serious?"

"I've never been more serious."

She was stunned. "Okay, um... Are you sure?"

"Yes. Not just because I want to be with you. But because I want you safe."

Cleo looked at him, her heart racing. The gesture was romantic—but also practical. And deeply revealing.

A thousand thoughts surged through her mind. Moving in with him would mean more than just love or proximity. It would mean crossing a threshold. She would be leaving behind the safety of her own space, her own rhythms, her independence—all for a man who, as much as she adored, still kept parts of himself shrouded in mystery. And then there was Pol. The whole situation reeked of something orchestrated, like she was a pawn on a board she didn't fully understand.

Was she walking into something... or being drawn in?

But then again, maybe it wasn't that complicated. Maybe it was just love.

Or maybe that's what made it so dangerous.

For Alek, the request was more than an invitation—it was a shield. The idea of her being far from him, vulnerable to Pol's manipulation, twisted something deep in his chest. If she stayed close, he could protect her, keep Pol's games from becoming anything more than whispers in the dark. Gods could fight each other, but Cleo? She was mortal. And Pol knew exactly where to strike.

"Let me think about it," she said.

"Don't take too long," Alek murmured, giving her a look that sent a shiver down her spine.

In that moment, surrounded by candlelight and shadows, Cleo felt the tectonic shift of something larger than either of them taking root. Something ancient. And irreversible.

Chapter 23

Cleo woke to the now-familiar sound of Alek's staff drawing back the bedroom curtains. The rustle of heavy fabric, the soft click of polished shoes on the marble floor—luxuries that still felt foreign to her. Golden morning light spilled in, warming the bedspread and brushing her bare skin with a gentle heat. For a moment, she lay still, wondering how long it would take for this strange new world to feel like her own. A faint smell of coffee and toast lingered in the air.

She slipped out from beneath the covers, pulled on a robe, and padded barefoot down the marble hallway to the dining room. There, Alek sat at the end of a long table, reading something on his phone with a half-eaten plate of eggs and toast in front of him.

"Good morning, beautiful," he said with a smile as she entered.

"Good morning. Why are you up so early?"

He put the phone down and smirked. "I was kept awake with anticipation."

She raised an eyebrow. "Of?"

"Your decision."

Cleo rolled her eyes. "I'll let you know tonight. It's a big one."

She leaned down and kissed him lightly. "Alright, I'm off. I need to stop by my place and change before work. I'll see you tonight."

As she turned to go, Alek called out, "Hopefully with a moving van!"

"Shut up," she called back with a laugh.

***

Driving through the city, Cleo wrestled with her thoughts. Moving in. The idea was both exhilarating and terrifying. She hadn't lived with anyone since college, and even then, it was different. This was real, intimate. Permanent. She loved Alek—that much she was beginning to accept—but the shadows that lingered around his past, especially when it came to Pol, made her hesitate.

As she pulled up in front of her apartment building, her breath caught. Pol was casually strolling down the sidewalk toward her, dressed impeccably as always. His smile unfurled like silk when he saw her.

"Cleo? What a pleasant surprise running into you this morning."

She stepped out of the car slowly. "Pol. What are you doing here?"

"Just exploring the city. Still fairly new to it, so I thought I'd wander. Beautiful day for it."

Cleo forced a polite tone. "Right, of course. Just caught me off guard, that's all."

"Late night? Or early morning?"

"Neither. Stayed at Alek's. Just came back to change before work."

Pol smiled wider, like her answer confirmed that she and Alek were growing closer, just as he had suspected. Cleo felt a flicker of unease—was he probing for cracks in their relationship, or simply cataloging facts for some larger, hidden agenda?

"Well, I won't keep you. Let me know what the board decides about the exhibit."

"Certainly," she said, offering a tight smile.

As soon as she was inside the building, Cleo rushed to her window and peered out. She watched as Pol leisurely turned the corner and disappeared down the block. A chill ran down her spine.

He knows where I live.

She'd never told him. Alek wouldn't have either. It was too coincidental. Too calculated.

What is he playing at?

***

She arrived at the museum flustered, her heart still pounding. As she ran through the lobby, the guard greeted her. "Morning, Dr. Tenner."

"Morning," she puffed.

Jasper was waiting just inside, glancing at his watch.

"Look at that—you beat yesterday's record. Still late, though," he grinned.

"Ha-ha, hilarious," she replied.

He followed her to her office.

"I wanted to tell you, I went ahead and emailed the board last night about Pol's proposal."

Cleo turned sharply. "I thought you said you'd wait."

"I did. Then I didn't," he said, shrugging. "The board said yes. They're greenlighting the whole thing."

"Even the part about him being involved?"

"Every detail. They loved it. Said it was an extraordinary opportunity. For you especially. If it goes well, you'll be on every museum's radar in the country."

Cleo sank into her chair. "That's what I'm afraid of."

"How did it go with Alek last night?"

Cleo hesitated for a moment, then glanced up. "He asked me to move in with him."

Jasper blinked. "Whoa. Really? Already?"

She gave a half-smile. "Yeah. He said it just makes sense since I'm there all the time anyway."

Jasper tilted his head, watching her carefully. "And how do you feel about that?"

"I don't know. That's the thing. It feels fast, and with everything going on... I just—I need to think it through."

"You definitely should," Jasper said, his tone soft but serious. "Just promise me you'll really think about it. Don't make any decisions because you feel swept up in the moment. You don't have to prove anything to him—or to yourself."

Cleo nodded, her fingers tracing the edge of her desk. "I know. It's just hard." Her mind flicked through every look Alek gave her, every secret he hadn't shared. There was love, yes, but also mystery—a heavy curtain she wasn't sure she had the strength to pull back. Was she stepping into something deeper than she could handle, or simply into a life she hadn't dared dream of? I care about him so much, but I also feel like I still don't know the full story.

"Did you tell Alek about Pol's proposal yet?" Jasper asked, watching her closely.

Cleo gave a small nod. "I did. I told him over dinner. His reaction was composed—calm on the outside—but I could tell it rattled him. He said Pol's probably setting something in motion, but he's not sure what. He just told me to be careful. He didn't push me or try to control the situation, but I could see it—something in his eyes changed the second I mentioned Pol."

"That must've been tough to bring up. What did he say when you told him about Pol's offer?"

"He wasn't surprised. Said Pol's likely up to something, but whatever it is, he doesn't know yet. He warned me to be careful."

Jasper frowned. "You trust him?"

"I trust Alek. But I also think there's a whole history between them that he hasn't told me."

She hesitated, then added, "There's more. I saw Pol this morning. Right outside my building."

Jasper sat up. "What?!"

"Said he was just walking around, learning the city. But I've never told him where I live. It's too much of a coincidence."

"You think he followed you?"

"I don't know. But it felt wrong. Like I was being watched."

Jasper nodded slowly. "Tell Alek. Tonight. Don't wait."

"I will. I just didn't want to mess with his day. He gets so cold when Pol comes up. It's like a switch flips and he turns into another person."

Jasper leaned against the wall, arms crossed. "Then you better be sure you're not moving in with a stranger wearing a familiar face."

Cleo didn't answer. She just stared at her desk, her fingers laced in her lap, her mind a whirlwind.

"Do you want me to call Pol and give him the good news?" Jasper asked.

She shook her head and reached for the phone.

"No," she said quietly. "I'll do it. Let's get it over with."

She began to dial, the receiver cold against her ear.

Outside her office window, clouds began to roll in, dark and low, curling like ink across the sky. The light in her office dimmed, and a faint pressure settled in the air, mirroring the heaviness that had taken root in her chest. A storm was coming—outside, and maybe inside too.

Chapter 24

Pol's phone began to ring. He pulled it from his pocket and smiled as the museum's number flashed across the screen.

"Hello, this is Pol," he answered smoothly.

"Yes, hello, this is Cleo Tenner from the museum. How are you?" she asked.

"Better now that I'm talking to you. Do you have some news for me?"

"I do, in fact. That's why I'm calling. We heard back from the board and they've agreed to your conditions. We'd like to move forward with the exhibit."

"Excellent. Would you be free this afternoon to go over a few of the details?"

"I am. How does three o'clock sound?"

"Perfect. I look forward to seeing you then."

Cleo ended the call and looked up at Jasper, who was still standing in her office.

"So it begins," Jasper said, raising his eyebrows.

Cleo smiled devilishly. "I don't know what you're smiling about—you're going to be there too."

"Oh, I have too much to do."

"No, you're not getting out of it that easily. You're the museum director, and even though I'm running point on this exhibit, you still need to be there. Besides, I'd feel more comfortable if you were there."

Jasper looked at her and sighed. "Fine."

"Great. That gives you a few hours to do whatever it is you do all day, and I'll get everything ready."

"I'm going to go now and do whatever it is I do all day—with your permission, of course," Jasper said sarcastically as he headed toward the door.

Cleo smiled and turned back to her computer, focusing on the exhibit proposal. Her phone buzzed. Two messages from Alek:

Alek: I'll pick you up from work tonight if you're okay with it.

Alek: I made reservations for us.

She smiled and typed a simple reply:

Cleo: OK.

***

The day slipped by as she dove into her work. Her desk phone rang, jolting her from her thoughts. She answered.

"Dr. Tenner, there's a Mr. Pol Cooper here to see you."

"Thank you, tell him I'll be right there."

She grabbed her laptop and printouts and headed to Jasper's office.

"Ready? He's here," she announced.

Jasper looked up from his desk. "Do I have a choice?"

They walked to the reception area where Pol was admiring a display.

"Pol," Cleo greeted.

He turned and smiled. "Good afternoon."

"I've asked Dr. Carrera to join us since he's the museum director."

Pol looked mildly surprised and possibly irritated. "That's not a problem. Good to see you again, Jasper."

"You too," Jasper replied, shaking Pol's hand.

"I have everything ready. Shall we?"

"Let's do it," Pol said enthusiastically.

As they walked, Jasper leaned toward Cleo. "Now I see why you wanted me here. Did you catch the look on his face when you said I'd be joining?"

"Yeah. Something doesn't sit right with me about him."

They entered the conference room—a grand space with high arched ceilings, classical busts lining the walls, and a long oval table that gleamed beneath the soft light of a vintage chandelier. Cleo laid her documents out across the table.

"I thought we'd begin with the history leading to the unification of Upper and Lower Egypt," Cleo began, clicking open her laptop. "We'll open the exhibit with an introduction to the pre-dynastic period and then move into the reign of Pharaoh Narmer—"

"He preferred Menes," Pol interjected.

Cleo paused, measured her breath. "Yes, also known as Menes. We'll include both names to provide context for visitors."

"But Menes should be the primary name. Out of respect."

Jasper raised an eyebrow. "You two on a first-name basis?"

Pol chuckled softly. "Of course. He was a good friend of mine," he said, not entirely joking, his tone straddling the line between jest and eerie conviction.

Cleo smiled tightly, masking her discomfort. There he goes again—like he's lived it. Just like Alek does at times. Like he was there.

She pressed on. "The exhibit will showcase artifacts from both Upper and Lower Egypt—flint knives, early hieroglyphic inscriptions, and some of the ivory tags associated with Narmer's reign. We're hoping to secure a replica of the Narmer Palette to explain the symbolic act of unification."

Pol leaned forward, folding his hands. "The original Palette is in Cairo, but I can reach out to some old colleagues there. They might be willing to loan it for the right diplomatic strings."

Cleo blinked. Old colleagues? Seriously? Does he just say these things to mess with me, or does he actually have these connections?

Jasper shot her a glance as if to say, Is he for real?

"That would be... phenomenal," Cleo replied cautiously. "Thank you."

She continued presenting her ideas, including interactive digital timelines, a reconstructed burial display, and an immersive audio-visual introduction narrated with ancient myths.

Pol nodded through it all, occasionally chiming in with oddly specific notes. "Make sure you feature Nekhen. It was the religious center before Memphis. Most people overlook it."

Why does he know that off the top of his head? Cleo thought. It's like he doesn't even need to research this stuff.

"I believe that covers everything," Cleo said finally. "Please write down any suggestions or questions. We'll meet again next Friday to finalize logistics."

Her phone buzzed. A message from Alek:

Alek: I'm waiting in the lobby. Take your time.

Cleo: On my way.

"Gentlemen, I have to run," she said, packing her materials.

"I'll walk you out," Pol offered. "I may know a few people at the Cairo museum who could help."

"Of course you do," Cleo murmured.

They walked through the museum's winding corridors. Pol continued listing names and institutions, speaking with an ease that unnerved her.

He's not just playing a role. He knows these people. He's not bluffing.

As they stepped into the lobby, Cleo spotted Alek.

"You didn't tell me my brother was here," Pol said, voice low.

"We have plans," Cleo replied.

Alek looked up. The second he saw Pol, his expression darkened—his jaw tensed, his eyes narrowed with an intensity that hinted at more than just sibling rivalry. A flicker of something older, more dangerous, passed behind his gaze. His spine straightened slightly, as if instinctively preparing for a confrontation he'd long expected but hoped to avoid.

"Alek! How nice to see you," Pol said, too cheerful.

"Pol," Alek replied, his voice flat.

"We just finished going over ideas for the exhibit," Cleo added quickly.

"I'm quite excited to see how it turns out," Pol said, flashing a smile.

"Nice seeing you. We need to be going," Alek said, wrapping a protective arm around Cleo. She could feel the tension radiating off him—the rigidness in his body, the quiet storm building just beneath the surface. Something in the air seemed to coil tighter with each second they stood there, like a thread about to snap.

Pol's smile didn't fade. "Yes, I'll see you soon."

"You can count on it," Cleo said politely.

But inside, her stomach turned. He wasn't just talking about the exhibit.

Chapter 25

Alek's sleek black Rolls-Royce glided to a stop in front of an opulent theatre tucked into a historic corner of downtown. The marquee lights cast a golden hue across the sidewalk, reflecting in the puddles left behind by an earlier rain. As always, the driver stepped out with polished precision and opened the door.

Cleo blinked against the warm glow spilling from the entryway, her tired gaze drifting to Alek as he exited behind her.

"Where are we?" she asked, her voice edged with fatigue.

"This, my dear," Alek said with a small smile, offering her his arm, "is a dinner theatre. We'll enjoy a four-course meal while watching a new rendition of A Streetcar Named Desire. But based on your tone, I find myself hoping I haven't miscalculated."

Cleo shook her head, managing a sheepish smile. "No, it sounds great. I didn't mean to sound ungrateful—I'm just a little worn out. Planning the new exhibit and dealing with your brother's endless suggestions has been... a lot."

Alek paused and turned to face her fully. "We can call it a night and head back to the estate. Truly, it's no trouble."

"No," she said quickly, reaching for his hand. "The show sounds like the perfect distraction. Honestly, I could use a drink and a few hours to forget about work."

Inside, the theatre shimmered with old-world charm. Ornate gold moldings curved along the ceiling, and a crimson velvet curtain swayed gently on stage. Crystal chandeliers hovered overhead like frozen fireworks, their light catching in Cleo's hair. An usher led them up a grand staircase to the second-story balcony, where a small table awaited— centered perfectly for an unobstructed view of the stage.

Alek pulled out her chair with quiet elegance. Cleo sat, smoothing her dress. She had long since stopped trying to argue with him about the extravagance. This was his world: seamless luxury and thoughtful excess.

At first, it had overwhelmed her—the quiet hum of wealth, the whispered promises of ease. But now, the velvet-lined walls and champagne flutes felt almost familiar.

She glanced sideways at him, watching the way he leaned back with casual grace, scanning the theatre below. There was no smugness in his demeanor, just comfort. This wasn't a performance for her benefit. It was simply who he was.

Still, uncertainty tugged at the edges of her thoughts. Was she losing something of herself by entering his world? Or was she gaining something she had always deserved?

She remembered her university days—how she'd scraped by, juggling late-night shifts and endless lectures. The weight of student loans still pressed against her every decision. She had built her independence brick by brick, never allowing herself to rely on anyone.

Now here she was, being offered something most would only dream of: love wrapped in silk sheets, devotion housed in a palatial estate.

But love was the part she couldn't measure.

As the lights dimmed and the first course arrived, Cleo found herself relaxing. The food was exceptional, the wine perfectly chilled. She let her fingers graze Alek's beneath the table. He turned to her, catching her glance, and smiled in that way that always made her breath catch.

Midway through the second act, during intermission, Cleo leaned closer. "I've been thinking... about moving in with you."

Alek straightened slightly, his attention narrowing. "And?"

"I think I will," she said, a soft blush creeping across her cheeks. "It makes sense. I'm there most nights anyway, and lugging my stuff back and forth every day is kind of ridiculous."

Alek's eyes glinted with amusement. "So, this is purely logistical? I suppose I'll take what I can get."

She nudged his shoulder playfully. "Don't let it go to your head."

"Shall I call a moving company while you're at work tomorrow?"

"No, no need. I'm not bringing everything just yet. I'll pack the essentials after work and bring them over. The rest can come gradually."

Alek hesitated, his tone light but his eyes serious. "So you're keeping the apartment?"

"For now," she admitted. "Maybe I'll sublease it later."

"I want you to be comfortable, Cleo. This isn't a test. Take the time you need. I just want you with me, in whatever way feels right to you."

Her shoulders softened. "Thank you."

As the curtain rose for the final act, Cleo felt something settle within her. Not certainty—but courage. Maybe this wasn't a step into something unknown. Maybe it was a step toward home.

Alek, sitting beside her, felt the same shift. He exhaled slowly, grounding himself in the knowledge that she had chosen to stay. But even as relief unfurled in his chest, another emotion bloomed—dread. Now that she would be living under his roof, it would be easier to watch over her, to shield her from whatever storm Pol was conjuring. But that same closeness could make her a more direct target. If Pol truly intended to strike, Cleo wouldn't just be caught in the middle—she'd be the catalyst. Alek clenched his jaw, the muscle ticking with restrained fury. This wasn't just about love anymore. It was about war. And Pol, ever the strategist, had just positioned Cleo squarely on the battlefield.

Because Pol's shadow was growing longer. And the real war, Alek feared, was only beginning. A war not just for revenge, but for dominion. Pol didn't merely want to punish Alek for what happened all those decades ago—he wanted to remake the world in his image. To pull the divine veil back over humanity, not to protect, but to rule. His ambition was ancient, twisted by time and solitude, and now he was dragging Cleo into the very heart of it. That, Alek could never allow.

Chapter 26

As the dinner show came to a close, the applause still echoing through the grand theatre hall, Alek and Cleo made their way out into the night and into the waiting embrace of Alek's Rolls-Royce. Rain had begun to fall again, light and misty, blurring the city lights into rivers of gold on the pavement.

The driver pulled out smoothly, guiding them onto the interstate.

"Did you enjoy the show?" Alek asked, his voice low and warm.

"I did," Cleo said, leaning back against the plush leather seat. "The food was incredible. Thank you."

"For what?" he asked, tilting his head toward her.

"For everything. For not pushing me about selling my apartment. For the evening. For just... being you."

He reached over, taking her hand gently in his. "You never need to thank me, Cleo. I love you. You deserve every kindness this world has to offer."

∎∎

Above the city, where the interstate carved through the sprawling dark like a silver vein, Pol stood on a service access ramp, cloaked in shadow.

His golden eyes glinted beneath the hood of his coat, fixed on a flatbed truck ahead. It rumbled forward, hauling massive reels of industrial cable, each one bound by thick chains and reinforced straps. Mortals and their flimsy precautions.

Pol raised one hand, his fingers splayed.

With a sharp flick of his fingers, the steel chains holding the spools snapped—silent to the human ear but deafening in the fabric of reality. Like threads cut from fate itself.

He didn't need to watch the chaos unfold. He could already see it.

The first spool broke loose.

The truck driver felt the sudden shift in weight too late.

The second roll slipped from its mooring, slamming into the side rail before bouncing back into traffic.

Screams. Brakes. Horns.

Pol smiled.

A slow, cold smile.

"Let's see how well the mighty Anu protects what he loves."

***

"I love—"

The car suddenly veered sharply right, cutting off Cleo's words.

Cleo was flung against the interior panel with a cry of pain as the vehicle lurched violently. Tires shrieked against wet asphalt. The driver's voice rose above the chaos. "Hold on!"

Outside, headlights spun, horns blared, and the shriek of twisting metal filled the air. A semi-truck ahead had lost control. Its massive load of industrial cable reels had broken free—several enormous rolls had bounced off the trailer and begun careening across lanes like runaway wrecking balls.

One of them barreled into a minivan in the center lane, caving in the roof and flipping it onto its side with a sickening crunch. Another collided with a guardrail and exploded into fragments, sending metal shards across the road like shrapnel.

The driver swerved hard, narrowly avoiding a rolling spool the size of a compact car. The Rolls-Royce jerked to the side, bounced once, and finally skidded to a halt on the shoulder with a jarring impact.

Alek whipped around, heart thundering. "Cleo!?"

She didn't answer.

"Cleo!" he shouted, panic slicing through his voice. She was slumped against the door, motionless.

He scrambled out of his seatbelt, sliding over to her. Her head had struck the interior panel. A thin ribbon of blood trickled down her temple.

"Cleo, please—"

Her eyes fluttered open, dazed. "What... what happened?"

"There was an accident. We avoided the worst of it, but you hit your head."

"I feel dizzy," she murmured.

"You need a hospital," Alek said firmly.

"No. Just take me home. I don't want the lights, the chaos. Please."

He hesitated, brushing her hair gently away from her face. "Alright. But I'm calling someone to come check you out at the estate."

"Fine."

The driver called back. "Sir, are you alright? We're clear—no damage to the car."

"Good. Let's get out of here."

The Rolls-Royce eased back onto the shoulder, weaving carefully around the wreckage. Ambulance sirens wailed in the distance. A police cruiser pulled up near the jackknifed semi. Flashing red and blue lights painted the surrounding vehicles in pulses of urgency.

As they passed the truck, Alek's senses prickled. There, standing casually near the chaos, was Pol. Hands in his pockets. Smiling.

Alek's jaw clenched.

Pol raised a hand and waved.

A taunt.

Alek turned his attention back to Cleo and squeezed her hand. She leaned her head gently against his shoulder. She didn't see the smirk. She didn't feel the fire roaring in his blood.

Back at the estate, the physician and nurse arrived moments after they did. Cleo was helped inside and led to the drawing room for examination.

Alek stood at the threshold, arms crossed, jaw clenched. The firelight from the nearby hearth flickered against his face, casting deep shadows under his eyes.

Pol didn't strike like a thunderbolt. He struck like a rumor. Like fear. He sowed chaos not just in blood but in anticipation—always the slow tightening of the noose.

The doctor emerged. "She'll be alright. Minor concussion. No stitches needed. Keep an eye on her tonight."

Alek offered a strained smile. "Thank you."

Cleo joined him in the foyer, her steps careful but steady.

"I told you I was fine," she said.

"I know," he murmured. "But seeing you like that..."

"I just want to sleep."

"You go. I'll be up soon."

Cleo nodded and ascended the stairs.

Alek retreated to the library, pouring himself a scotch he barely touched. The fire crackled, but the warmth didn't reach him.

Pol's message had been loud and clear: I can reach her any time I want.

And worst of all, Alek knew Pol wasn't finished. This was only the beginning.

He wanted more than revenge.

He wanted rule.

To drag the divine back into dominion over mankind. To unveil the gods not as myth, but as masters.

And Cleo—brilliant, beloved Cleo—was no longer just in the line of fire.

She was the lever.

She was the thing Pol believed would break him.

But Pol was wrong.

Alek wouldn't break.

He would burn.

Chapter 27

The library had never felt more like a cage. Its vaulted ceiling and towering shelves of books offered no wisdom that could still Alek's turbulent thoughts. He paced, arms folded tightly, brows furrowed, as the storm outside lashed rain against the windows like ghostly fingers.

Pol. That bastard.

Last night should have been a quiet celebration. Instead, it turned into a warning shot from the one person Alek could never trust, yet couldn't fully destroy. He clenched his jaw as the image of Cleo's blood appeared again in his mind—a flash of red on porcelain skin.

He stopped pacing and stared into the fire. The flames reminded him of Pol's smile—bright, consuming, cruel. Was Cleo in immediate danger? Or was this another game? And what would happen if Pol escalated?

Alek could barely breathe under the weight of his restraint. He had kept the truth from Cleo to protect her. Now he feared that very silence might cost her everything.

He pulled his phone from his pocket and dialed. It rang only once.

"Hello, brother," Pol's voice came, dripping with feigned civility.

"We need to talk," Alek said, tight.

"Ominous. But fine. Meet me at the bluffs just outside the city."

The call ended.

Alek looked down at the phone's screen—it had fractured from his grip. A second later, his body vanished in a crackle of light.

***

The bluffs outside the city loomed high and jagged above the crashing ocean. The wind howled across the rocky ledge, whipping Alek's coat around his legs as he appeared in a flare of lightning.

Pol stood near the edge, arms folded, a ghost of amusement tugging at his lips.

"Hello, Anu."

"It's Alek now."

Pol rolled his eyes. "Yes, yes. Your mortal identity. Forgive me if I find it... quaint."

"Why did you do it?" Alek asked without preamble.

"Do what? Watch a truck lose its cargo? Mortals build such fragile machines."

"Don't lie to me. You orchestrated that accident."

Pol chuckled. "And if I did?"

"She could have died."

"So what if she had? She's just a mortal," Pol said with a slow, deliberate shrug. Then he paused, watching Alek's reaction with a gleam of recognition in his eye. "Unless..." A grin spread across his face. "So it is true then, you do love her."

Alek didn't answer.

Pol stepped forward. "You turned the others against me. You judged me for guiding history—for being the spark that set the world ablaze."

"You sparked war. You fed on chaos."

"And you fed on their adoration," Pol snapped. "Their prayers, their temples. Don't pretend you didn't revel in it."

"We made a pact. We protect humanity. We guide, not control."

Pol hissed. "You set the rules. You call the meetings. You punish those who step out of line."

Alek narrowed his eyes. "What do you want?"

Pol's smile faded into something colder, more resolute. "I want the world to remember what it means to fear the divine. I want to walk among mortals, not as a shadow, but as a god—and I want them to kneel. And I need your help to do it."

Alek stared at him, incredulous. "You want me to help you conquer humanity?"

"Think about it, brother," Pol said, stepping closer. "You and I—together again. The creators reborn as rulers. No more hiding, no more pretending. We were worshipped once, we can be worshipped again. All it takes is one spark. One show of power. I know the humans. They'll fall in line. They always do."

Alek's voice turned to ice. "And Cleo?"

Pol gave a lazy shrug. "She lives. Untouched. Unbothered. I walk away from her forever. I won't say a word to the others about your... violation of the pact. But only if you stand with me. Help me retake the world."

"You want me to trade her life for your empire."

Pol's grin returned. "I want you to choose your family. I want you to choose power."

Alek's jaw clenched. For a moment, silence stretched between them, the wind screaming in their ears.

Then Alek spoke, calm and unflinching. "No."

Pol's face twitched. "Think about what you're saying. If you stand against me, I won't hold back."

"Then don't. But you will leave Cleo out of this."

"I don't take orders from you anymore," Pol sneered.

"Then this is war."

"So be it," Pol said, and vanished in a burst of golden smoke.

***

Alek stood alone on the cliff, fists clenched, the storm answering the storm within. The wind ripped around him in a deafening roar, his long coat snapping like a banner in battle. He trembled—not with fear, but with rage.

His breath hitched as the fury overcame him. He threw his head back and roared—a raw, thunderous sound that split the sky. Lightning surged around him in jagged arcs. His feet cracked the stone beneath him. Thunder echoed over the ocean like the war drums of old.

He raised his hands to the heavens, palms splayed, and a bolt of lightning, blinding and pure, exploded from the clouds, striking the very place Pol had stood.

Another, and another, until the entire bluff was illuminated in a strobe of celestial fire.

When the light finally died and the wind began to settle, Alek stood panting in the silence, smoke rising from the scorched stone around him.

"So be it," he whispered. "War it is."

And with that, he vanished in a final crack of thunder.

Chapter 28

Alek reached for his cell phone and typed a message to the one person he knew he could trust—the one who had stood by his side through eons of wars, exiles, and reckonings. "I need your help. Can we talk?"

The moment he pressed send, a gust of wind swirled behind him, brushing the drapes as if the house itself exhaled. The air thickened, tinged with the sharp scent of pine and wildflowers. He turned just in time to see a young woman reclining—casually and confidently—across the velvet chaise lounge. She looked as though she had been born of moonlight.

Her dark hair tumbled over her shoulders in tousled waves, glinting with streaks of silver that shimmered subtly under the lamplight. She wore a sleek leather jacket over a fitted black top and jeans, an anachronistic blend of streetwise style and timeless grace. Around her neck hung a delicate crescent moon pendant that pulsed faintly with celestial energy. Her eyes—piercing and silver-flecked—sparkled with mischief but held the steely clarity of someone who had hunted gods and monsters alike. A band of carved obsidian, inlaid with starlight, circled her wrist, and at her side lay a quiver of ethereal arrows, only half-glimpsed—fading in and out of the mortal realm.

This was who mortals had once known as Artemis—the Huntress, daughter of Zeus and Leto, twin sister to Apollo. Guardian of the wilderness, mistress of beasts, protector of the innocent and the wild. Her presence exuded the quiet power of ancient forests and moonlit glades. Once worshipped in marble temples and sacred groves, she now drifted through the modern world cloaked in leather and shadow, equally at home with a bow or a smartphone.

"Al! Long time no see!" she chirped with a radiant grin, kicking one booted foot over the other with feline ease.

"Artemis," Alek breathed, the tension in his voice softening. "That was quick."

"Well," she said, twirling a silver ring around her finger, "when one gets a message from the great and mighty Anu, one doesn't dawdle. Also, it's Ari now. Modern name for a modern world. So, what's up?"

Alek sank beside her, his hands clasped tightly between his knees. His shoulders sagged under the weight of his thoughts.

"Oh no," Ari said, her tone shifting. "This is serious."

"I made a mistake," he admitted. "A big one."

She raised an eyebrow. "You? The architect of laws, guardian of humanity? What kind of mistake are we talking about?"

He exhaled slowly, the words thick with meaning. "I fell in love with a human."

Ari blinked. "Wait—what? Okay, but that's not illegal. Well, I mean, it is... technically. Loving a human isn't a violation unless you're actually in a relationship with them and then decide to do what Eros did. That's when it crosses the line."

"I am in a relationship," he said quietly but firmly. "But I would never do what Eros did. Ever."

She sat back with a nod. "Okay. So just be careful and don't let the others find out. Problem solved—unless there's another problem?"

"Pol," he growled. "He knows. And he's going to use her to get to me."

Ari's mouth twisted. "That wanker. Still nursing a grudge from the forties, huh?"

"This isn't just about revenge. He wants more than retribution. He wants humanity to worship us again. He wants power. Fear. And he sees Cleo as my weakness—his leverage."

"Would he actually hurt her?" she asked, her voice tightening.

"Yes," Alek said without hesitation. "He won't stop unless I join him—or until he breaks me."

Ari's expression darkened. For a moment, the goddess of the hunt was silent, calculating. The air around her shimmered faintly, like moonlight on water.

"We all know Pol can be irrational and extreme— especially when he feels wronged. You really think he'd hurt this Cleo?"

"I do. I spoke with him earlier—begged him to leave her alone. He said there's no chance unless I help him with his latest world domination scheme."

"I believe you. So how can I help?" Ari asked.

"I need someone to watch over her when she's not with me. I obviously can't tell her who I really am or what's happening, but she needs protection. Someone to watch for anything Pol might try—accidents, manipulation, fate itself. Can you do that while I deal with him?"

"Of course I'll help you," she said without hesitation. "You're my favorite brother, after all. And besides, I owe you for helping me with that, uh, thing that one time." Her form shimmered, the crescent moon pendant glowing brighter. "I've guarded mortals before. I can do it again. Besides," she added with a sly smile, "I never liked Pol anyway."

She leaned in, voice low and sincere. "Now tell me everything I need to know about this mortal."

Chapter 29

Cleo sat at her desk the next morning, forehead bandaged, fingers dancing across her keyboard. The museum was quiet, save for the faint hum of fluorescent lights and distant chatter from the atrium.

Jasper leaned into the doorway, coffee in hand. "So... what happened to your head?"

Cleo sighed, looking up. "Alek and I were driving home and had to swerve to avoid an accident. I smacked my head pretty hard against the side of the car."

"Damn. That sounds rough. You okay?"

"Alek had a doctor come over last night and check me out. He insisted. He practically carried me inside and wouldn't let me move until the doctor arrived. Sat right beside me the whole time, arms crossed like some kind of immovable statue, glaring at the poor doctor like he might miss something. He said I'd be fine—just a mild concussion, apparently. But honestly, I think Alek needed to hear it more than I did."

She hesitated, then glanced around before lowering her voice. "There's something else, though. When I came to—

I could've sworn I saw Pol standing along the side of the road."

Jasper blinked. "Pol? Like, Pol Cooper?"

She nodded slowly. "But I think it must've been in my head. I mean, I was concussed, and after everything that had happened earlier that day... It had to be a hallucination."

Jasper didn't respond right away. He sipped his coffee, watching her with a thoughtful expression.

"Yeah," he said finally. "Probably just your brain playing tricks on you. But I'm not gonna lie to you, I don't like the guy either—he seems shady as hell. If anything feels off with him while you guys are working on the exhibit, let me know right away, okay?"

Cleo nodded. "I will."

But as she turned back to her computer, her thoughts churned behind her eyes.

What if it hadn't been a hallucination? What if Pol had really been there? She could still see him in her mind's eye— standing calmly in the chaos, watching her with that eerie, knowing smile.

Maybe it was nothing. Maybe Jasper was right.

Still, the unease didn't fade. It had burrowed into her chest, gnawing quietly with each passing hour. Pol's presence, real or imagined, lingered in the corners of her thoughts like a shadow that wouldn't leave.

And as she resumed work on the exhibit, she couldn't shake the feeling that something was coming.

Something she wasn't ready for.

Later that afternoon, as the sun dipped lower in the sky and the museum began to empty out, Cleo tried to refocus on the exhibit timeline.

"How's the exhibit coming along?" Jasper asked from Cleo's doorway.

Startled, Cleo jumped in her seat. "Jesus, Jasper! Give a girl some warning." She tossed a pen across the office at him.

"It's coming along just fine, not looking forward to having to take criticism from Pol Cooper for the next several months but it is what it is."

"Ha, yeah, happy I am not you right now. Anyway, I planned on stopping for a quick drink down the street after we close up here if you are interested, unless you have some grand ball or something you need to be at tonight?" Jasper poked.

"Very funny, but you know what, I think I will have a drink. I could use it." Cleo closed down her computer for the day and crammed her paperwork into her bag.

The streets outside were awash in golden light, the sun casting long shadows over the sidewalk as Cleo and Jasper stepped out of the museum. The air was crisp and smelled faintly of orange blossoms from the planters lining the boulevard. Storefronts glowed under warm light, and the occasional clink of glasses and low murmur of conversation drifted from nearby cafés.

They passed a street musician playing a soft tune on a violin, his case open for tips, and a couple walking a golden retriever that wagged enthusiastically at every passerby.

As they walked the short distance to their favorite saloon, Bootleggers, Cleo typed a quick message to Alek letting him know what she was up to.

"Look at you, being all considerate and like relationshippy and such, texting Alek that you will be home late. I never thought I would see the day," Jasper joked.

"Oh, you are so very fun..." Cleo walked right into a young woman coming out of a small shop, knocking her phone out of her hands.

"I am so sorry, that was all my fault," the young woman said.

"No, I'm so clumsy, I should have been paying attention," Cleo insisted.

The young woman bent down and picked up Cleo's phone.

Handing it back, she said, "I'm Ari by the way, nice to meet you."

"I'm Cleo, nice to meet you too and thank you." Cleo took her phone back and continued down the sidewalk with Jasper.

Bootleggers loomed ahead, just across the street, its vintage neon sign flickering gently against the encroaching twilight. The smell of aged whiskey and warm wood greeted them before they even reached the door. Inside, laughter and the clatter of pool balls echoed in cozy harmony.

Chapter 30

Pol watched from across the street as Cleo and Jasper waited at the crosswalk. With a subtle wave of his hand, the illuminated sign flickered and changed, signaling it was safe to cross. As they stepped off the curb, a horn blared—Cleo froze, paralyzed by the sudden danger. Tires screeched. A hand reached out and yanked her back to safety.

"Holy shit!" Jasper shouted, his arm protectively across Cleo.

Cleo turned to see who had saved her. It was Ari—the same young woman she'd bumped into moments ago.

"Oh my god, are you okay?" Ari asked, breathless.

"I... I think so. Thank you," Cleo managed.

Ari grinned. "We meet again."

Cleo laughed weakly. "Apparently, I need to watch where I'm going. First, I almost knock you over, now I almost walk into traffic."

"You do seem a bit accident-prone," Ari teased.

"Confirmed," Jasper added.

Cleo shook her head, still rattled. "But the sign said it was safe..."

"People drive like maniacs. Probably texting or something," Ari offered casually.

Cleo nodded slowly, unsettled.

"We were heading to Bootleggers for a drink. Let me buy you one for saving my life," Cleo offered.

"Yeah, come on," Jasper added. "Unless you've got something pressing?"

"Why not? I've got time to kill," Ari agreed.

They crossed safely this time and stepped into Bootleggers. The bar was buzzing, more packed than usual. Warm lamplight spilled over dark wood and brass fixtures, while the scent of whiskey and citrus drifted through the air.

They snagged a recently vacated high-top table near the back, the scuffed wood sticky with traces of citrus and spilled whiskey. Jasper flagged down a bartender and ordered drinks: a whiskey sour for himself, a gin and tonic for Cleo, and let Ari choose her poison.

"Old fashioned," she said smoothly. "Heavy on the bitters."

Jasper raised his eyebrows. "Classic. Mysterious. I approve."

Ari grinned. "I aim to keep people guessing."

"Thanks again," Cleo said, settling onto a stool. "I'm Cleo, this is Jasper—we work up the street at the museum."

"Nice to officially meet you. I'm Ari. Currently unemployed—on purpose," she added with a wry smile. "Call it a soul sabbatical."

"Jealous," Cleo groaned. "I'd kill for a break like that."

"You could probably afford one," Jasper said, nudging her. "Your guy owns a literal fortress and a car that costs more than our salaries combined."

Cleo rolled her eyes. "His money. Not mine. I still use coupons at Trader Joe's."

"I respect that," Ari said. "Though I wouldn't turn down a five-star weekend in Paris. Just saying."

Jasper tilted his head. "So what do you do when you're not pulling people out of traffic?"

"Lately? Art. Walking. Eating pastries. Crashing into people, apparently." She sipped her drink and leaned slightly toward him. "I follow the energy. If it feels right, I stay. If it doesn't, I move on."

"Sounds like freedom," Cleo said wistfully.

"Sounds like witchcraft," Jasper countered, flashing a grin. "No wonder you showed up out of nowhere. You probably have a broom parked outside."

"Oh, I do," Ari said smoothly, eyes twinkling. "It's a Vespa now, though. Got tired of splinters."

Cleo laughed. "Okay, you two are ridiculous."

"I'm trying to keep up," Jasper said, now clearly intrigued. "So if you're not working, how do you afford old fashioneds and vintage boots?"

"I trade in secrets," Ari replied, cryptic.

He blinked. "That's... kind of hot."

Cleo snorted into her drink. "God, Jasper, subtlety is a thing."

"I'm just being honest!" he said, turning to Ari. "Look, you're sharp, cool under pressure, possibly magic, and you saved my friend's life. I'm impressed."

Ari tilted her head, smiling. "Flattery noted."

"Is it working?"

She sipped her drink slowly, eyes never leaving his. "Almost."

"Oh come on," Jasper said. "At least tell me what kind of art you do."

"Mixed media. Found objects, street salvage, natural pigments. I like to make ugly things beautiful again. Sometimes they stay ugly, but meaningful. Life's like that."

"That's... actually pretty awesome," he said, more genuinely now.

Cleo watched them, amused. "Wow. I didn't expect to be the third wheel tonight."

"I should go," Ari said, glancing at her phone. "It's getting late."

"Wait," Jasper said, half-rising. "Can I call you sometime?"

Ari looked at him. "Maybe."

He grinned. "Could I get your number?"

"No."

He blinked. "So I can't call you?"

"I didn't say that."

"I'm so confused."

Cleo shook her head. "That means she likes you."

Ari stood and pulled on her jacket. "You work at the museum, right?"

"Yeah."

"Then I'll find you when I decide you've earned it."

She slid her drink napkin across the table, revealing a single red lipstick kiss mark on it. "Hold onto that. Might be worth something someday."

Cleo laughed and gave Ari a high five as she stood. "Come on, walk me out before Jasper implodes."

As they stepped into the cool night air, Ari nudged Cleo with her elbow. "He's cute."

"He's also going to overanalyze that kiss mark for the next week."

"Good. Let him."

Cleo grinned. "We should do this again."

"Absolutely. Here—give me your phone." Ari typed in her number. "Just don't give it to museum boy. Let him earn it."

A cab rolled up, headlights sweeping across the pavement. Ari waved as Cleo climbed in.

"Try not to get run over again!" she called.

"No promises!"

As the cab pulled away, Ari turned slightly.

Across the street, Pol stood in the shadows, arms crossed, face unreadable.

Ari gave a small, two-fingered salute.

He smiled.

Chapter 31

In a flash, Ari transported herself across the street, appearing beside Pol in a shimmer of energy too swift for mortal eyes to catch. The night hummed with the low buzz of streetlights and distant traffic, but around them, time felt oddly still.

"How are you doing, Pol?" she asked, her voice light, but her eyes watchful.

Pol didn't look at her right away. His gaze lingered on the spot where Cleo's cab had disappeared. "Never better, sister."

Ari raised a brow. "You must've been watching for a while."

"I like to keep an eye on things that matter." He turned slowly, offering her a grin that didn't reach his eyes. "I see you've been talking to Alek."

"I have," Ari said, folding her arms. "I hear you two are having a bit of a row."

"No, I wouldn't say that." Pol's voice took on a mocking edge. "A row implies something petty. This is... biblical."

Ari narrowed her eyes. "Dramatic as always."

"You say that like I'm the unreasonable one," he snapped. "He made his choice."

"And you made yours," she countered. "But this doesn't have to end in blood, Pol."

Pol laughed bitterly. "You think this is about blood? No. It's about loyalty. About what was owed."

"He's not your enemy."

"He is now."

Ari's jaw tensed. "Come on now, can't you two work it out?"

"It will be worked out when he pays for his betrayal and decides to make amends by joining me," Pol said. "I would ask you to choose sides, but we already know where your loyalties lie."

She stared at him. "Don't do this."

"Why not?" His voice dropped, colder now. "Because it makes you uncomfortable? Because you think you can guilt me out of what needs to be done?"

"You know I can't stay out of it," she said, her tone quieter but resolute.

Pol's expression shifted, something like regret flickering behind his eyes. "I do. I saw you earlier today— pulling the human out of harm's way."

"She didn't deserve to be caught in the middle of your tantrum."

He laughed again, harsher this time. "Tantrum? Oh, Ari. You always did love to moralize. Always the little mediator, pretending the world can be balanced if you just try hard enough."

She didn't flinch. "I'm not pretending. I'm choosing. There's a difference."

"I wish you'd choose yourself, for once," he muttered. "Before this breaks you, too."

The air between them crackled with unspoken history. Then, as if the weight of the moment became too much to bear, Pol's form shimmered, edges bleeding into shadow.

"I wish you'd stay out of this... for your sake," he said softly—almost genuinely.

Then, with a pulse of cold and shadow, he vanished into the night, leaving Ari alone beneath the flickering glow of a broken streetlamp.

Chapter 32

The night deepened over Los Angeles, stars faint against the glow of city lights as Alek remained on the patio, the weight of the evening pressing down on his shoulders. The scotch in his hand had long since lost its chill, but he barely noticed. The air carried a distant hum of sirens and the occasional bark of a dog, but here, in this quiet slice of his estate, it almost felt like the world had paused.

Alek turned around at the sound of Ari appearing on his patio. "Ari, how did it go?"

"You were right to be concerned. Pol is definitely after Cleo; he managed to manipulate a walk sign and almost got her run over. If I hadn't been there, we would be having a very different conversation."

Alek wiped his brow. "Shit, that's twice in two days. Thank you, Ari."

"So, what's our next move?" she asked.

"I don't know. I can't just outright go after him, not without raising the attention of the others," Alek explained.

"True, but would anyone really care if something happened to Pol?"

"Honestly, probably not. But I'm still hoping I can talk some sense into him. Settle this like adults."

"Alek?" Cleo called from the foyer. "Are you out there?"

"Quick, you better go before she sees you," Alek insisted.

"Just be careful," Ari said as she vanished in a shimmer of light.

"I'm out here," Alek called to Cleo from the patio.

Cleo found him standing next to the bar with a glass of scotch in his hand.

"Nightcap?" he asked.

"No, thank you. I had enough with Jasper at Bootleggers."

"How was your day, then? Go on, tell me all about it," he insisted.

"Very tiring and a little stressful, with all the work going into the new exhibit. Then there was me not paying attention and almost walking into traffic."

"What?!" Alek exclaimed, his voice sharp with concern.

"Yeah. Thankfully the woman standing behind me at the crosswalk was paying more attention than I was and she grabbed me before anything happened. Jasper and I ended up having drinks with her after, and she seemed really nice. I think Jasper has a bit of a crush on her. We're actually talking about getting together again sometime soon." She laughed softly.

"Leave it to you to make friends by almost dying," Alek said.

Cleo laughed. "I think I'm going to head off to bed. I'm exhausted. You don't mind, do you?"

"No, absolutely not. I'll be up in a bit. I'm just going to sit out here for a while longer and take in a little of the night air."

Cleo gave him a quick kiss. "Good night."

"Good night."

Alek leaned against the railing, staring into the dark garden below. The conversation with Ari haunted him. Pol's descent into vengeance wasn't just dangerous—it was personal. And Cleo, unknowingly caught in the middle, had nearly paid the price. Twice.

He turned the glass in his hand and sighed. How long could he keep her safe without telling her the truth?

The door creaked softly behind him. For a moment, Alek thought Cleo had returned, but when he turned, it was Viktor, his house manager and longtime confidant. The man stepped onto the patio with the silent ease of someone who'd done it a thousand times.

"You're still up," Viktor said.

"You're one to talk."

Viktor's eyes flicked to the empty glass. "Pol made a move?"

Alek nodded. "Ari intervened. Just in time."

Viktor's jaw tightened. "He's escalating."

"I know. I'm just not sure what his endgame is. Revenge? Retribution? He won't stop until he gets me to agree to join him. And if I don't, he'll kill her out of spite."

"With Pol, it's all of the above. He doesn't make idle threats, Alek. And he doesn't forgive."

Alek rubbed his temples. "We need to be ready. But until then, I want her kept out of it. No more close calls."

Viktor inclined his head. "I'll tighten the perimeter. Quietly. No alerts unless it's necessary."

Alek nodded, grateful. "And Viktor?"

"Yes?"

"Thank you."

Viktor gave a curt nod and disappeared back into the house.

Alone again, Alek looked toward the upstairs windows. One of them was dark—Cleo's. He imagined her curled beneath the covers, hair tousled, her breathing slow and even. Peaceful. Unaware.

But for how long?

The silence stretched around him, a fragile bubble he knew wouldn't hold forever. Pol was coming. And next time, he might not miss. It might not be another warning shot.

Alek tightened his grip on the railing, jaw clenched.

Let him come.

But he wouldn't touch her again.

Chapter 33

Alek looked at the notification on his phone.

Pol: Tick Tock brother, its time to make a decision

Alek: My answer remains unchanged.

Pol: We will see about that.

Chapter 34

"Good morning, Jasper. Did you hear anything back from the museum in Cairo about our loan request?" Cleo asked.

"Good morning to you too. What are you doing here so early?"

"What do you mean early? I'm here on time," she rebuked.

"Exactly. You're never here on time!" Jasper teased.

"Anyway, did you?" she asked.

"Did I what?"

"Hear back from Cairo?"

"I did. They're still considering our request."

"Still! We're never going to get this exhibit open by the deadline if they keep dragging their feet," Cleo said, exasperated.

She hated how powerless she felt. Every delay was another stone stacked on her chest, another reminder that so much of her work depended on forces beyond her control. She had done everything right—secured funding, curated the pieces, even rewritten the exhibit copy herself. And still, Cairo held the keys.

"Why don't you ask Pol to make a call? Didn't he say he knew people there?" Jasper urged.

"He did, but I was hoping I wouldn't have to rely on him. I just don't like the guy."

Her voice was steady, but her stomach twisted. It wasn't just dislike. There was something deeper—an instinctive wariness. Pol Cooper was the kind of man who wore charm like armor. Every smile had weight. Every compliment, a motive.

"I get that. But I don't think we have much of a choice if we want to make the deadline. Let him throw his weight and money around a little. The guy will probably get off on it anyway."

"Fine, you're right," Cleo said begrudgingly. "I'll give him a call."

She pulled out her phone, feeling the slight tremor in her fingers. The screen blurred for a moment as her mind raced. She had a list of people she trusted. Pol wasn't on it.

The call rang once before he answered.

"Why hello, my dear. What can I do for you?"

"Good morning, Mr. Cooper. I was wondering if you could reach out to your contacts at the museum in Cairo. We've been having trouble making progress on the antiquities loan for the new exhibit."

Jasper leaned back in his chair, trying to look nonchalant as Cleo continued.

"I'd be more than happy to," Pol replied. "Say, why don't we meet this evening to discuss the details before I trouble anyone there?"

She felt her jaw tighten. He was always turning favors into obligations. Always converting requests into games.

"Oh, I don't think that will be necessary. Cairo knows what we're looking for—they have our list. We just need them to approve it," she explained, trying to hold firm.

"Nonsense. It'll give us a chance to catch up on the exhibit—and on my dear brother. I insist."

Of course you do, she thought.

"You know what, why not."

"Excellent. I know a lovely French restaurant downtown called Le Divin. Shall we say seven o'clock?"

"That would be fine. I'll see you then."

"Great. Oh, and bring your appetite."

She ended the call and slid the phone back into her pocket.

"So?" Jasper asked.

"He wants to have dinner and discuss it before he'll make any calls," she replied, irritated.

"That's not so bad, is it?"

"We'll see. He always has an angle. But I don't have any other option if we want this exhibit to open on time."

There was that feeling again—like she was walking a tightrope and couldn't see the other side. She hated that she'd been backed into this.

"Yeah, that sucks for you," Jasper said sympathetically.

Cleo shook her head. "I'm going to my office."

"Don't hurt yourself," Jasper joked.

She flipped him the bird on her way out and pulled her phone out again to text Alek:

Cleo: Going to be home late, have a meeting about the new exhibit XO

Alek: No worries. See you tonight.

Alek didn't just understand her work—he respected it. And that was rare. She often felt like she had to shrink parts of herself to make room for others, but not with him. With Alek, she could be whole.

The day passed quickly as Cleo immersed herself in work. She welcomed it—she could control her office, her notes, the exhibit flowcharts. Here, in the quiet hum of focused effort, the rest of the world fell away.

When her alarm buzzed, she packed up and left her office. "Good night," she said to the guard at the front desk.

"Cleo!" a voice called from behind.

She turned. "Ari? What are you doing here?"

"Spared Jasper another round of torment and gave him my number," Ari said proudly.

Cleo laughed. "Done for the day, then?"

"I wish. I have to meet an investor downtown about a favor for our new exhibit," Cleo replied.

"Ouch. Sounds tedious."

"Normally it wouldn't be, but I don't like the guy."

That was putting it mildly. She felt like she was walking into a room with too many mirrors. Everything about Pol reflected something back at her—none of it true.

"Want to share a ride? I'm heading downtown anyway. You can tell me all about why you don't like him."

"Why not."

As they climbed into the car, Ari asked, "What's the new exhibit about?"

"Early dynasties of ancient Egypt," Cleo replied.

Talking about the exhibit helped. It grounded her. This was where her passion lived—in dusty artifacts, forgotten lineages, and the quiet thrill of resurrecting history.

"Sounds interesting. Why don't you like the investor?"

"He's actually my boyfriend's brother."

"Really? Complicated."

"A little. But mostly, he's always playing some angle and seems to enjoy causing trouble for Alek. Anyway, I called him to ask for help with a museum loan and now he wants dinner before making any calls."

"Instead of just making the call?" Ari asked as they arrived at Le Divin.

"Exactly."

Cleo's eyes drifted over the restaurant's facade. Elegant. Expensive. Controlled. Everything Pol liked to wrap around himself like a second skin.

As they approached the entrance, two men stepped out—one in a hood, the other was Pol.

"Pol, how are you? This is my friend Ari. We shared a ride. Are you ready?" Cleo asked.

"Yes. We've met," Pol said with a devious smile.

Cleo looked puzzled. "You two know each other?"

"Unfortunately," Ari said flatly.

Something sharp moved through her chest. This wasn't a coincidence. Something was wrong.

"Take her," Pol ordered.

The hooded man lunged. Ari struck him square in the chest with a flash of light, sending him flying backward through the air. Cleo's breath caught in her throat. The impact cratered the sidewalk.

Before she could move, Pol conjured a ball of pulsing blue energy and hurled it at Ari. Ari countered with a blast of golden flame. The energies collided midair in a thunderous shockwave, knocking over a streetlamp and shattering nearby windows.

Cleo stood frozen, her mind fracturing under the weight of the impossible. This was real. It was happening. She was watching people—no, beings—tear reality open in front of her.

"That was excessive—even for you, sister," Pol snarled, forming another energy sphere in his hand.

"Sister? What's going on?" Cleo stammered.

The word hit her like ice water. Sister. What the hell did that mean?

"Get out of here! Get to Alek. He'll explain everything!" Ari shouted, unleashing another wave of energy that sent Pol stumbling back.

Her body moved before her mind caught up. She ran, her heels clacking against the pavement, her breath ragged. Nothing made sense. Every law she knew had shattered. She felt like she'd fallen into someone else's nightmare.

She turned just in time to see Pol vanish in a shimmer of light—only to reappear in front of her.

Cleo screamed. Her legs faltered. Logic screamed for a foothold, but her world had no anchor anymore. Her thoughts spiraled: Who were they? What were they? What did that make Alek?

Another burst of golden light as Ari reappeared, slamming into Pol with explosive force.

"What the fuck is going on?! Who and what the fuck are you people?!" Cleo cried, her voice raw.

"Go, Cleo!" Ari shouted.

She ran again, tears blurring her vision. But Pol was faster. He lunged and caught her. The world blinked out in a sphere of blinding white.

Ari screamed, her voice a furious storm. The streetlights exploded in cascading sparks. Fury radiated from her in waves.

She shot into the sky, trailing fire. Her hands glowed with incandescent light, energy crackling between her fingers. She traced the remnants of Pol's signature through the ether.

The war had begun.

Chapter 35

Ari rematerialized just outside the gates of Alek's estate, stumbling slightly as displaced energy crackled around her. The iron gate creaked open as she approached, sensing the urgency radiating from her body.

Alek was already at the entrance, eyes fixed on her. One look at her face and his world narrowed.

"What happened?" he asked, his voice sharp, urgent.

Ari's lips were tight. "It's Cleo," she said. "He's got her."

Alek stood still for a moment, frozen. His chest rose slowly, then faster, and something primal flickered behind his eyes.

"Alek..." Ari stepped closer, cautiously. "What do you want to do?"

"We're going to find her," he said, his voice low. "We're going to bring her back before Pol has the chance to do anything."

"You think he'll wait?"

Alek nodded grimly. "He'll want to draw it out. He wants me to feel it. He always savors the suffering."

A deeper note of fury entered his voice. "He'll use her to try to pull me back. Make her a bargaining chip. If I refuse, he'll punish her for it. That's how he works."

Even saying it made his hands tremble. Not from fear—but from the effort it took not to tear the world apart in that moment.

Ari looked away, jaw clenched. "Even if we get her back..."

"We will get her back," Alek said, his voice like iron. His eyes flashed—two searing, white-hot points of light. "And when we do, I'll make sure he never lays a hand on anyone again."

Alek raised his hands, calling on the deeper senses that connected him to Cleo—the soul-thread formed by love and trust and time. He reached inward, searching for her. But what should have been a bright beacon was dulled, smothered, buried beneath a veil of shadow.

"He's cloaking her," Alek said through gritted teeth. "I can feel the interference. It's dense... like smoke soaked in old magic."

"Let me help," Ari said, stepping in beside him.

Together they focused, their energies overlapping—his glowing white, hers a golden radiance. Their connection fanned out across the metaphysical threads of the world, piercing the veil in bursts and flares. Pol was strong, but so were they.

"There," Ari whispered. "Do you feel that ripple?"

Alek's brow furrowed. "Yes. Hold it—just a second longer—"

And then he saw her. Briefly. A flicker, a breath. Cleo, standing alone in a stone chamber lit by torchlight. Symbols carved into the walls. Ancient air. The smell of time and reverence.

Alek recoiled, his breath catching.

"What did you see?" Ari asked.

"I know where she is," Alek said. His voice was quiet now, but laced with something sharp. "It's one of the temples the ancients built... for me."

Ari's brows knit together. "Pol took her there?"

"He's trying to shake me. He knows I'll recognize it. He wants me to remember everything. The adoration. The weight. The loneliness of it."

He exhaled slowly, controlled.

"He chose that place so I'd be off balance. So I'd feel like the past was breathing down my neck."

"Then we won't let it."

Alek looked at her, something resolute settling into his expression. "No. We won't."

He turned toward the horizon, already moving.

"She's waiting. And I'm done playing his games."

Ari stepped beside him, her golden light coalescing around her fists. Her voice was fierce, steady.

"Then let's go get her back."

Chapter 36

Cleo started to slowly open her eyes. Her head throbbed. Her limbs felt heavy and distant, like they belonged to someone else. "Where... am I? What happened?"

"Look who's finally woken up," came a voice—smooth, mocking.

Pol.

She tried to raise her hands to rub her eyes, but panic surged through her when they didn't move. Her wrists were bound tightly. So were her ankles. She was tied to a chair.

No, no, no—

She yanked against the restraints, but they only bit deeper into her skin.

The memories crashed in like a wave. Ari—fighting that hooded man. Pol—stepping from the shadows. Running. Ari shouting her name. And then... nothing. Darkness.

"What's going on!" she yelled, eyes wide, heart slamming against her ribs.

Pol laughed at her panic, clearly enjoying the chaos blooming inside her. "You really have no idea what you've gotten yourself into, do you?"

"What are you talking about?" Cleo asked, her voice cracking, tears rising. "What did I do?"

"My brother—your sweet, soft-spoken boyfriend— owes me a debt," he said, circling her chair. "A very old debt."

"I don't understand!" she cried, her voice breaking, hot tears slipping down her cheeks. "What does that have to do with me?"

Pol leaned in, his voice low and condescending. "Now, now, don't cry. You're not in danger. At least... not yet."

She flinched as he reached out and wiped a tear from her cheek with the back of his hand. It was more terrifying than any threat—like he was touching a piece of glass he planned to shatter later.

"No," he continued with a twisted smile, "I'm not going to hurt you. Eventually, sure—I'll snuff you out like a candle. But first, you're going to help me."

"Help you? Why would I help you, you psychopath?!"

"Oh, my dear," he said with mock affection, "you won't have a choice."

Cleo's breathing slowed as she tried to force herself into clarity. She scanned the space around her—dim light, dry air, the scent of old stone and ancient dust. Pillars loomed around the room's edge. She couldn't see their tops in the shadows above, but she could tell they were carved. There were windows, but heavy curtains draped across them, letting in only threads of light that painted golden stripes across the floor.

This wasn't a modern building. This wasn't even a ruin. This place felt... alive. Timeless.

She looked Pol straight in the eye, her voice steadying. "Where am I? And what are you?"

Pol's grin widened. "Oh, my dear girl. We are in Babylon. The ancient city itself."

Her eyes widened. "Babylon? Mesopotamia? That's not possible... How did we get here? How long have I been out? And you never answered me. What are you?"

He chuckled, clearly pleased with her confusion. "We got here with a little magic. As for what I am..." He stepped back and spread his arms. "I'm a god. A real one. Flesh and blood, immortal and magnificent."

He snapped his fingers.

The curtains snapped open in unison with a low, thunderous boom. Sunlight flooded the chamber. Cleo winced as her eyes adjusted.

She gasped.

Outside the towering windows, she saw a sprawling harbor, ancient stone docks, strange vessels rocking on the river. The skyline of an ancient world framed in heat haze. Domes and towers. An otherworldly beauty preserved through time.

Pol turned to her and bowed with mock grandeur. "Let me reintroduce myself. My name is Pol. Though you may know me better by names like Loki... or Seth. I've worn many faces over the centuries. Trickster, storm god, harbinger of chaos. It's a crowded résumé and before you ask, no we didn't travel through time but I am showing you through a little illusion what this place looked like, once upon a time."

Cleo stared at him. The words didn't make sense. They echoed, hollow, disconnected from reality. She could feel herself trembling, could feel the dryness in her throat and the way her chest struggled to rise and fall.

And yet she believed him.

Because deep down... something had always felt off.

Pol walked to the center of the room and ran his fingers along the stone wall. "This temple... it was once devoted to your boyfriend's worship."

The floor seemed to shift under her.

"What?" she whispered.

He smiled like a serpent. "Before Alek was pretending to be human, to be harmless, he was someone great. People built this temple in his name. They came here to praise him. To beg him for mercy. He was worshiped."

"No," she breathed. "No, you're lying."

But her eyes betrayed her. The carvings on the walls, the inscriptions etched in languages she didn't know yet somehow stirred something primal in her. The central dais, worn from centuries of footfalls. This place wasn't for Pol. It radiated reverence. It hummed with Alek's presence.

Her mind reeled.

He never told me this. He never told me any of it.

She felt sick. She wanted to cry again, but she couldn't—she didn't even know what she was grieving yet. The man she loved had a history measured in millennia, and he'd kept it from her. The truth wasn't just buried—it had been mythologized.

Pol leaned down, lips nearly at her ear. "He'll come for you, of course. That's the point. This place will call to him. And when he sees it—when he remembers the centuries he's tried to forget—it will break him. That's when I'll strike."

Cleo closed her eyes, her pulse thundering in her ears.

She felt like a thread pulled too tight.

What am I to him, really? What am I to any of them?

She couldn't answer. But she knew this: she wasn't just afraid of Pol.

She was afraid of how much she didn't know.

Pol straightened and clapped his hands once. "Now, if you'll excuse me, I have a call to make."

From the shadows behind one of the columns, a hulking figure stepped forward.

"This is my associate, Bob. He'll keep an eye on you."

Cleo squinted against the light, trying to see who he meant—until she saw the horned silhouette. The face.

Not a face.

A snout. Deep-set black eyes. Curved horns rising from a massive head.

It wasn't a man.

It was a minotaur.

She froze. Her skin crawled. "Oh my god—"

The creature said nothing. Just watched her, muscles taut beneath thick leather armor.

Pol laughed at her expression. "Don't worry, my dear. He won't hurt you—unless you try to escape. Or I tell him to."

With a flash of light, Pol vanished, leaving behind only dust motes dancing in the air—and the sound of her own shaky breathing.

Cleo stared at the minotaur, heart in her throat. This wasn't a nightmare.

She was in Babylon.

In an ancient temple.

A prisoner of gods.

And utterly alone.

"This can't be real," she whispered.

But it was.

And she knew—if Alek didn't come soon—she might never leave.

Chapter 37

Alek stood before the roaring fire in the library of his estate, the flames casting flickering shadows across the room's carved wooden walls and ancient tomes. The scent of aged paper, smoke, and old magic lingered in the air. His fingers curled tightly around the back of an armchair, knuckles white.

Behind him, Ari poured herself a drink from the side table with more force than finesse. The decanter clinked sharply against the glass. "You're going to break something if you keep pacing like that," she said, taking a steadying sip.

"I might break something anyway," Alek muttered. "We don't have time for this."

Ari lowered her glass, watching him carefully. "Do you have a plan? Any idea where Pol could have taken her?"

"Not yet," Alek admitted, spinning toward the fire. "He could have her anywhere in the world. But Pol—he wouldn't hide her randomly. This is a performance. A game. He wants me to chase him."

Ari nodded, sitting on the edge of the sofa. "He'd pick a place that meant something. Something symbolic. That's how he operates—layers of meaning and cruelty."

Alek ran a hand through his hair, frustration flaring. "He said he wanted me to suffer. That he'd use her to turn me. And if I don't join him—he'll hurt her."

A long silence stretched between them.

"We have to be smarter than him," Ari said finally. "He mentioned returning to the old ways. The gods worshiped openly. That narrows the list. Greece, Egypt, Mesopotamia..."

Alek's eyes narrowed. "Wait. When he showed us the vision of Cleo, tied to the chair—did you see the stonework behind her? The ziggurat carvings. The columns. That was one of the temples."

"The ones built for you," Ari said slowly. "Babylon."

Alek nodded. "Pol took her to one of the first temples humans ever built in my honor. He wants me to remember what it felt like to be worshipped. To crave it again."

Ari exhaled sharply. "So we know where. Now we need to figure out how."

Alek turned from the fire and moved to the large circular table at the room's center, sweeping aside old scrolls and blueprints of celestial architecture. With a wave of his hand, a magical map flared to life across its surface—a starry globe hovering inches above the table, threaded with golden ley lines.

He placed his palm over Mesopotamia. "Babylon is cloaked. He's woven concealment wards across the city, embedded in the very stones. But this temple—it was once mine. I can still feel the remnants of devotion etched into its walls. That thread is enough for me to tether to."

Ari stepped closer. "A back door, then. Can you anchor a portal?"

"Yes. But it won't be stable for long," Alek said. "Once we enter, we'll have minutes—maybe less—before Pol senses us."

"Then we make it count." She summoned a blade of starlight into her hand, the weapon humming softly with raw divine energy. "I'll take the minotaur. You focus on Cleo. Is she still tethered to you?"

Alek closed his eyes, reaching with his mind. "Faintly. She's frightened. I can feel her heartbeat—like thunder beneath stone."

"She'll hold on until we get there," Ari said gently. "Now tell me the rest of the plan."

"We drop in fast," Alek said. "You distract the minotaur, keep him away from Cleo. I'll get her loose, and if Pol is there—"

"You deal with him," Ari finished. "We don't fight unless we have to."

"I won't risk her life in a duel," Alek agreed. "If he sees us coming, we retreat and regroup."

"What about barriers? You said Pol layered the place with magic."

"I'll weave a counter-charm into the portal," Alek said, already forming glyphs with a wave of his fingers. Glowing sigils spun into the air like embers. "It'll disrupt the outer shell for a moment—enough time for us to break through."

Ari nodded. "Alright. What about after? You think he'll retaliate?"

"He will," Alek said darkly. "But I'll be ready."

Ari stepped back and crossed her arms. "So, to recap: you weave the tether and get us in. I keep the beast occupied. You grab Cleo. If Pol shows up, we get out. No heroics."

"Exactly."

She met his glowing eyes. "We've done crazier things."

"Not with this much at stake," Alek murmured.

A soft hum filled the room as Alek began his work. The air shimmered, the scent of ozone and myrrh rising as divine energy swirled into a thin spiral in the center of the room. The spell circle beneath their feet pulsed with gold and sapphire light, anchoring itself between worlds.

"Ready?" Ari asked, flexing her fingers around her starlight blade.

Alek turned toward her, his face hard and radiant, eyes gleaming like twin suns. "Let's bring her home."

With a final pulse of light, the portal snapped open, and they stepped through—vanishing into the crackling storm of magic between worlds.

Chapter 38

Cleo stood trembling, her wrists raw from the ropes that had bound her. Her eyes darted between Alek and Ari, the air dense with tension. She took a staggering step back from Alek's outstretched hands.

"Don't touch me," she snapped. "Not until you tell me what the hell just happened!"

"Cleo, please—" Alek started.

"No," she cut him off. "You don't get to 'Cleo, please' me! I was kidnapped by your brother—who calls himself a god, by the way. I was in a place that looked like ancient Babylon with a literal minotaur standing over me, and I watched the two of you throw magic at each other like something out of a nightmare. What the hell is going on?!"

Alek's face was drawn, worry carving deeper into his features. "Cleo, I know how this looks—how it feels—but we don't have time to explain everything right now. Pol knows we got you out. He'll come for you again."

"You expect me to just trust that?" she shouted, eyes wild. "You're both talking about gods and ancient temples and realms—what am I supposed to believe? That this is all real? That you're real?" Her voice cracked, and her gaze bounced helplessly from Alek to Ari. "You—you're telling me that you're actual gods? That all those myths, all those stories—they're not just stories? That you've been alive for thousands of years? How is that even possible?!"

Her voice trembled with disbelief, but it was the look in her eyes—betrayal mixed with awe and terror—that shattered Alek's heart. She ran a shaking hand through her hair, trying to ground herself, to will logic back into her world.

"I studied this stuff," she said, more to herself than to them. "Mythology, ancient cultures, lost civilizations. It was all supposed to be metaphor and symbolism—not real."

"I never lied," Alek said gently, stepping closer. "I didn't tell you everything—but I never lied. I love you. And I will explain, I swear it. Just not here. This place—it's not safe."

"We're already exposed," Ari added, scanning the windows, her voice low and urgent. "Every second we stay here, we're risking Pol tracking us. He's fast. And he's angry."

Cleo turned her wide eyes on her. "You're telling me he can track us like some divine bloodhound?"

Ari's tone sharpened. "Pol isn't just a god—he's vindictive, powerful, and desperate. He's already shown he's willing to cross lines we never thought he'd cross. Do you really want to be here if he decides to try again?"

Alek stepped in. "He won't just knock this time, Cleo. He'll tear through reality to get to you."

Cleo's breath hitched. She blinked rapidly, heart thundering, as if her body could sweat out the unreality of it all. But it wouldn't go. The image of Pol's burning eyes, the minotaur's inhuman face, the way Alek's hands had glowed with lightning—none of it was fading.

"I—I don't understand," she whispered. "This doesn't make any sense…"

"I know," Alek said. "I know how much this is to take in. But we'll explain everything—every last detail—as soon as we get somewhere secure."

Cleo's hands shook at her sides. "You have one chance. Both of you. If you lie to me again, I walk. I don't care what realm we're in."

"You have my word," Alek said.

Ari moved quickly, grabbing both of their arms. "No more arguing. We leave now."

"Wait—where are we going?" Cleo protested, voice catching with panic.

"Someplace even Pol won't be able to follow. Close your eyes," Ari instructed, eyes flaring with golden light. "And hold on."

Before Cleo could object again, the library vanished in a blinding burst of radiance.

Chapter 39

"Where are we?" she asked, her voice hoarse.

"My villa in Italy. No one knows about it," Ari assured her. "It's heavily warded, layered with ancient protections—charms and glyphs that hide us from the eyes of gods and mortals alike. No one can track us here. Not even Pol. We're safe."

Cleo took a step toward Alek, who stood a few feet away. He opened his arms, hoping to comfort her after the trauma she'd endured. But instead of the embrace he anticipated, Cleo drew her arm back and slapped him across the face with all the strength she could muster.

The blow landed squarely, but Alek didn't so much as flinch. It was like striking stone. Cleo recoiled, cradling her throbbing hand.

"Ouch! Fuck, that hurt!" she exclaimed.

Alek didn't react. "I deserved that," he said quietly.

"Tell me what the hell is happening—right now!" Cleo shouted.

"Alright," he nodded solemnly. "But first—what did Pol tell you while he held you?"

Cleo's eyes narrowed, her breathing still ragged. "He said you owe him a debt and that he's a god. But that can't be true, can it? I feel like I'm losing my mind. This... this can't be real!"

"It's okay," Alek said gently. "You're not losing your mind. You've just seen the veil pulled back. Let's go up to the house. It'll be easier to explain everything where we can sit down."

"Fine," she muttered.

Ari led the way through the olive and lemon trees lining the path to the villa. The estate was vast, built in a classic Italian style, warm stone walls draped in ivy, with broad balconies and archways open to the sea breeze. Magical sigils shimmered faintly along the columns and fountains, pulsing gently with protective energy.

The garden was a wonderland of native flowers and twisting grape vines. Crystal spheres floated lazily above a reflecting pool, humming with latent energy. Birds, seemingly unaffected by the divine magic cloaking the villa, flitted from branch to branch.

They reached a large stone gazebo near the villa's edge—a circular structure supported by Roman columns, each one wrapped in silk that danced in the breeze. A domed roof offered cool shade from the sun.

Inside, plush seating was arranged in a circle around a low table inlaid with constellations that glowed softly when touched. Cleo sat down stiffly, arms crossed. Alek took a seat across from her. Ari sat at his side.

"Alright. Explain," Cleo demanded.

Alek leaned forward, his elbows resting on his knees. He let out a slow breath. "What Pol told you is true—

partially. He is a god. And he believes I owe him a debt. I disagree."

Cleo's voice wavered. "So... you're all gods? You? Ari? Pol? This is insane. I must be going insane."

"You're not crazy," Ari said gently. "You've just seen more than most humans ever do."

"If you're all gods, who are you really? Pol mentioned Loki and Seth... And why does he want me?"

"He wants to use you to get to me," Alek said. "He's angry with me for something that happened long ago. He hoped to force my hand by threatening someone I care about."

Cleo blinked. Her scholar's mind began to assert itself. "Okay... so what is he angry about? What law did you break? But first—who are you? Each of you?"

Alek chuckled dryly. "One question at a time."

"This isn't funny!" Cleo snapped. "You've been lying to me the entire time we've been together. I can't believe I trusted you."

"You have every right to be angry," Alek said. "I am sorry. But ask yourself this—if I'd told you who I really was, would you have believed me?"

She hesitated. Then, begrudgingly, "I guess I would've thought you were just some delusional, self-obsessed billionaire with a god complex."

"Not a complex," Ari interjected. Alek shot her a sharp look.

"If you want answers, I'll give them to you. Ask."

Cleo stared at him. "Who are you? I mean really. Which god are you?"

Alek's eyes glowed faintly with celestial light. "I've had many names. The Mesopotamians called me Anu. The Egyptians, Ra. The Greeks, Zeus. The Norse, Odin."

Cleo's jaw fell slightly open. Her world cracked again.

Alek continued. "Ari, you may know best as Artemis."

"Hi. That's me," Ari said with a quick wave.

"And Pol?"

Alek's face darkened. "Pol is known by many names too—most commonly as Loki, or the Egyptian god Seth."

Cleo stood up suddenly and started pacing. "When we first met—at the garden—you talked about how ancient gods were the same beings across different cultures. You weren't speculating. You were telling me the truth."

"Yes."

"All your theories... they weren't theories. You know all of it because you were there."

"Yes," Alek said again.

"How old are you? What am I even asking—you're a god. You're probably as old as time."

Alek met her eyes. "Older. I was here before time had a name. Before the stars were counted. Before humanity had words."

Cleo staggered back a step, the enormity of it pressing down on her. Her lips parted, but no sound came out. It was too much. Too big.

"I... I can't handle this right now," she whispered. Then she turned and ran from the gazebo, disappearing down the path through the gardens.

"Cleo, wait!" Alek stood to follow her.

Ari caught his arm. "Wait. Let me talk to her. She's overwhelmed. She's been through hell—abducted, threatened, lied to, dragged into a divine war she never asked for. She's grieving the world she thought she knew."

Alek clenched his jaw, but nodded.

Ari gave him a reassuring look and then turned, heading after Cleo.

Chapter 40

Cleo sat beneath an olive tree, eyes closed, the warm sun on her face, listening to the sound of the waves crash against the rocky shore below, desperately trying to convince herself that she wasn't insane. She heard footsteps approaching from behind, startled and traumatized from the events that led her here she jumped to her feet, turning around defensively to identify the source of the approaching footsteps. Her eyes were once again filled with tears from the emotions of the day.

Through her tears she was able to make out Ari cautiously approaching, and as she came closer, Cleo could no longer contain herself as more tears formed in her eyes and she started to sob. "Oh, my dear girl," Ari said as Cleo dropped to the ground, covering her face with her hands. Ari raced over and dropped to her knees to wrap Cleo in a comforting embrace. "It's okay, I know it's a lot to take in, you just let it all out," Ari assured her as she continued to release the events of the day into Ari's arms.

"I don't know how all of this can be true. With everything that has happened in the last few days I know it is, but I feel like I am losing my mind," Cleo said.

"I know dear, it's a lot to handle, but you are strong, and you will make it through this," Ari assured her.

"You know, the thing that hurts the most is finding out that Alek had been lying to me, hiding all of this from me. Before you say anything, I know why he did it and I do understand. Like he said earlier, I never would have believed him. But the truth is, it still hurts," Cleo said. Ari rubbed Cleo's back before releasing her.

"I understand, but he didn't keep all of this from you just because you wouldn't believe him, he did it to protect you," Ari explained.

"Protect me from what, Pol? I feel like I would have been better equipped to handle that lunatic had I known who I was dealing with," Cleo argued.

"There's more to it than just that, a lot more," Ari said. Cleo wiped her face dry, now calm from the relief that the tears had brought.

"Listen, Alek loves you. In all my years, I have never seen him love someone like he loves you—especially not a human," Ari explained.

"We gods are not without our own faults. We created humanity to mirror us, with that, a lot of the same faults that you humans have, we do as well. Because we are not without fault, we decided eons ago to put in place rules or laws, if you will. As time goes on, the need for new rules and laws comes up from time to time. One of the more recent ones—well, recent for us anyway—is that we do not allow ourselves to get too emotionally attached to humans. We are allowed to interact with them, obviously, but not to reveal what, who, we are to them," Ari explained.

"Why? What's the danger in letting humanity know that you exist—all the good that you could do?" Cleo asked.

"As humanity evolved and developed, we started giving them more and more freedom. As a result, they started needing us less and less. Their prayers slowly faded to nothing more than a whisper of what they once were. So, seeing the progress they were making, the advancement in technology and medicine, we decided, collectively, that we should take a step back from humanity. Think of it as a parent with a child: when the child is young, they need their parents. They depend on them for everything—food, shelter, clothing. But as they grow, as they reach adulthood, they no longer depend on their parents. They move out of their parents' home and start a life of their own, have children of their own. Do you understand?" Ari asked.

"Actually, I do," Cleo said.

"It was easier for a lot of us to step back from humanity, to move on with our own lives and continue on our own paths, than it was for others."

"You mean Pol... or Seth... or whoever?" Cleo interrupted. She found herself no longer filled with the fear and betrayal she felt earlier. Instead, she found herself to be intrigued now, yearning to understand.

While the situation was still terrifying, to say the least, the academic in her was starting to realize what an opportunity this was. She had the chance to sit down and talk with actual gods. She had spent her entire life researching, trying to understand and interpret ancient religions and cultures, understand the connection between humanity and the gods. Right now, she realized, she had the opportunity to get the truth from the actual gods that she had spent years studying—an opportunity to obtain knowledge and information that no one has ever had.

Ari continued, "Especially him, but a few others as well. Most of them did eventually come to terms with it. But Pol—remember when I said we gods had our flaws? Well, Pol's is his need for attention. Pol wishes to return to a world where humanity worshiped him, prayed to him, made sacrifices in his honor. He wants to be worshiped and served again. I would be lying if I said I didn't miss it from time to time myself."

"But why does he need Alek for that? Why not just see if he can get the other gods that were not happy with the change to help him?" Cleo asked, her intrigue continuing to grow.

"Because Pol knows that a move like this would start a war. A war that he has no chance of winning without Alek. You see, as powerful as Pol is—as all of us are—the collective of gods that Pol would be up against would still be more powerful. Pol by himself, or maybe half a dozen others combined, would not stand a chance. They would be defeated in no time at all. But with Alek, no—with Alek this would be a very different story."

"What do you mean?" Cleo asked.

"Alek is different from the rest of us," Ari hesitated.

"How so?" Cleo asked, a quizzical look coming across her face.

Ari took a deep breath and exhaled. "It is because Alek is the first of us. He is also the most powerful of us."

"How powerful? I mean, obviously he's a god so there is that, but in terms of compared to the rest of you?" Cleo asked.

"Let's just say that Alek is the architect of creation. We all played a hand in the design of it, but it was Alek who actually made it happen. When it comes to the general hierarchy of us gods, Alek is the god with the big G," Ari continued.

"So did Alek create all of you, or how were you created?" Cleo asked.

"We were not created, per se. We have always just been. A very long time ago, we existed as energy. We can create and manipulate matter and energy, and over time we learned to materialize ourselves into the form you see us in now. Our ability to create and manipulate matter and energy is what allowed us to create the world you live in today, along with other planes of reality."

"So, if Alek and all of you are so powerful, why doesn't one of you just blink Pol out of existence or something, solve everyone's problem?" Cleo asked.

Ari laughed. "Oh my dear, if only it worked that easily. No, since the beginning of time no one god has ever had the power to do something like that. It can't be done, and trust me, it has been attempted."

Cleo looked down at the ground, disappointed at Ari's answer and slightly embarrassed by the question.

"Thank you, Ari, for explaining all of this to me. For helping me understand. There is still one more question I have. Why are gods not allowed to have relationships with humans?" Cleo asked.

"It's not that we are not allowed to have relationships with humans or to love humanity. We are not allowed to fall in love with humans—to get emotionally attached to any specific one. That is what Pol is trying to blackmail Alek with," Ari explained.

"So Pol took me because he knows Alek broke that rule."

"Exactly," Ari said gently. "And he's trying to blackmail Alek—manipulate him into joining his cause by using you as leverage. He knows Alek's love for you is his vulnerability, and he's exploiting it in the cruelest way."

Cleo swallowed, hard. "So what happens now?"

Ari smiled at Cleo for a long moment. "If you are feeling up to it, why don't we make our way back up to the garden, and I will let Alek tell that story. We should get you something to eat as well, you must be famished."

Cleo took a deep breath and wiped what remained of the half-dried tears from her cheeks and nodded in agreement. "I think I would like that," Cleo said as Ari reached for her hand and they started their way back toward the garden.

Chapter 41

Alek stood anxiously as Cleo and Ari approached the gazebo. Cleo walked straight toward him. As she neared, Alek opened his arms. Without a word, Cleo stepped into his embrace. They held each other tightly for several long moments, the tension slowly easing from her body as she relaxed in his arms.

"I love you," Alek whispered.

"I love you too," she said softly.

Ari cleared her throat audibly. "If you two are finished, we really need to get some food in her."

She turned to walk toward the villa. "I'll have one of the staff prepare something. In the meantime, Alek, Cleo has a question for you."

Alek looked at Cleo, still holding her close. "Whatever you want to know."

"Ari explained a lot, but I was wondering..." Cleo trailed off as they took seats across from one another beneath the shade of the silk-draped gazebo. "Why aren't gods allowed to fall in love with humans?"

Alek sighed, leaning forward, his elbows resting on his knees. "There was a time, not so long ago—for us, anyway—when that wasn't forbidden. Many of us did fall in love with mortals, even knowing that a human life is a blink of an eye to us. We loved them anyway, knowing full well it would end in grief. But we believed love was worth the pain."

He paused as Ari returned, holding a plate with a gyro in one hand and a tall glass of lemonade in the other. "Here you go, my dear. Don't let me interrupt," she said cheerfully, setting the food down for Cleo before taking a seat beside Alek.

"As I was saying," Alek continued, "it was permitted—until Eros and Anthansia."

"Who are they?" Cleo asked, intrigued.

"Eros," Alek said, "is our brother. He fell in love with a young woman named Anthansia from the island of Santorini. He loved her so deeply he couldn't bear the thought of losing her to time. As she aged, he grew desperate."

"And one day," Ari cut in, "he asked the rest of us for help. Using the combined power of the gods, he did something that had never been done before."

"He turned her into a god," Alek said gravely.

Cleo's eyes widened. "He actually made her immortal?"

"Yes," Ari confirmed. "And at first, it was perfect. They were happy. In love. But power—it's a dangerous thing. Especially to someone who hasn't spent millennia learning to wield it."

"She couldn't handle it," Alek said. "At first, it was small. Little manipulations. Then came the punishments. Her mortal memories twisted her perceptions. She saw enemies where there were none. She turned her anger on innocent people."

Ari's face darkened. "Eventually, she destroyed Santorini. She ripped the earth open. The eruption buried the city in fire and ash. Thousands died."

Cleo dropped her gyro, stunned. "Wait—that was her? The Minoan eruption?"

Alek nodded. "Yes. Eros tried to stop her. But in the end, it took a dozen of us to subdue her. We bound her powers and locked her away in a prison only gods can enter."

"What happened to Eros?"

"He asked to be imprisoned with her. He couldn't bear to live without her."

Cleo sat in silence, absorbing it all. "It's... tragic. Beautiful. Terrifying."

Alek nodded. "That's why the law was created. No god is permitted to fall in love with a human. We can care, admire, even guide—but not love. Not like that. Not again."

"That's what Pol is threatening you with," Cleo realized aloud. "He's accusing you of falling in love with me."

Ari nodded. "Exactly. He's trying to blackmail Alek— use you as leverage to force him to join his rebellion."

"But we haven't done anything wrong," Cleo said. "We're not starting a war."

"The law doesn't care about intent. Only precedent," Alek said bitterly.

Cleo pushed to her feet and began to pace. "Then we have to go to the others. Tell them what Pol is planning. He's dangerous. If he pulls this off, it won't just be about us—it'll be the end of everything."

Alek stood, tension returning to his shoulders. "You don't understand, Cleo. If the others suspect how much I care for you, they won't ask questions. They'll act."

"Then lie," she said fiercely. "Tell them you saw his plan. That he tried to sway you. That you refused. Keep me out of it."

"They might not believe me."

"But some will," Ari said, joining them. "Especially Helena and Theo. They're already suspicious of Pol."

Alek looked between them. "What if they find out the truth?"

"Then we deal with it," Cleo said. "But letting Pol get stronger, letting him manipulate you—me—everyone... we can't allow that. The world deserves the truth. The other gods deserve to know what he's planning."

"She's right," Ari added. "If we wait too long, the damage could be irreversible."

"I'm not going to let him use me as a weapon against humanity," Cleo said firmly. "I might not have divine power, but I still have a voice—and I'll use it."

Alek looked at her, his expression unreadable. Then he sighed, rubbing the bridge of his nose. "You're both right. But if anything happens to you—"

"Then it happens," Cleo interrupted. "But if we do nothing, worse will happen. Billions could suffer. Civilizations could fall. Do you really want that blood on your hands?"

"No," he admitted quietly. "I don't."

A heavy silence settled between them. Then Alek nodded, his voice steady.

"Tomorrow morning, we go to the Council."

Cleo let out a breath she hadn't realized she was holding. Ari smiled faintly.

"We'll prepare everything tonight," she said. "Wards, protections, the proper words. And Alek..." she looked at her brother carefully, "we do this together."

"Yes," he said. "Together."

Cleo sat back down, exhausted but determined. She looked at Alek, her voice barely above a whisper.

"No more lies. No more running. We face this—head-on."

He took her hand. "No more lies. I promise."

Outside the gazebo, the Mediterranean breeze whispered through the garden as the sun dipped lower into the sea.

Tomorrow, the gods would gather.

And everything would change.

Chapter 42

The sky had just begun to bloom with gold and rose above the sea, the earliest fingers of light brushing the waves. Beneath the ancient olive tree on the cliff's edge, Cleo lay in Alek's arms. The wind carried the scent of salt and wildflowers, and the leaves rustled softly overhead, whispering through the branches as if echoing the secrets of the gods.

Cleo tilted her face up toward Alek, her fingers brushing along his jaw. The warmth in his eyes anchored her, steadied her in a world that had tilted so violently off its axis. He stroked her cheek with the back of his fingers, then leaned in and kissed her—slowly at first, as if asking for permission. Her answer came in the way her lips parted beneath his, in the way her hand slid to the back of his neck to pull him closer.

The kiss deepened, breathless and hungry now, not just with desire but with the ache of everything they had endured, everything they might lose. Their movements were unhurried but deliberate, each touch a reassurance, each sigh a promise. When Alek lowered her gently onto the sun-warmed grass beneath the tree, her breath caught in her throat—not from fear but from the weight of wanting him, all of him, here and now.

His hands explored her slowly, reverently, as though he were learning her anew. He kissed her collarbone, the soft hollow beneath her throat, down to the curve of her ribs. She arched beneath him, fingers tangled in his hair, whispering his name like a prayer.

They undressed each other in pieces, not tearing or rushing, but peeling away layers of cloth and fear until nothing separated them but the last shreds of uncertainty. When he paused, eyes searching hers for hesitation, she reached up and touched his cheek. "I want this," she said. "I want you."

He entered her slowly, the sensation a mixture of heat and heartache, of something too powerful to be contained. She gasped softly, her hands pressing against his back, anchoring herself to him. They moved together, their bodies in rhythm with the sea and the wind and the pulse of the earth itself.

Alek held her as though he feared she might vanish. Every kiss, every movement was threaded with a fierce tenderness. He whispered her name against her shoulder, her throat, her lips, again and again, as if speaking it aloud might bind them closer.

She moaned softly, her body trembling beneath his, overwhelmed not just by the physical pleasure but by the sense of being fully seen, fully cherished. "Don't stop," she whispered. "Please."

They climaxed together, a soft cry slipping from her lips, a groan deep in his throat, the world momentarily fading into white light and warmth and nothing else. He collapsed beside her, chest heaving, arm pulling her close.

For a long while they lay there, skin slick with sweat, limbs entangled. The wind cooled them, carrying away the last of their urgency and leaving only a lingering, gentle ache—the kind that came from loving someone so deeply it hurt.

"I wish we could stay here," Cleo whispered.

"So do I," Alek said, brushing damp hair from her cheek. "But this world has a terrible way of interrupting moments like this."

And just as he spoke, a familiar voice called out across the garden.

"Alek, we should go," Ari said, approaching with purpose in her step and warning in her voice.

Cleo sat up, pulling her linen dress over her shoulders. Alek helped her to her feet and embraced her one final time, resting his forehead against hers. "I'll be back. I promise."

"I know," she said softly, touching his chest. "Just... come back to me."

"I will."

Then, with one last look between them, he turned to Ari. "Alright," he said.

And in a flash of light, they vanished.

Chapter 43

"It's been a long time since I was last here," Alek said as he and Ari stood at the gates of the radiant city of the gods.

"I assure you, not much has changed," Ari replied dryly.

They approached the massive entrance, and the gates opened at their arrival with a sound like shifting tectonic plates, resonant and deep, as if the city itself acknowledged the return of one of its eldest.

"Remind me again why we didn't just materialize in the Grand Hall?" Ari asked.

Alek shrugged. "To delay the inevitable, I suppose. And... I wanted to see the city again."

The golden streets beneath their feet shimmered with threads of starlight woven into the stone. Towers spiraled like living vines up into the eternal sky, and ethereal bridges floated between them. Winged guardians of celestial flame circled high above, casting jeweled light through the morning haze.

As they made their way toward the Council Citadel at the city's center, the silence of the divine realm shifted. Gods turned their heads, some halting in mid-step, others whispering with unmistakable disbelief: Anu had returned. The whispers spread like fire through dry grass. By the time they reached the arched obsidian doors of the citadel, the Council was already buzzing with speculation.

Inside the Grand Hall, Helena turned toward the entrance as the first murmurs reached her. Theo followed her gaze and immediately straightened.

"Alek," Theo said with surprise as the pair entered. "And Ari."

"What brings you here, my brother?" Helena asked. "It's been an age."

"It's Pol," Alek said simply, gravely.

"I warned you he wouldn't leave you alone," Helena said, her tone hardening.

Alek nodded. "It's worse than I feared. He's planning to reveal our existence to humanity. To reignite worship. To reclaim dominion."

"That's impossible," Theo said. "Even Pol wouldn't dare risk a conflict that catastrophic."

"He's not acting alone," Ari added. "He's trying to rally others. And... he asked Alek to join him."

Helena's expression faltered, and the gods who had drawn closer in curiosity now recoiled, stunned. "You?"

"You know why," Alek said, his gaze cast low.

Theo exchanged a wary glance with Helena. "Then you came to stop him."

"I need your help," Alek said. "To stop this before it becomes a war. But without... drawing attention to certain complications."

Helena's eyes searched his face and then nodded in quiet understanding. "I'll call the Council."

Moments later, they stood in the soaring chamber of the High Council. Towering columns of moonstone formed a perfect circle, vanishing into the misty vault above. The walls shimmered with woven glyphs of cosmic law, each inscribed by gods long since faded into legend. Crystal orbs floated in concentric circles overhead, their movements keeping divine time.

The gods assembled at the round table, each taking their place—elders and new voices alike, glowing with their own power and spheres of dominion. The room filled with the rustle of robes, low murmurs, and the faint hum of celestial energies.

Theo rose from his seat. "Brothers. Sisters. We are summoned by troubling news. Our brother Pol has begun to conspire once more. I yield the floor to Alek."

Alek stepped forward, the light from the vaulted ceiling framing him in golden fire.

"Pol came to me directly," he began. "He spoke of bringing humanity back under divine rule. He believes our time of seclusion was a mistake—that mortals should know who we are again. Worship us. Fear us."

Gasps erupted across the chamber.

"He's assembling allies," Alek continued. "He wants to reshape the mortal world in our image. He asked me to join him. I refused."

"He asked you to join him?" cried Bellona, war goddess of the early empires. "He dared?"

"Because of your power," said Ishtar, her voice edged with both awe and suspicion. "He thought if he had you, the rest of us would follow."

"He always was bold," muttered Thor from his seat of frost and ravens. "But this? This borders on madness."

"We gave up dominion over humanity for a reason," said Amaterasu, radiant as the rising sun. "Has he forgotten the chaos we left behind?"

"He hasn't forgotten," Alek said. "He rejects it. He believes we grew weak by turning away. That our strength lies in being feared and followed."

The room broke into furious discourse—voices raised, some in fear, others in defiance. Thunder cracked outside though the skies had been clear.

"Order!" Theo called.

Ares stood, his armor clinking like broken chains. "If Pol means to undermine our compact with the mortal world, we must act swiftly. Not to eliminate him, but to contain and stop him before this escalates."

"We cannot destroy him," Helena reminded. "Even if we wished to. Our essence resists destruction. No god can kill another."

"Then bind him," Ares retorted. "Seal his power as we once did to others who betrayed the balance."

"We must proceed cautiously," Theo said. "Our laws are clear. To restrain one of our own requires consensus—and evidence. Not just fear."

"He's trying to provoke us into breaking the laws ourselves," Ari said. "If we lash out without proof, we become the tyrants he claims we've become."

"Then we gather proof," said Hermes, perched casually on the railing above his seat. "We watch. We test. If he's building an army, it won't stay hidden forever."

More voices joined in—Athena, Isis, Quetzalcoatl—each offering fragments of wisdom, warnings from past epochs when god fought god and the mortal world burned in the crossfire.

Eventually, the noise ebbed.

"We will deliberate," Theo said. "But no action can be taken without agreement. Not yet."

"We understand," Ari said. "We'll return to my villa in Italy while you debate. You know how to reach us."

Helena approached Ari quietly as the Council began to murmur once more.

"We'll do what we can to protect the girl," Helena whispered. "Theo and I both."

"Thank you," Ari replied with quiet gratitude. She rejoined Alek, who eyed her curiously.

"What was that about?" he asked.

"Nothing important," Ari said briskly. "Let's go. Before someone asks a question you won't want to answer."

The two of them vanished in a ripple of starlight.

Chapter 44

The village spread before them like something conjured from memory and dream. Narrow stairways climbed steep hillsides lined with whitewashed stone homes whose red tile roofs curved gently under the sun's golden touch. Clusters of lavender spilled over garden walls. Lanterns, unlit in the daylight, dangled between crooked iron balconies wrapped in vines of blooming wisteria.

They moved slowly now, the weight of the conversation thick in the summer air. Cleo glanced at Alek, studying the solemn set of his jaw.

"You said Pol won't stop looking for me," she said quietly. "What does he actually want, Alek? What's the endgame?"

Alek hesitated, his gaze traveling to the sea. "Power. Recognition. Worship."

"But gods don't need worship to survive, right?"

"No," he said, "but some still crave it. Some believe it defines them."

He paused beside a cracked mural on an old stucco wall—faded but still vivid with gold leaf and indigo pigment.

It depicted a robed figure with many arms standing between two burning towers. Below him, men and women knelt, arms raised in devotion.

"It started eighty years ago," he said. "Pol saw the world changing. Humanity had already turned away from us. They believed themselves to be gods of their own making—scientists, soldiers, rulers."

Cleo's breath caught. "World War II."

Alek nodded slowly. "He didn't start it with a rifle or a speech. He seeded unrest. Whispered into ears. Pushed at fault lines until the world cracked open."

"And then?"

"He tried to end it. In one final act of so-called mercy, he planned to reveal himself—destroy the tyrants he helped elevate, stop the suffering... and rise as humanity's savior. Their god."

Cleo stared at him. "Why didn't it work?"

"Because I stopped him," Alek said simply. "Before he could make his 'divine' entrance. Before he could rewrite the end of the war and script his legacy."

She was quiet for a long moment. "He never forgave you."

"No," Alek said. "And now he's trying again. This time with a new angle. A new vengeance."

They reached a low stone wall overlooking the harbor, where fishing boats rocked in the tide, their painted hulls bright against the darkening sea. Seagulls circled above, crying into the sky.

Cleo leaned on the wall. "This place feels like it doesn't belong to the world. Like it's holding its breath."

"It is," Alek said. "Ari constructed it with intent. The wards here not only protect, they preserve. This village exists in a pocket of reality, shaped by divine will. It moves slightly out of sync with the world around it. Time flows differently."

She looked around, wide-eyed. "That's why it feels like something from another age."

"It is. And the people here, the ones who can sense that difference—they're part of the veil. Some are descendants of those we once protected. Some are simply drawn here, never quite knowing why."

A wind stirred the lemon trees. Distant church bells rang out the hour.

"I can feel it now," Cleo whispered. "Like the village itself is watching us. Waiting."

"It is," Alek said. "The gods are always watching."

From beneath the folds of her worry, Cleo felt a flicker of awe. She stood beside a man older than history, in a place hidden from the world, on the edge of a war between immortals.

And she was not afraid.

Not entirely.

Alek's phone chimed again.

"They're at the villa," he said.

Cleo didn't speak. She simply took his hand. "Let's go."

The shadows of evening deepened as they stepped back into the alley. With a shimmer of golden light, the village blurred away—folded into memory—and the scent of stone, rosemary, and sea salt was replaced by the stillness of Ari's sanctuary, where fate now awaited them.

As the golden haze of the hidden village dissolved, the familiar scent of jasmine and cypress folded around them. Cleo blinked as the shimmering passage resolved into the tranquil courtyard of Ari's villa. The marble colonnades stood bathed in the amber light of early evening, their surfaces glowing like bone warmed by fire. A breeze stirred the olive branches overhead, their silver-green leaves whispering like the hush before a storm.

Cleo instinctively stepped closer to Alek. There was a stillness in the air—expectant, like the gods themselves were holding their breath.

At the edge of the veranda, beneath Ari's domed gazebo, stood Theo and Helena.

They looked like figures from legend come to life. Helena's gown shimmered like starlight against the pale marble. Her skin, smooth as porcelain, bore a luminescent glow. Theo, regal and solemn, radiated quiet gravity. The siblings stood side by side—two halves of a divine axis, their presence as unsettling as it was awe-inspiring.

Cleo slowed, her fingers tightening around Alek's.

"Why, hello, my dear girl," Helena said, her voice lilting like music over water.

"Um... hello," Cleo managed, her voice barely more than breath. "I—I'm not sure what I'm supposed to do. Should I bow, or...?"

A soft laugh escaped Theo, kind but amused. "No, child. You're not a subject. Just a guest."

Behind them, Ari emerged from the shadows of the pergola, barefoot and composed as always, arms crossed loosely. "What's the word?" she asked, wasting no time on ceremony.

Helena exchanged a glance with her brother, then said, "The Council has agreed to send a representative. Pol will be given a chance to stand down—warned of the consequences if he refuses."

"And you think he'll listen?" Ari asked, one brow arching like a crescent moon.

"We hope," Theo replied. "But we're not fools. Contingencies are already in motion. If Pol rejects diplomacy, the Council is prepared to act."

Cleo watched them with wide, searching eyes. "Act... how?"

"Containment," Helena answered softly. "Nothing more, if it can be helped. He is still one of us."

"And if it can't be helped?" Cleo asked, voice catching.

Helena didn't answer.

Instead, she stepped forward and laid a hand on Cleo's shoulder. Her touch was cold and impossibly light, like a snowflake resting on skin.

"You have courage," she said quietly. "And that will matter, in the days to come."

Cleo swallowed hard. "Thank you. I think."

Theo's eyes flicked to Alek. "You're playing a dangerous game, brother."

"I didn't choose the board," Alek said, voice hard as flint.

Theo gave a slight nod. "Then may the Fates be kind."

With a flare of silver light, the twins vanished, leaving only the faint shimmer of displaced air and the lingering scent of myrrh.

Silence fell again. Ari stepped up beside Cleo, watching the space where Theo and Helena had stood.

"They won't protect you if this goes too far," Ari said quietly.

Cleo looked at her. "They said they'd try."

"Yes. They'll try. But Pol knows how to twist the truth. And he has nothing left to lose."

Alek's jaw tensed. "He won't get to her."

"He already has," Ari said, turning to face him. "Not with chains or threats—but with fear. With leverage. The more you love her, the more power he holds."

Cleo stepped forward, chin lifted. "Then take it away."

Ari blinked. "What?"

"Take away the fear," Cleo said. "Tell me what I need to know. Show me how to fight back. I'm done hiding."

The sun had vanished beyond the western cliffs now, leaving only twilight and the first glimmers of starlight.

Alek studied her face, caught between admiration and dread.

Ari exhaled slowly. "Then come inside. We have work to do."

And as the three of them turned toward the villa's shadowed archways, the wind stirred once more—rustling the olive branches like an ancient warning, as night fell on a world that would never be the same.

Chapter 45

Twilight burned across the sky as Cleo and Alek stepped through the garden gate of Ari's hidden villa. The wards shimmered faintly as they passed, invisible to most, but now perceptible to Cleo—like a soft humming at the edge of her senses. The path wound through ancient olive groves, their silver leaves rustling in a wind that smelled of salt and sage.

Despite the warm Mediterranean dusk, the tension in Cleo's shoulders never loosened. She was still adjusting to what she had learned—about Alek, about the gods walking hidden among mortals, and about Pol, who had taken her as a pawn in a game she couldn't yet see the rules to.

"This village," she said quietly, breaking the silence, "it's protected."

Alek nodded. "Ari set the wards herself centuries ago. This place isn't on any map. Not even divine ones. As long as we're here, Pol can't see us. Not without revealing himself."

Cleo took that in as they passed a weathered stone wall carved with faded Greek runes. Somewhere nearby, the bell of a chapel tolled softly, echoing like memory.

"But he will try, won't he?" she asked.

"Yes," Alek said, glancing toward the sea. "He already has."

They turned down a narrow lane where vines clung to stucco facades and lanterns flickered like distant stars. "The Council sent Theo and Helena?" Cleo asked.

Alek nodded. "They're upstairs with Ari now. They brought the Council's decision."

"What did they say?"

"That they'll send a representative to speak with Pol. A warning. A chance to back down."

"And if he doesn't?"

Alek's jaw clenched. "Then we act. But only if he forces it."

They came to a small courtyard where citrus trees cast long shadows and vines hung heavy with dusk-blushed flowers. A wrought-iron table waited beneath the pergola. Ari sat there, flanked by Theo and Helena, their divine presence subtle but unmistakable. Where mortals might have appeared relaxed, the three of them radiated coiled readiness—like archers before battle.

"You're back," Ari said, standing. "Good. We need to talk."

Helena gave Cleo a gentle nod. "How are you holding up?"

"I've stopped waiting to wake up," Cleo replied. "It's getting easier to believe this is real."

Theo's silver eyes flicked to Alek. "Then it's time we're all honest."

Ari leaned over the table, tapping the map between them. "Pol's already made his next move. That fire-wrapped threat he sent to Alek wasn't just theater—it was strategy. He wants to provoke a response."

"To push you," Theo added, looking at Alek. "To make you act first. So the Council will have cause to step in. And when they do, he'll cry injustice."

"He's not doing this alone," Helena said. "He's reaching out. Whispering to others. We've heard the undercurrents—rumors."

Ari frowned. "Gods who once feared the Council's authority are remembering what it felt like to be revered. To rule."

Cleo folded her arms. "You think they'll follow him?"

"They won't need many," Alek said. "A handful could do it. If they move through the thin places—temples, ruins, forgotten sanctums—they'll have the power to bring the veil between the celestial and mortal world down."

Ari gestured to a glowing mark on the map. "And if they do, humanity will see them. Worship may follow. Fear definitely will. And once the world remembers... it won't forget again."

Cleo's throat tightened. "He tried this before. During World War II."

"Yes," Alek said. "He stirred empires. Whispered in leaders' ears. Stoked fear and ambition and fire. His plan was to end the war himself—in divine spectacle. To force belief back into the world."

"The Council stopped him," Ari added. "But the only punishment he received was exile from the mortal world. Not imprisonment. Not judgment. Just distance."

Theo's expression darkened. "He obeyed. For a time. But never forgot."

Helena turned to Cleo. "We tell you this not to frighten you, but so you understand: Pol isn't simply dangerous. He's deliberate. And now that he knows what you mean to Alek, he will use you."

Cleo exhaled slowly. "He already has."

Alek reached for her hand across the table. "I won't let him again."

Ari looked between them. "We have a night to prepare. The Council won't act unless forced. That means it's up to us."

"Then we strike first?" Cleo asked.

"No," Theo said. "But we watch. We listen. And if he tries anything again—we don't hesitate."

Helena touched Cleo's shoulder. "We'll keep your secret. For now. But if the Council finds out about your bond... if they confirm it..."

"They'll act," Alek said.

"And not just against you," Ari added. "Against her."

The silence that followed was heavy, laced with centuries of precedent and pain.

Cleo squared her shoulders. "Then we don't give them the chance."

Alek turned to the others. "If we're doing this, we do it now. Together."

They all nodded.

Outside the courtyard, the winds shifted. The olive branches whispered.

And in the distance, thunder rolled—not from the sky, but from something older, stirring beneath the earth.

Chapter 46

The ruins of Babylon breathed with silence, the kind only gods noticed—layers of forgotten prayers, crumbled monuments, and the weight of centuries drifting like dust through the desert air.

Pol stood beneath the shattered bones of the Ishtar Gate, arms folded, eyes turned skyward. Moonlight etched sharp angles across his face. His fingers drummed idly against his sleeve as firelight from the summoned braziers danced across broken stone.

He had chosen this place for a reason.

Let the gods remember what they abandoned.

Then came the sound—low, distant, unmistakable.

Thunder.

It rolled across the night like a slow exhale of the sky itself, deep and old. The braziers flickered. The wind stilled.

And without warning, Thor was there.

No footsteps. No flash of power. Just presence—solid, absolute. As if the world had always meant for him to arrive at that precise moment.

He stood a few paces away; a silhouette forged from storm clouds and carved from ancient stone. A broad figure clad in dark leathers and iron-threaded cloth, Mjölnir slung across his back like a slumbering beast. His beard was coarse with silver, his eyes gray storms that held no humor tonight.

"Pol," he said, his voice like the echo of a distant mountain cracking in two.

Pol smirked. "Now that's an entrance."

Thor didn't respond. He walked forward, slow and grounded, until he stood just inside the ring of firelight.

"They sent you," Pol said. "How quaint. Did the Council think thunder would frighten me?"

"They thought I'd speak plainly," Thor replied. "And end it quickly if I needed to."

Pol made a small, theatrical bow. "By all means, then—let's be plain."

"You've begun to move," Thor said. "Not just whispers. Not just symbols. You're stirring the world again."

"I never stopped," Pol replied. "Only slept, like the rest of you. But sleep is no longer sustainable, is it?"

Thor's jaw tightened. "The Council wants clarity. You'll give it."

Pol stepped closer, firelight casting flickering shadows across his face. "You know what's happening. The memory of gods is thinning. Even you are fading, Thor."

muscle ticked in Thor's jaw.

Pol's voice lowered, almost intimate. "You were once worshipped in thunder and blood. Now you're a myth sold in comic books and film. A name spoken for entertainment. How long before even that fades?"

"I'm still here," Thor said evenly. "Still standing."

"For now," Pol said. "But you feel it—don't you? The drift. The irrelevance. The slow death of meaning."

He stepped around one of the crumbling stones, voice gaining weight. "We were never meant to vanish. We were meant to be eternal. The world doesn't forget gods on its own. It forgets when the gods forget themselves."

"You mistake humility for weakness."

"I mistake nothing," Pol snapped. "I remember exactly what we were. And I intend to become it again."

"You want worship."

"I want truth."

There was silence—thick and sharp.

"I walked away once," Pol said. "Obeyed their sentence. No extended time in the mortal world. And what did it accomplish? Amnesia. Diminishment. We let them forget us. I will not let them forget again."

"You're playing with fire."

"I am fire."

Thor's voice darkened. "If you act—if you cross lines—you will face the gods. And you will face me."

Pol smiled slowly. "Then bring them. Bring all of them. But remember—storms pass. Memory doesn't."

He stepped back, then paused, almost as if in afterthought. "Tell me something, though—was it Alek who came crawling to the Council with this information?"

Thor didn't answer immediately.

Pol's smirk deepened. "Well. That's rich coming from him."

Thor's eyes narrowed. "What are you implying?"

Pol tilted his head. "Why doesn't the Council ask him about his little mortal lover?"

Thor blinked, the faintest flicker of surprise tightening his face before he masked it. "You're lying."

"Oh, I'm many things," Pol murmured. "But not wrong."

Thor said nothing, but Pol could feel the shift in his stance—tense now, wary. The kind of quiet a warrior makes before deciding whether or not to draw blood.

"I'll see you again soon," Pol said. "When the thunder's no longer metaphor."

Then he vanished—quiet as smoke, final as ash.

The fire cracked and hissed in the silence left behind.

Pol remained in the ruins.

He stood still in the dark, breathing in the old dust of fallen empires and broken oaths. The silence wrapped around him like a crown.

I already gave them the seed. If the Council acts accordingly with the knowledge of Cleo, they will take Alek off the board for me. He won't be able to get in my way this time.

He smiled again, slower now, colder.

His expression darkened.

And as for the girl... she dies. Sooner or later. By my hand if not by the Council's. But I will end her one way or another. No hesitation.

Because that is how you destroy a god like Alek.

Not in battle.

But in grief.

He turned his back to the firelight and walked deeper into the bones of Babylon, the ruins swallowing him whole.

Chapter 47

The Celestial Hall was carved into starlight and silence.

Columns rose like pillars of time itself, woven with constellations that moved of their own accord. The marble underfoot was veined with memory—every step echoing with the decisions of countless epochs. High above, a vaulted dome shimmered with shifting skies: dusk, dawn, eclipse, eternity. In the center, the Council waited.

They sat in a circle of thrones, each shaped by legacy. Athena's seat, wrapped in bronze and wisdom. Amaterasu's, golden and radiant. Horus, shadowed in obsidian feathers. And at the apex, Helena and Theo—guardians of balance.

The gates at the far end opened.

Thunder walked in.

Thor's heavy stride carried the weight of the storm still lingering on his shoulders. The dust of Babylon clung faintly to his boots. He wore no armor, but the tension in his form spoke of restraint—of something held in check.

Helena stood. "Report."

He gave a respectful nod. "I spoke with Pol."

A pause. The air tightened.

Theo leaned forward. "Did he deny the accusations?"

"No," Thor said. "He was proud of them."

A murmur ran through the chamber.

"He's not hiding," Thor continued. "Not scheming in secret. He wants us to see. He wants us to respond. Everything he's doing is a provocation."

"Did he issue any direct threat?" Athena asked, voice cool and precise.

"Not in words," Thor replied. "But his intent is clear. He believes the time of hidden gods is over. That we've faded too far. He sees this as correction. Restoration."

"Madness," muttered Ogun, his voice like grinding iron. "He would drag the world into fire to feel important again."

Thor's expression remained unreadable. "He also... said something else."

The room stilled.

"He implied that Alek is compromised. That he's formed a bond with a mortal. A romantic one."

Several heads turned sharply. Helena's face went still as glass.

"Alek?" Theo asked, slowly.

Thor nodded once. "Pol was mocking. But not uncertain. He knew something."

"And you believe him?" came Athena's sharp challenge.

"I believe he believes it," Thor said. "And if there's even a chance that it's true, it complicates everything."

"It's a violation of one of our most sacred rules," murmured Amaterasu. "No god may fall in love with a mortal."

"It's not just a taboo," Theo said grimly. "It's a risk to the entire world."

"We haven't seen Alek in defiance before," Athena said. "But if Pol is telling the truth... then Alek may no longer be fit to stand against him."

"No," Helena said. "Alek is our strongest barrier. If we lose him now—"

Finally, Thor spoke. "We need to speak with Alek. Directly. Privately."

A heavy silence followed.

"If Pol won't back down," Athena said slowly, "then we must prepare for the possibility he escalates."

"It won't be possibility much longer," Ogun said. "He wants a return to divine rule. He'll use chaos to make it happen."

"A warning won't be enough," Amaterasu added. "We have to consider what comes next. How we contain him—if he forces our hand."

Thor's expression darkened. "Containment will not come easily. He's stronger now. More deliberate. We will need old magic—older than most of us remember."

"We may also need unity," Theo said. "Which we no longer have."

A silence fell again, heavier than before.

"And Alek?" Athena asked.

Thor's eyes narrowed. "We question him. Soon. And if the girl is real—if he has broken faith—then we face another choice altogether."

None spoke.

The war they had hoped to avoid was beginning to breathe.

And in the high dome above them, the sky flickered—not with stars, but with gathering stormlight.

Chapter 48

The morning air in the hills of northern Italy was cool and quiet, filled with birdsong and the distant toll of chapel bells. Cleo sat alone on the edge of Ari's terrace, wrapped in a shawl and nursing a lukewarm cup of tea. Below her, the olive trees rippled gently in the breeze, silver leaves flashing like blades.

But peace was a thin veil now. She wore it like a borrowed dress—ill-fitting, temporary. Her body was back in the villa. Her mind was still in Babylon.

Alek hadn't spoken much since their return. He walked the grounds like a haunted general, constantly watching the horizon. Ari stayed inside, sharpening blades no one could see.

Cleo didn't know what she was supposed to feel anymore. She had asked for the truth—and gotten more than she ever could have imagined.

She turned her gaze upward. The sky was cloudless. Too serene for what she knew was coming.

Then came a shift in the wind.

It wasn't loud. It didn't rattle windows or stir trees. It was subtler than that—an atmospheric ripple, like reality inhaling.

They arrived without footsteps. Without a sound.

Theo and Helena stepped into the courtyard from nowhere.

Helena's robes shimmered like ice caught in sunlight. Theo looked more grounded, but no less unearthly, his expression unreadable as always.

Cleo stood as Ari emerged from the villa, already tense. Alek followed close behind her, his face unreadable until he saw them—and stopped.

Theo offered Cleo a polite nod, then looked to Alek. "We don't have much time. The Council has made its decision."

Cleo's chest tightened. "About what?"

"About Pol," Helena said. "And about you."

That silenced everyone.

Ari's eyes flicked toward Alek, who said nothing. His jaw was set like granite.

Helena continued. "Pol will not back down. He's made that clear. The Council will prepare for open confrontation. But war is no longer a distant possibility. It's a probability."

Theo added, "They will not act yet. But when they do, it will be swift. Final. Alliances will be tested."

"And us?" Alek asked, voice low.

Helena hesitated.

Then Theo spoke. "They're coming. Not in force. Not yet. But they suspect."

A beat of silence passed.

"What do they suspect?" Cleo asked.

Helena looked at her with a strange kind of pity. "That you are not simply mortal. That Alek is not simply loyal."

Cleo swallowed hard.

Theo looked at Alek. "Pol said something during his meeting with Thor. Something... specific. He implied you were compromised by your affection for a mortal woman."

"He did more than imply," Helena said. "He planted doubt. And now the Council is acting on it."

Cleo looked at Alek, who remained very still.

Ari's voice was tight with fury. "And you're warning us why?"

"Because we believe Pol is manipulating them," Theo said. "And if he succeeds, Alek could be removed from the equation altogether."

"Exiled?" Ari asked.

"Or worse," Helena said quietly.

Cleo stepped closer to Alek. "What do we do?"

"We don't give them proof," Alek said. "We protect you. And when they come—we stand our ground."

Theo glanced toward the tree line, as if sensing the first tremor of something distant.

"They won't strike yet," he said. "But be ready. They will come with questions. And they will be watching everything."

Helena met Cleo's eyes. "Don't give them a reason."

And with a shimmer of light, they were gone.

The courtyard was silent again—but the air felt thinner.

War was no longer just a word. It was a direction. A wind. And it was moving toward them.

Chapter 49

The villa had grown quiet again. The kind of silence that wrapped around the walls like fog—not peaceful, but waiting.

Cleo stood at the edge of the olive grove, the trees casting dappled shade over her shoulders. The wind carried the scent of thyme and stone and distant sea. She listened for movement, for wings, for thunder, for anything that might signal the Council's arrival. But all she heard was her own breathing.

She didn't turn when Alek approached. She could feel him—his presence was unmistakable now, heavy and golden, like the sun resting on her back.

"They'll come soon," she said.

"Yes," Alek replied, stepping beside her.

She looked up at him. "And you'll lie to them?"

"I'll protect you," he said. "In whatever way I must."

There was a beat of silence.

Then he reached into the folds of his coat and withdrew a small object wrapped in velvet. He held it out, palm open.

"I made this for you," he said.

Cleo unwrapped it slowly.

Inside was a necklace—delicate, ancient, and impossibly bright. A gold disc no larger than a coin, etched with strange runes that shimmered faintly in the light. The chain was impossibly fine, but strong as steel beneath her fingers. The charm hummed when she touched it, like it knew her already.

"What is it?" she asked softly.

"A ward. A weapon," Alek said. "It carries part of my essence. Enough to stop anything—anyone—that tries to harm you."

Cleo blinked. "How does it work?"

"If you're in danger," he said, "touch it. Think of me. It will release a blast of my power—enough to knock back even a god. It won't kill. But it will give you a chance to run."

She stared at it, this fragile, glowing piece of him. "You gave me part of your power."

"I'd give you all of it, if I could."

He moved behind her and fastened the chain around her neck. His fingers brushed her skin—warm, reverent. She felt it settle against her collarbone like a second heartbeat.

Cleo turned to face him. "You're not scared of the Council?"

"I'm terrified," he said honestly. "But not of them. Of losing you."

Before she could speak, Ari's voice cut through the grove.

"Well, if we're all done being romantic and tragic," she said, emerging from the trees, "we've got bigger problems than divine fashion accessories."

Alek didn't flinch. "You heard them. The Council will come. Pol won't stop. And we're caught in the middle."

"Which is why we need to plan," Ari said. "We need layers of defense. Magical, physical, psychological. If they come for Cleo, they'll expect obedience. We give them defiance instead."

"We need misdirection," Alek added. "Enough to buy time."

"And routes of escape," Ari said. "If things go wrong, Cleo has to be able to disappear. Not just physically—magically."

Cleo stepped forward. "You want me to run?"

"No," Ari said. "We want you to survive."

Alek nodded. "If the Council turns against us, they'll come for me first. If I fall—"

"You won't," Cleo said quickly.

"If I fall," he repeated gently, "you have to go. You use the necklace. You go where Ari sends you. You trust her. Promise me."

Cleo hesitated. Then nodded. "I promise."

Ari knelt on the earth and began sketching lines in the dirt—sigils, escape paths, power centers on the land.

"We'll reinforce the villa's wards. I'll call in some old favors. I know gods who owe me—some still remember what Pol did during the war. And I'll teach Cleo a few new tricks. She won't be defenseless."

Cleo looked between them—two beings older than empires, readying themselves for war because she had become something more than a witness.

She had become a reason.

And that made her dangerous.

Chapter 50

The courtyard was quiet again, but not still.

Cleo stood barefoot in the warm dirt, the sun high and golden above her, the olive trees casting shifting shadows around the perimeter. A circle had been marked on the ground with salt, ash, and crushed petals—old symbols Ari had drawn by hand. At its center stood a life-sized mannequin carved from dark wood and iron, humanoid in shape but faceless, rune-scribed joints glowing faintly. It breathed no air, but it moved—twitching slightly, tilting as if it were listening to Cleo's heartbeat.

Ari stood at the edge of the circle, arms crossed, eyes sharp.

"Again."

Cleo exhaled, sweat tracing a path down her spine. Her arms ached, her legs were beginning to tremble—but she nodded and stepped forward. In her hand was a small dagger, weighted strangely—like it didn't want to be held.

"Focus on the connection," Ari said. "Not the form. You're not a soldier. You're something older than that. Something quicker."

Cleo tightened her grip and moved. The blade whirled once, then twice—but the mannequin shifted, spinning on its base with unnatural grace. Its shoulder dipped and dodged the arc of her strike. Before she could react, its arm snapped outward with a fluid motion, catching her squarely in the side and knocking her flat onto the packed earth.

The breath slammed out of her. Dust clouded around her face as she lay stunned on the ground.

"Again," Ari said.

But Cleo didn't move.

She sat up slowly, chest heaving, eyes burning—not from the hit, but from something deeper. The frustration she'd been trying to smother all morning cracked through her chest.

"I don't know if I can do this," she said, her voice rough. "I'm not like you. I'm not like Alek. I'm just—me. I can't do this."

The silence that followed was sharp.

Ari didn't kneel. Didn't rush to comfort. She stepped to the edge of the circle and looked down at her, face unreadable.

"You're right," she said. "You're not like us."

Cleo looked up, ashamed and angry all at once.

"You're something rarer," Ari continued. "You're a mortal who hasn't run. You're a woman who watched gods fight in the street, was kidnapped by one, and still came back swinging. That doesn't require divinity. That requires grit."

She tossed the dagger back down into the circle.

"You're allowed to fall. You're just not allowed to stay there."

Cleo stared at the dagger. Then she stood.

The mannequin reactivated as she stepped forward, turning toward her, arms rising like a marionette on strings.

Cleo inhaled. Closed her eyes.

This time when she moved, the air shifted around her—not just heat, but pressure. The dagger became an extension of her will, not her fear. As she stepped into the arc of motion, the mannequin twisted with supernatural speed, arms sweeping to deflect her—but she adjusted mid-strike. Her blade cut a line through the space where its chest had been an instant before. Metal sparked. Runes flared and dimmed.

Ari smiled. "Better."

They trained until the sun dipped low and the breeze turned cool. Cleo's muscles throbbed, but something within her had begun to settle—a quiet center she hadn't known she was missing.

As they took a break beneath the fig tree at the edge of the courtyard, Ari passed her a flask of cold water.

"You've come farther than I expected," she said. "Even for someone as stubborn as you."

Cleo leaned back against the tree trunk, catching her breath. "What happens if I'm not ready when they come?"

Ari shrugged. "Then we buy time. Or we lie. Or we bleed a little."

"That's comforting."

"No, this is comforting—" Ari leaned forward, her tone suddenly soft. "They underestimated you the second you stepped into this world. Pol, the Council, maybe even Alek. That's your weapon. Use it."

Cleo looked down at the necklace resting against her chest, its gold disk warm against her skin.

"I will."

From the shadows of the villa, Alek watched them—arms folded, eyes unreadable. Not with fear, but with something heavier: awe.

She wasn't ready.

She was becoming ready.

Chapter 51

They came just after sunrise.

No sound announced them—no chariots in the sky, no shattering of clouds, no thunder. Just a tightening of the air. A stillness that ran through the olive trees like a held breath. The birds stopped singing. The breeze forgot to move.

Ari felt it first. She stood on the villa's southern balcony, eyes on the distant ridge, where light had begun to warp—subtly, like heat mirage. Then came the shimmer. The ripple.

She didn't blink.

"They're here," she said.

Inside, Cleo stood in the atrium, already dressed in neutral tones, her hair pulled back. The dagger rested in its sheath beneath her coat. The necklace lay against her chest like a glowing coin beneath her heartbeat.

She touched it once—lightly—not to activate it, but to remind herself it was real.

Alek emerged from the hallway behind her, his expression unreadable, his steps soundless on the marble. Since the Council's warning, he hadn't slept much. He hadn't needed to. Gods didn't tire the way mortals did, but something in his silence had the weight of exhaustion. Or restraint.

The front gates creaked open of their own accord.

And the gods walked in.

They were four this time:

Athena, clad in bronze that gleamed like burnished judgment, her eyes hard and clear and sharp as strategy.

Theo, composed as always, every movement minimal, controlled, precise. The diplomat. The observer.

Amaterasu, radiant and cool, her presence like sunlight behind clouds—beautiful, but distant. Her robes whispered with power.

And Thor, who needed no fanfare. He was the storm held in check, broad-shouldered and silent, Mjölnir slung behind him like a slumbering threat. He scanned the villa like a sentry entering enemy ground.

No introductions. No pageantry. Just arrival.

Ari met them at the top of the marble steps with her arms folded and one brow raised. "This is private land."

"This is Council business," Athena replied without pause.

Cleo stepped forward from the atrium, her heartbeat pounding louder with every footfall the gods made. The olive trees behind her swayed as though trying to hide her. She didn't let them.

She made herself visible.

Theo studied her, his gaze neither kind nor cruel. "You are Cleo Tenner."

"I am," she said.

"We have questions," Amaterasu said, "for both of you."

Alek moved beside Cleo, calm but watchful, as if weighing every breath for consequence. "Then ask them here."

The gods exchanged glances. Athena stepped forward first—her movements precise, rehearsed, like a general crossing into disputed territory. She stopped just short of Cleo. Close enough for intimidation, not enough for provocation.

"Are you in love with her?" Athena asked Alek directly.

The courtyard went silent.

Cleo's breath caught—but Alek didn't flinch.

"You came here for answers," he said. "Not accusations."

Athena stared at him. "That was an answer."

Theo stepped forward now. "Alek, the Council has been made aware of certain... concerns. Namely, that your judgment may be compromised."

"Because I protected her?" Alek asked, voice cool.

"Because you acted alone," Amaterasu said. "Because you may have broken one of our most sacred boundaries."

"He already did," Ari interjected, her voice like a drawn bowstring. "Pol took her. Tortured her. Left a message behind in blood and fire. And Alek did what none of you were willing to do—he brought her home."

Theo's voice didn't change. "And Alek intervened—personally. That alone puts his judgment into question."

Before Alek could answer, Thor's voice cut in, calm and grave. "He acted under duress. Pol forced his hand. Anyone here would have done the same."

Theo turned toward him. "Would you?"

Thor's answer was immediate. "If Pol had stolen something under my protection? Yes."

There was a pause.

"Intent is what matters," Amaterasu said, glancing toward Cleo. "And intent is difficult to prove."

Cleo stepped forward before anyone else could. "I didn't ask for this," she said. "I didn't seek out any of this. But I'm here now—and I'm not running."

"You claim Pol is using you," Athena said.

"He is," Cleo replied. "But only as long as I'm weak. As long as I'm seen as something to be taken."

Athena's eyes shifted to Alek. "And if you are the reason she is vulnerable?"

Alek's jaw tightened. "Then I'll be the reason she's not."

The words hung in the air like iron in water.

Thor's gaze narrowed, but he said nothing. Theo looked at Amaterasu. Amaterasu watched Cleo for a heartbeat longer, then turned her attention back to the courtyard.

The gods had what they came for.

Theo turned toward the steps. "The Council has not passed judgment. Not yet. But if Pol rises and we find that your actions have endangered the veil—or the balance between our worlds"

"We won't," Alek said flatly.

Thor gave him one last look. "See that you don't."

And just like that—no spell, no flash of light—the gods vanished.

The courtyard was suddenly too quiet.

The breeze returned.

Cleo realized her fists were clenched. She released them slowly. Her fingers trembled.

"I didn't breathe," she whispered.

Alek placed a hand lightly on her back. "You held your ground. That's what matters."

But even he was still staring at the space where the gods had stood—where their judgment had not yet fallen, but now hovered like thunder just beyond the hills.

Chapter 52

The gods were gone.

But they'd left something behind. Not dust, not fire—just pressure. Like the air had grown heavier around the villa, infused with all the things they hadn't said aloud.

Cleo didn't speak at first. She stood in the shadow of the olive trees, arms crossed over her chest, staring at the gravel path the Council had walked. Her breathing was shallow, but measured. She hadn't cried. She hadn't broken.

She had simply endured.

Alek stood beside her in silence.

"They already knew," she said at last, her voice small but steady. "About us. Or they suspect it. I could feel it."

"They didn't have proof," Alek replied. "They still don't."

"They came looking for it."

His eyes shifted toward her, golden and calm. "And you didn't give it to them."

Cleo looked up at him. "That question... when Athena asked if you loved me. You didn't answer."

"I gave her exactly what she wanted," he said. "An opening to doubt without confirmation. They want hesitation more than truth. It lets them delay judgment."

She nodded slowly. "So we're living on borrowed time."

He stepped closer, brushing his fingers lightly along her arm. "We always were."

The words should have chilled her. Instead, they settled in her chest like gravity—real, heavy, and strangely grounding.

A rustle came from the far side of the garden. Ari emerged from the shade of a cypress, arms folded, face unreadable.

"Well," she said dryly, "that could've gone worse."

Cleo let out a laugh that sounded too much like disbelief. "That could've gone worse?"

"They didn't summon a tribunal. They didn't detain Alek. They didn't call for Cleo's immediate containment or questioning. And Thor didn't throw his hammer through our walls. That's a win in my book."

Alek arched a brow. "You're hard to impress."

"I'm realistic," Ari replied. "They didn't come to pass judgment. They came to test the waters. You bought us time."

"How much?" Cleo asked.

"Days, maybe. A week if we're lucky. They'll argue, posture, and delay. Theo's voice carries, but Athena's pride slows her hand. And Thor—" she paused "—he's conflicted. You saw it."

"He doesn't want to fight me," Alek said.

"No," Ari agreed. "But he will, if it comes to that. Which means we need to be ready before they make up their minds."

Alek's gaze narrowed. "They want delay. Not just because they doubt—but because they need me. They won't take me off the board until Pol is dealt with."

"Exactly," Ari said. "You're still their best weapon. And they know it. But the second Pol falls—"

"They'll come for me," Alek finished.

Cleo's breath hitched. "Even after everything?"

"They're not sentimental," Ari said. "They're strategic. And right now, Alek is useful. But when he stops being useful—when the war ends—they won't hesitate."

Cleo looked between them. "So we're just... what? Stalling?"

"No," Ari said. "We're using their stall to prepare. Because once Pol's no longer the distraction, you'll be."

"And me?" Cleo asked, voice quiet.

"You're the fulcrum," Ari said. "To Pol. To Alek. To all of this. If they ever confirm what you are to him—what he's become because of you—there will be no more doubt. Only decree."

Alek's hand found hers. "Then we don't let them see it."

"Or," Ari added, "we make it so powerful they won't dare touch it."

Cleo exhaled slowly. "What does that mean?"

"It means more training. Fallback plans. Figuring out what Pol's next move will be before he makes it. Because once the Council decides, they'll move fast. And so will he."

Alek nodded. "And we move first."

Ari gave him a thin smile. "Now you're talking like a god again."

Chapter 53

The ruins whispered.

Not with wind—but with memory. With rage. With prophecy.

Pol stood in the crumbling heart of ancient Carthage, beneath a temple long buried and now unearthed by hands both mortal and divine. The light here was not sunlight, but firelight—deep red and low, cast from ever-burning braziers carved from volcanic stone. Shadows writhed along the cracked columns, their movements slow, serpentine.

He had felt the shift in the world the moment it happened.

The Council had moved. Visited the villa. Confronted Alek.

He smiled.

"They're predictable," he murmured to the flames. "Soft. Hesitant. Still clinging to the illusion of balance."

A figure stepped out from the darkness behind him, cloaked in oil-black silk, their face hidden beneath a jackal mask.

"They didn't strike?"

Pol didn't turn. "Of course not. They want Alek to clean up their mess. Just like always. Let him fight their wars, shoulder their fear. And when he bleeds enough—then they'll decide he's dangerous."

The masked figure moved closer. "And the girl?"

"They still don't know what she is to him. Not entirely. But suspicion is a fuse." Pol's smile twisted. "All I had to do was light it."

Another shape emerged from the edge of the firelight. This one shimmered unnaturally, her skin the color of onyx and her eyes like frozen stars. She was barefoot, adorned in chains that didn't bind but sang when she moved.

"They bought time," she said. "He bought time."

Pol turned toward her, admiring her elegance—the way her very presence disrupted gravity.

"Time is good," he said. "Time gives me options."

He gestured toward the broken altar behind him. "Summon the others. Quietly. I want all pieces on the board before the Council makes their next move."

The masked one tilted their head. "Even the Old One?"

Pol's smile darkened. "Especially the Old One. If Alek is going to bleed, I want him to bleed in front of those who still remember what he was. What he failed to protect."

The woman's voice was smooth as oil. "And when Cleo stands beside him?"

"She won't," Pol said coldly. "Not for long. Once the Council makes its decision, they'll strip him of protection. And if they hesitate—"

"You'll finish it yourself."

Pol nodded. "I already planted the seed. If they take him down, he won't be there to stop me. And if they don't... I will kill her myself."

He stepped closer to the fire.

"Because that's how you destroy a god like Alek. Not in battle. Not with power. But in grief."

The brazier flared as if in answer.

He turned to the gathering shadows. "Tell the others: we don't wait. We don't hope. We don't believe in mercy. The Council showed its fear today—and fear makes them weak. We press now. While they argue."

One by one, the others appeared—figures from all corners of forgotten pantheons, those who had once ruled rivers, deserts, stars, and storms. Betrayers, exiles, hungry things wrapped in skin and myth.

Pol stepped onto the fractured dais and raised one hand.

"The end of the age of silence begins now."

Chapter 54

The council of traitors had dispersed, but the fire still whispered.

It crackled low in the shattered hearth of the forgotten temple, casting long, broken shadows against walls etched with languages no mortal tongue remembered. Carthage had fallen a hundred times, yet the bones of this place endured—buried deep beneath the ruins where history couldn't find them. Only gods with long memories and longer grudges still knew the way.

Selene stayed behind.

She stood like a statue carved from shadow and obsidian, unmoving as the heat flickered over her skin. Her chains glinted dully—not ornamental, but sacred. Each link had been forged in a different age, each one a memory, a vow, a blade dulled by betrayal. They shimmered faintly with runes only gods could see, and hummed as if they still remembered how to sing in the tongues of stars.

The others had gone. Pol with his glee. The jackal-masked assassin with her silence. The mountain god with his hunger. All fools, eager to set fire to a world they could no longer rule.

Only Selene remained in the ash-swept hall, her bare feet stirring no dust as she approached the altar. The carved lions on its corners had long since lost their faces, worn away by time and blood. She knelt before it, not in reverence—but in ritual.

Then she whispered a word.

One word.

It was not a word mortals could pronounce. It was a frequency of thought, the memory of silence shaped into form. It slipped between the cracks of stone, through the glowing veins of magic still buried in the foundations of the world.

The air held its breath.

A low ripple answered from beneath the earth, like the temple itself had exhaled. A circle of soot within the altar's center began to pulse with faint silver light. The glow intensified, congealing into a disc of glassy shadow.

A mirror.

Its surface shimmered, then stilled.

And within it: Helena.

Her face, serene as always. Ageless. Pale as moonlight on stone. Her golden eyes narrowed, seeing not only Selene, but the sacred darkness wrapped around her like a veil.

"Speak," Helena said. Her voice was quiet thunder— impossibly soft, yet undeniably commanding.

Selene bowed her head. Her chains whispered.

"They've begun," she said, her voice low and rich, smooth as blackwater. "Pol has summoned his broken court. He is assembling his storm."

Helena's image didn't react, but the mirror grew colder around the edges.

"He plans to strike before your Council can reach consensus. Before you stop debating and start acting."

"We expected that," Helena replied. "Anything else?"

"He knows the Council won't remove Alek. Not yet. Not until Pol is dealt with."

Helena's expression tightened by a fraction. "He's correct."

Selene's dark eyes flicked upward. "So he was right to plant the seed. You will use Alek. Until he's no longer necessary."

Helena didn't flinch. "We don't have the luxury of purity. Alek is the sword we need—until the moment that sword becomes too dangerous to hold."

Selene gave a quiet nod, as if that answer was both expected and damning.

"And the girl?" Helena asked.

Selene's voice dropped further. "Cleo is not as fragile as she appears. She learns quickly. There's fire in her—not Alek's gift, but something older. Something mortal. That's what makes her dangerous."

"Or valuable," Helena said.

"If she survives."

Helena's eyes narrowed slightly. "She must."

"And if she doesn't?"

Helena's tone hardened like steel cooling. "Then we lose Alek. And the veil collapses."

For a moment, there was only the low hiss of fire.

Selene turned her gaze back to the mirror. "Do you trust me?"

"No," Helena said simply. "But I believe you."

A pause.

"Send your next message at the turning moon. Until then—watch Pol. Watch the cracks in his court. And Selene?"

The chains around her arms glowed faintly, as if acknowledging Helena's voice.

"Be careful. Pol doesn't forgive betrayal."

Selene rose slowly, like smoke drawn upward. "Neither do I."

The mirror dimmed. The silver light dissolved into ash. The shadows reclaimed the altar.

Selene stood for a moment longer in the dying heat, staring at the embers where Helena's reflection had been. Then she turned and walked into the darkened colonnade— back to the deep chambers, where Pol's creatures slept and dreamed of slaughter.

The mask would go back on.

The smile.

The lie.

But beneath the silk and stone and silver, Selene's mind was already turning.

She would serve. She would watch. She would wait.

And when the moment came—

She would strike.

Chapter 55

The sky above Ari's villa had turned molten with sunset.

Cleo stood alone near the edge of the hill, where the olive grove gave way to cliffs that looked out over the sea. The sky had gone blood-orange, with veins of violet threading through the clouds like bruises. Waves broke in rhythm far below, a slow, steady crashing that made the world feel both ancient and small.

She didn't hear Alek approach.

But she felt him.

His presence no longer startled her—it warmed and steadied her, like gravity leaning in her favor. She glanced sideways and saw him there, hands in his coat pockets, golden light catching in his dark hair.

"Didn't think you'd be this quiet after the gods came knocking," she said, trying to make it light. It came out a little too honest.

Alek studied the horizon. "There's a kind of silence that comes before war. This feels like that."

She nodded. "And what comes after?"

"Graves," he said softly. "Sometimes peace. But usually more silence."

They stood there a moment, the wind tugging gently at her sleeves.

"Do you regret it?" she asked. "Bringing me into all of this?"

He turned to her fully. "No."

"But if the Council decides to act... if Thor is the one sent to stop you—"

"I'll face him," Alek said.

"What if you lose?"

He hesitated. Then said, "Then I lose."

But he didn't just mean the battle. If he lost to Thor— if the Council took him down—he would lose her. And that was the part that mattered. Whatever punishment they had in store for him—exile, imprisonment, silence—it wouldn't compare to the weight of losing Cleo. Because a life without her wouldn't be life at all. It would be memory. And torment.

Cleo looked down at the necklace around her neck, the gold charm now warm against her skin as if reacting to the conversation.

"I keep wondering," she murmured, "if they're right. If you're different because of me. If I've made you weaker."

Alek stepped closer. "No."

His voice was low, but firm. "You haven't made me weaker. You've made me choose. That's what they're afraid of—not that I'll break rules. But that I'll break away from them."

Cleo looked up, and there was something so open in his expression it almost hurt.

"I wasn't supposed to feel this," he said. "Not in this life."

"They think love makes gods reckless," he continued. "And maybe it does. But it also makes them willing to fight for something more than power."

Her throat tightened. She tried to respond, but the words caught in her chest.

Alek stepped forward, gently brushing her hair back behind her ear.

"If the Council comes for me, you run. You vanish. Use the necklace. Use Ari's wards. Don't wait for me."

"No," Cleo said, voice shaking. "I'm not running again."

"Cleo—"

"I won't lose you and live like it never happened. If they come for you, I fight."

Alek stared at her, his gaze raw and ancient and aching.

"You weren't supposed to be part of this world," he whispered. "But now that you are... I can't imagine surviving it without you."

She touched his hand.

"You won't have to."

They stood like that as the sun bled into the sea, and night rose to claim the world again.

Behind them, the villa lights flickered on, and from inside, Ari's voice rang out—sharp, practical, determined.

"Get inside, lovers. We've got a war to plan."

***

The main hall had been cleared. The antique tables were pushed against the walls, candles floated above a wide map etched into the tiled floor. Not a paper map, but a glowing constellation of runes, ley lines, and pulse points— each flickering softly in response to Ari's magic.

The room smelled of lavender oil and iron.

Ari stood at the center, barefoot, her sleeves rolled, blades laid out like surgical tools on a velvet cloth beside her. She looked less like a goddess and more like a war general in the skin of a scholar.

"Close the door," she said without looking up.

Alek shut it behind them.

Cleo stepped carefully around the glowing lines on the floor, eyeing the map. "What am I looking at?"

"Potential staging grounds," Ari said. "Places Pol has been quietly setting up operations. Strongholds. Storage caches. Passageways between realms. Some old, some newly claimed."

She waved a hand. The glowing points pulsed, some red, some gold, one pulsing dark like a wound.

"What's that?" Cleo asked, pointing to the black mark near the Mediterranean basin.

"Babylon," Ari said. "Still bleeding. We think it's become a hub. He's using it to coordinate his movements."

"And if we don't move fast?" Alek asked.

"Then those dots connect," Ari said. "And we end up boxed in."

Alek crossed his arms. "We disrupt before he consolidates."

Ari nodded. "Exactly. We strike early. Shut down movement. Cripple communication. And make sure he never feels safe."

She turned to Cleo. "You're the key to half of this. Not because you're divine—but because you're not."

Cleo frowned. "What does that mean?"

"You're not divine. You can cross many of the wards that would keep us out. You carry mortal unpredictability. That makes you the perfect infiltrator."

"And what do I do once I'm in?"

Ari smiled grimly. "Anything you want."

Alek frowned. "He's not working alone."

"No," Ari said. "He's building a new court. Old gods, dangerous relics, forgotten things with nothing left to lose. We've confirmed at least four. If we isolate and eliminate them, we cut his teeth before he gets to bite."

"Who's first?" Alek asked.

"One of Pol's allies. He's positioned in the Balkans, moving fast, gathering muscle. We won't wait for him to mobilize."

"How do you know all this?" Cleo asked.

Ari hesitated, then said, "Helena's been speaking to me. Quietly. Off record."

That gave Alek pause. "Since when?"

"Since before the Council left. She has a contact—a double agent inside Pol's court. Someone close enough to report movements, gather signs, warn us."

"You trust this agent?" Cleo asked.

"I trust Helena," Ari said. "And I trust that she wouldn't risk leaking intel unless she knew it was real. That's how we know where many of these strongholds are—and how we know Rome can't wait."

Cleo looked to the dark pulse on the map again. "Then that's where we go."

Ari's expression hardened. "We shut it down. Fast. Before it becomes the first major strike."

She turned to Cleo. "This is your first deployment. You'll be shadowed, guarded—but I need your instincts sharp. If you sense anything strange, we act on it."

Cleo nodded. "What's the objective?"

"Shut down the stronghold. And if possible—draw them out."

Cleo's eyes narrowed. "A trap?"

Ari smiled. "If we're lucky."

Silence followed.

Then Cleo stepped forward. "Let's make sure they regret underestimating us."

Ari's smile sharpened like a blade being drawn.

"Now you're talking like a god."

Chapter 56

The air in Ari's villa buzzed with a quiet urgency.

Alek moved through the halls in silence, packing only what he needed: an old dagger that had seen wars in three continents, a silver ring forged during the fall of Atlantis, and a sliver of obsidian etched with protective sigils. Tools, not weapons. Symbols of resolve, not fear.

Cleo stood by the window, lacing her boots.

The necklace Alek had given her pulsed faintly, like it could sense the approaching storm. Her fingers brushed it once—an unconscious habit now. She hadn't spoken much since the planning session. Not out of doubt, but focus. Her mind was already there, in the dark beneath Rome, running the steps.

Ari entered without knocking, a compact satchel slung over one shoulder. "Ward tokens, cloaking dust, three backup blades, and a lockstone," she said. "We leave in an hour."

"Where do we land?" Alek asked.

"Old catacombs outside the Aventine. Quiet, sacred. Still tethered to old routes. We'll cross there."

"And the Council?" Cleo asked.

"They won't follow," Ari replied. "Not yet. They're still 'deliberating.'"

The sarcasm was sharp.

She turned to Cleo. "You sure you're ready?"

Cleo met her gaze. "I'm already gone."

Far beneath the bones of Carthage, Pol stood at the edge of a reflection pool that had long since dried to ash. The chamber was round and rough-hewn, its walls streaked with iron and soot. Fires crackled low in the corners, casting golden patterns that danced like serpents across the stone.

One of his lieutenants emerged from the shadows—Skae, the one who wore a hundred faces but never his own. Tonight, he looked like a Roman senator. Elegant. Imperious. Hollow-eyed.

"If your decoy works," Skae said, "they'll strike Rome first."

Pol didn't turn. "Of course they will. They're so predictable it's pathetic."

He stepped forward and traced a finger through the air—marking a new path, one unseen by the rest of the world. His illusions shimmered to life: an identical copy of the Rome stronghold, mirrored in appearance, but hollow beneath.

"They'll find nothing but ruins," Pol said. "And the little surprise I left for them."

Meanwhile, en route to Rome...

The sky above the Italian countryside was overcast, the clouds hanging like bruises across the horizon. Ari stood at the edge of the Threshold site, her eyes narrowed as she extended one hand toward the air.

The ground trembled faintly in response.

With nothing but intent—no words, no gesture beyond thought—the space before them fractured with light. A vertical seam of gold split the air, widening with a pulse like a heartbeat.

A thunderclap of pressure. Then, a blinding flash.

Cleo vanished first, caught in the flare.

There was no sensation of walking or stepping—only the instant, jarring shift as the world inverted.

When her vision cleared, she stood in silence.

Stone. Cold. Wet. The underground smelled of dust and time.

Alek and Ari appeared beside her an instant later, the air snapping closed behind them.

"It's quiet," Cleo said.

"Too quiet," Alek murmured.

Ari held up the map—the same glowing constellation they'd reviewed back at the villa. One of the points dimmed slightly as if receding. The black pulse that had marked Rome now blinked—once—then stilled.

"This isn't right," she said.

A distant echo reached them.

Not a footstep. Not wind.

A laugh.

Cleo's hand went to the dagger at her belt. "Trap?"

"Maybe," Ari said. "But if it is... it's not for us."

The catacombs beneath Aventine Hill were wrong.

The silence wasn't reverent. It was staged.

The air smelled like damp stone and burnt copper. The flickering torches Ari conjured danced across faded frescoes and carved archways that looked too clean, too preserved, as if the decay had been... paused. Or painted on.

Ahead, the corridor opened into a massive domed chamber. Ari led the way, blades drawn, cloak trailing like a shadow with intent. In the center of the chamber stood a crude altar—a patchwork of old Roman marble, shattered statues, and burned offerings that hadn't been lit for centuries.

And there—perched atop the broken altar—was a creature.

It crouched low on all fours, skeletal in shape but pulsing with thick, ink-like muscle. Its skin shimmered like obsidian soaked in oil, and its tail was barbed and twitching. Its head—twisted and elongated—resembled that of a basilisk carved from ancient bone, with golden etchings seared into its skull like a crown. Its tongue forked and smoked with shadow.

"What the hell is that?" Cleo breathed.

"Shadow-born," Alek said grimly. "A basilisk bred in the Underwilds. They shouldn't even exist anymore."

The creature snapped its head toward them—no eyes, only pits of golden heat—and shrieked.

Then it launched.

Alek moved first, sword drawn and glowing. The creature struck faster than expected, slamming into him and sending him skidding across the stone. Sparks erupted as his blade scraped the floor.

Ari spun, blades up. Her stance was effortless, precise—but the creature moved with the rage of a storm. Its tail whipped toward her. She ducked low and slashed across its front limb. The blow only slowed it.

It turned toward Cleo.

Her fingers brushed the necklace.

The golden pulse burst forward, slamming into the creature and throwing it against a column. Cracks spiderwebbed through the stone, dust and shards raining down. The beast rolled, rose again.

"Its hide's too thick," Alek growled.

Cleo darted in. She ducked under a swipe of its clawed limb and slashed across its chest with Ari's enchanted dagger. The blade sank in—not deep, but enough to make it stagger.

The basilisk hissed and lunged—

But it never reached her.

Ari moved like lightning.

She crossed the distance in a blur—bare feet sliding over ancient dust, both blades drawn. She didn't yell. Didn't hesitate.

She leapt.

One blade drove into the base of the creature's skull.

The other swept in a clean arc through the softened neck where Cleo had struck.

A crack. A collapse.

The basilisk hit the ground in a heap of smoke and bone, its black ichor sizzling on the stone.

Ari landed beside the corpse and turned to the altar.

"It's a distraction," she said. "All of this. A noisy illusion to keep us here."

Cleo slowly stood. "To keep us looking in the wrong direction?"

Alek's expression darkened. "Make us watch his right hand while the left makes the real move."

"And if the creature killed me in the meantime..." Cleo said quietly.

"Then that's a bonus for him," Ari finished.

They looked around the room again. The crude altar. The mimicry of power. The deliberate performance of menace.

"It's not war yet," Alek said. "It's sleight of hand. And we just fell for it."

Cleo stared at the basilisk's body, her grip tightening around the dagger.

Chapter 57

The lower chambers beneath Babylon were colder now.

Selene moved through them with the ease of habit, but not peace. Shadows clung tighter to the archways. The torches burned low, guttering in bowls carved from obsidian and bone. The deeper she walked, the more she felt it—the sense of being watched not just by guards or gods, but by something older, patient, and amused.

She kept her pace measured. Her expression neutral. But something was wrong.

Everything Pol had told her about Rome, about the ritual sites, about his "reconstruction efforts" had led her to think he was laying the groundwork for domination. Anchoring power. Taking cities one by one.

But now...

Now she saw the pattern differently.

Too clean. Too legible.

Pol never played straightforward games.

She reached the reliquary vaults and paused, hand on the edge of a sealed iron door that should have been dormant.

It was open.

Just slightly.

Selene stepped inside, the door groaning faintly behind her. The room beyond was dim—only one torch lit on the far wall. What should have been a sanctuary of silence was filled with movement. Murmurs echoed from the next corridor. She edged closer.

Two of Pol's followers stood at a granite table, unfolding scrolls marked in gold ink. The words were old—dangerously old—recorded in a dialect that hadn't been spoken in over a thousand years.

But Selene didn't need translation.

They were maps.

Not of Rome.

Not even of Prague.

They were of Delphi, Alexandria, and something marked only as "The Deep Place."

A breath caught in her throat.

Everything she'd been told—everything she'd reported—was wrong.

And Pol had known she would report it.

He hadn't missed her glances. Her secret movements. Her silences at the wrong moments. No, he'd seen through her from the start. And he had let her play her part. Not to mislead him—but to mislead everyone else.

She backed away, slowly.

Then froze.

Someone stood behind her.

"You're not nearly as subtle as you think, Selene,"
Skae murmured. He no longer wore a Roman face. This one
was jagged. Familiar. Cruel.

She didn't speak.

Didn't run.

Just lifted her chin and asked, "Is this the part where
he breaks me?"

Skae smiled. "No. He's done enough. The rest... you'll
do to yourself."

Then he vanished, the air whispering closed behind
him.

The torches dimmed.

The vault door slammed shut.

Selene moved.

In a blur, she turned toward the corridor and drew
the silver sickle blade at her hip. She hadn't used it in years—
because she hadn't needed to. But now it gleamed in her
hand, runes along the edge burning like winter fire.

Footsteps pounded behind her.

Two of Pol's co-conspirators entered, faces shrouded,
hands already weaving sigils meant to bind and silence. She
didn't wait.

She summoned a burst of raw power from her core
and flung it down the corridor. It struck like lightning—
white-blue and searing. The air cracked. The floor glowed.
The first follower stumbled, blinded, hands to his face. The
second tried to shield himself—she was already on him,
blade drawn.

She struck fast and clean, knocking him to the
ground. The other lunged, and she blasted him back with a

second surge, his body slamming into the wall hard enough to leave a crack.

She ran.

Through the vaults. Past chambers of false knowledge and dust-thick lies. The alarm tones deepened, the very stone beneath her feet pulsing with the weight of a god's wrath closing in.

At the outer wall, she skidded to a stop, lifted one hand, and let go.

A blast of raw divine force surged from her palm— blue-white, radiant, laced with fury.

The wall exploded outward in a shockwave of shattered stone and searing light.

Guards shouted. Too late.

She stepped through the smoke, already turning into speed and light and memory.

She vanished into the bones of Babylon.

Chapter 58

Selene appeared in a burst of white fire at the edge of the Celestial Hall, her cloak scorched, silver blade still slick with ash. The guards nearby stepped back—not in fear, but in recognition. A god returning not victorious, but furious.

Helena was already waiting at the steps.

The Matron of Dusk looked regal as ever, her silken armor gleaming like starlight soaked in shadow. But her eyes narrowed the moment she saw Selene's state. No words were exchanged until they were inside the marble corridors, the veil of silence behind them.

"What happened?" Helena asked.

Selene didn't pause. "He knew. The whole time."

Helena's expression hardened.

"I saw the scrolls. Not Rome. Not Prague. He planted those for me to find. He's after Delphi. Alexandria. And something older—something he called the Deep Place."

Helena's breath caught, but she masked it with a turn of her head. "You're certain?"

"I watched his followers reading the maps. I wasn't meant to see the real plan—I was meant to deliver the false one. Pol's been playing all of us."

"And the others?"

"Trying to bind me," Selene said simply. "Trap me before I could warn anyone. I didn't stay to see what else they had planned."

Helena closed her eyes for a long beat. "The Council will need to hear this. Immediately."

Selene raised a brow. "And will they listen this time?"

"They'll have no choice."

***

The Great Hall

The Hall stood colder than usual.

Light poured in from nowhere and everywhere—high above, the dome shimmered with celestial fire that refused to flicker. Columns of marble and obsidian ringed the circular chamber, and at its center, the gods gathered, restless and waiting.

Theo sat with his hands steepled. Helena stood beside him. Ares leaned forward on the edge of his throne like a soldier who smelled blood but didn't know where it was coming from. Thor paced, shoulders tense. Artemis stood silent behind her brother, arms crossed and gaze sharp.

Selene entered the circle.

She was still streaked with ash and shadow. Still smelled faintly of smoke and shattered stone. But her presence silenced the room. No one mistook her for weak—not now.

Helena spoke first. "Selene has returned from Pol's stronghold. She brings new intelligence—and a correction to what we believed."

Murmurs flickered like sparks through the chamber.

Theo's voice followed. "Speak."

Selene didn't bow. She didn't need to.

"Pol knew I was feeding information to Helena," she said. "He let me. Because the information was false—deliberately planted. He constructed a decoy campaign. Rome. Prague. Ritual sites and relic activity. All believable. All designed to waste our time."

Artemis frowned. "And the real targets?"

"Delphi. Alexandria. And something referred to only as the Deep Place. There were no coordinates, no sigils—just a name. Intentionally vague. Which means it wasn't for his followers."

Thor stopped pacing. "The Deep Place. That name hasn't been spoken in an age."

"It's not a location," Theo said slowly. "It's a concept. A warning. A term we used in the early days to refer to any realm or event that couldn't be charted or contained. Unmaking. Collapse. Places where divine order failed."

"Pol doesn't want a throne," Selene said, her voice colder now. "He wants a reckoning. And he's moving differently. He's not stirring mortals into war like before. He's not interested in worship anymore. Not even power in the traditional sense."

"Then what is he after?" Ares snapped.

"Control," Selene said. "Or erasure."

Murmurs rose again.

"He's destabilizing the architecture of divine reality," she continued. "Targeting sites where the divine and mortal realms once touched—before they were sealed, veiled, ordered. If he ruptures those points—"

"He could collapse the separation between worlds," Helena finished quietly. "And undo everything we've tried to preserve."

Artemis' voice was sharp. "He wants the veil to fall."

"Or to become irrelevant," Selene said. "He believes the old ways were a mistake. That division weakens us. That if we return fully—without masks, without laws—we'll ascend beyond what we were. Or burn the world in the attempt."

Thor's jaw flexed. "That's not ambition. That's madness."

"Not to him," Theo said. "To him, it's restoration."

Selene looked around the room. "You wanted to know what he's planning. That's your answer. Not a war to win. A line to erase. And if he succeeds, there won't be gods and mortals anymore. There will only be ruin. Or dominion."

For a long moment, no one spoke.

Then Ares leaned forward, voice sharp. "And what of Alek?"

The name echoed like a thrown blade.

"He went after the girl. We all know it."

Thor frowned. "What's become of her?"

A brief glance passed between gods.

Helena turned, voice cool and measured. "Perhaps now isn't the moment—"

But Ares cut her off. "It's exactly the moment. We need to be clear on where every player stands."

All eyes shifted to Artemis.

Ari's expression didn't waver. "She's under Alek's protection. That's all that needs saying."

Helena spoke again, her tone diplomatic. "She was targeted by Pol. The Council has already agreed she warranted shielding."

Ares wasn't convinced. "And his connection to her? You're saying he just happened to rescue her? Nothing more?"

"He intervened," Ari said, voice edged now. "He's done it before for less. And we have more pressing threats than hypotheticals."

Ares leaned back, slow and deliberate. "If there's something more—if affection has crossed into something deeper—we all know what that means."

Helena stepped in smoothly. "Let's not confuse rumor with proof. Alek has always walked close to the edges of our laws—but he has not stepped across. Not yet."

"Not that we've seen," Ares muttered.

Ari snapped, "He's the only one—as far as we know— that Pol tried and failed to recruit before turning to war. And the only one Pol truly feared. You want to fracture our defenses now? Just because you're uncomfortable with what you think you see?"

Thor's voice cut through the tension, calm but unyielding.

"We are watching him. We may have bigger issues at the moment, but if he goes too far—we will act. Regardless of the situation with Pol, Alek is not immune to our laws."

Helena added softly, "And until then, we would do well to focus on the god actively trying to unravel the world."

The tension hung in the chamber like a drawn bowstring.

Selene could feel it—tightening around them all. Not just the weight of Pol's return, but the uneasy, splintering trust inside the divine ranks.

The Council would act.

But cracks had already formed.

And once those opened—nothing held would stay contained

Chapter 59

The olive groves beyond Ari's villa were quiet, but the silence had changed.

It was the kind that held its breath.

Alek stood at the edge of the veranda, gaze fixed on the hills, as if watching for a threat that had yet to take shape. The light around him was golden, but his shadow stretched long—darker than it should have.

"They've met," he said, not turning.

Ari joined him. "We felt it too."

A pulse, low and distant, had passed through the fabric of divine space just hours ago—a tremor in the Great Hall. A decision was made. Not final. But something had shifted. Eyes had turned. And now... they were watching.

Cleo stood farther back, arms folded. Her posture was strong, but her face was tight with unease.

"What did they decide?" she asked.

"They didn't have to speak it aloud," Ari said. "Not yet. But the tide's turning. They're afraid. And when gods are afraid, they sharpen blades."

Alek's jaw tightened. "They don't trust me."

"Not entirely," Ari said. "But they still need you. That's the only thing holding them back."

"For now," he muttered.

He glanced back at Cleo, his expression softening. But beneath that gentleness was a war. Not of emotion—of calculation. Every moment she stood beside him made the Council more uneasy. Every breath she took as his equal, more dangerous.

"They'll come," Cleo said quietly. "Eventually. The Council. Or Pol. Or both."

Alek nodded. "I know."

She stepped forward, her fingers brushing his hand. "Then we make sure we're ready."

Far Below, Beneath Ruined Stone

Pol moved through the subterranean chambers like a storm barely leashed. The creature he had unleashed in Rome was gone—killed. The trap had failed. Ari's blade had torn through it, and Cleo had walked away stronger than before.

He had underestimated the girl.

He wouldn't make that mistake again.

Skae knelt in the center of the chamber, sifting through relics pulled from sealed coffers: amulets of binding, serpents coiled in gold, a fragment of a forgotten oath carved into obsidian.

Pol didn't look at him. "It's time."

Skae rose. "Another creature?"

Pol shook his head. "No. A team. Hands that can think. Adapt. Improvise."

He extended his hand toward a map scrawled on the stone floor—a mark over Italy glowing faintly red.

"I want her taken. Not killed. Not yet."

Skae narrowed his eyes. "Again with the girl."

Pol's gaze flicked to him, dangerous and flat.

"You have something to say?"

"Yes," Skae replied. "You're letting your obsession with Alek and the mortal distract you."

Pol's expression didn't change, but the air shifted—denser now.

"You talk of bringing down the veil and returning us to our former glory—better than before even. But everything we do circles back to her. To him. You claim strategy, but I see fixation. Personal vendetta."

Silence.

Then—

The fire roared upward.

Pol didn't raise his voice, but his wrath spilled out like heat.

"You think I've forgotten the plan?" he said, eyes gleaming. "You think I would abandon it for sentiment? For spite?"

He stalked forward. Skae stood his ground.

"I am the plan," Pol growled. "I wrote it when the stars still burned with meaning. I carved the first path into the Deep. I was the one who bled when the Council turned their backs."

He paused, breath coiled with fire.

"But Alek made it personal. He made it personal when he chose her."

Skae's mouth tightened. "And if you break yourself chasing vengeance, you'll never finish what you started."

Pol was still now, stone-carved and terrible.

Then, slowly, he turned back to the map.

"I won't break," he said. "I'll make him bend."

A cold smile curved his lips.

"And when she screams for him—when he arrives too late—I'll show him what grief really looks like. Then I'll finish what we began."

He gestured again—this time to the spiral etched deeper into the stone.

"Call them," he said. "The hollow-eyed. The drowned queen. The ones who owe me from before the fall. I want every loyal shadow brought into the light."

Skae straightened, jaw tense. "And if they refuse you? After all this time?"

Pol turned his head slightly, a smile curling with something cruel.

"Then remind them who they feared before they feared the Council."

He paced to a second altar near the back of the chamber—a stone slab etched with ancient circles, each one glowing faintly.

"This world will not be ruled," he said, more to himself than Skae. "It will be rewritten. Their veil is weakness. Their order is a cage."

He placed a hand on the slab. Power rippled outward, touching the edges of the map.

"I'll make the mortal realm divine again," Pol whispered. "Not with temples. Not with prayers. With fear. With memory. When the sky opens and the gods walk freely—unchallenged, untethered—the world will remember who we were."

He smiled, teeth sharp in the firelight.

"And then they'll kneel. Or burn."

Chapter 60

The sky over the Italian villa dimmed into dusk, shadows stretching long across the courtyard as Ari laid out the maps. Three sets of coordinates were circled in deep red.

"He's moving again," she said. "Subtle, but deliberate. These sites aren't random. They're aligned with ley lines—ancient ones. Ones older than any recorded city."

Alek stood over her shoulder, arms crossed. "Strongholds. Not just points of power."

Cleo stepped into the lamplight, brow furrowed. "So he's setting up a base in each one?"

"Or activating what's left behind," Ari said. She tapped the map with two fingers. "Most of the old temples and cities were built on ley lines—places where the veil between the celestial realm and the mortal world was weakest. Divine power leaked through in those places, saturating the ground. That's why oracles saw more clearly there. Why gods walked more freely."

She paused, her gaze darkening. "I think he's using these sites in two ways. First, the veil will be weakest there. Even with limited help from the gods who still follow him, he could try to tear open the divide. It took many of us to create the veil. Tearing it down won't be easy—but in these places, it's possible."

She looked to Alek. "And second... it's symbolic. These are places where we were worshipped. Where offerings were made in our names. He's not just reclaiming power—he's reclaiming memory."

Alek tapped one of the marked sites. "This one in Thessaly—it's near where the old Oracle once stood. If he breaches that site, it could unbind protections woven before the Council even formed."

Cleo looked up. "Then we don't let him."

A moment passed between them—silent, urgent.

Then a pulse of energy washed through the villa like a breath exhaled by the earth itself.

Alek's head lifted. "Did you feel that?"

Ari went still. "That wasn't Pol."

Cleo stepped closer. "Then what was it?"

Alek's voice was tight. "Something powerful. Ancient. Something that doesn't belong here anymore."

Ari's eyes scanned the horizon. "Something just crossed the veil. Not Pol. Not the Council. Something else entirely."

They exchanged a glance, and the weight of it was clear—whatever had entered their realm, it wasn't meant to exist here anymore.

***

In the Shadows of Armenia

A cave temple lost to time flickered with returning life as Pol's chosen began to arrive.

A figure cloaked in feathers and bones emerged first, her face hidden behind a mask of sharpened ivory. The hollow-eyed. Once a high priestess of forgotten rites, now half-wraith, her allegiance to Pol had never truly ended.

The drowned queen came next—dripping salt and river light, crowned with broken pearls. Her smile held no warmth. Her voice had not been heard in centuries.

More followed: warriors out of step with time, beasts disguised as men, seers who had once blinded themselves to better see.

Skae watched as they circled, kneeling one by one before the blood-lit altar.

Pol raised his hand.

"You are not bound by faith," he said. "You are here to correct—to finish what was started before the veil was ever lifted."

A murmur passed through them—rasping, inhuman.

"There is a girl," Pol continued, stepping forward, "and a god who would tear the heavens open for her. Take her. Bring her to me. Do not kill her unless you must."

He turned slowly, facing each of them. "You've stalked the edges of empires. Burned down kingdoms in my name. And now I call you back to purpose."

A beast with curling horns snarled softly. Another, with eyes like burning coals, nodded once.

"If Alek comes," Pol added, voice sharpening, "do not face him head on. Delay him. Bleed him. Break him if you can. But I will end him myself."

He stepped down from the dais, cloak trailing like smoke behind him.

"The Council watches. The world sleeps. But I have awakened you. Go now—into the gaps between memory. Into the veins of the earth. And bring me the key to breaking him."

He paused, and his voice dropped lower.

"He cannot protect her forever. The longer she breathes, the weaker he becomes. They've given him something to lose. And we will take it from him."

The shadows moved.

And war crept forward in silence.

Chapter 61

The Italian villa hummed with restless energy. Night had fully fallen, yet no one slept. The pulse they had felt earlier had left something behind—like ash in the air, a tension that hadn't existed before.

Ari moved through the villa's main room, tracing sigils in the air with a glowing fingertip. "I've reinforced every layer of the wards," she said. "But if that thing we felt decides to come for us, these won't stop it. They'll only slow it down."

Cleo sat near the hearth, legs drawn up beneath her. She didn't look afraid—but focused, her gaze sharp with purpose. "Then we make sure it doesn't get that far."

Alek stood near the open doors to the garden, arms folded, silent. The starlight hit his face in hard angles. He hadn't spoken since the pulse.

"You recognize it, don't you?" Ari asked gently.

He nodded. "Not by name. But by weight. Whatever crossed over... it's not a servant. It's not a trick. It's old. Ancient like us—but darker. Forgotten for a reason."

"Do you think it's one of his?" Cleo asked.

Alek finally turned. "No. Pol would have announced it. Made a spectacle. This was quiet. Precise. Like it knew how to avoid notice. But it couldn't avoid us."

Ari joined him. "Then it wasn't meant for the mortal world. Not yet. Which means we're ahead of it—barely."

Alek's jaw tightened. "We need to find where it came through. If it left a mark on the veil, we might be able to track it."

Cleo stood. "Then we go together. Wherever this thing came in—we meet it there. Before it finds us first."

Ari gave a grim smile. "Now you're thinking like a god."

***

By morning, the trio had crossed into the high ridges overlooking an ancient forest in northern Italy. The land here was older than the maps that claimed to know it—dense with secrets, thick with fog.

Alek moved ahead, eyes scanning invisible threads in the air, threads only gods could see. "There," he said, pointing to a ruined shrine barely held together by time and vine. "The veil is thinnest here. It's recent."

Cleo stepped forward, placing her hand against the air just above the moss-covered stones. A static charge pulsed through her fingertips.

"It's like something pushed through, but didn't bother hiding the breach," she whispered.

"Or wanted us to find it," Ari muttered.

A sudden gust swept the ridge—and then the world turned.

Shadows dropped from the treeline.

Figures cloaked in smoke and hunger. Too many. Faster than they should've been.

Pol's followers.

The first wave hit with brutal force. Cleo ducked beneath a blade of obsidian, only to be knocked aside by something that wore a man's face but moved like a predator. One had wings of matted feathers and a tail made of writhing flame. Another hissed in a forgotten tongue, its form shifting like smoke.

Alek roared, lightning flashing from his hands, tearing the hillside open. The shockwave sent creatures flying, but for every one that fell, two more surged forward. Ari's arrows found their marks—bursting through skulls, pinning limbs to the trees—but they kept coming, screeching with glee.

"Cleo! Stay close to me!" Alek shouted, his voice thunder through the chaos.

Cleo tried—dodging and weaving—but the terrain turned against her. Rocks slid underfoot, branches whipped her face, and the fog grew thicker.

Then the mist thickened. A wall of water surged upward from the ground itself. From within it stepped the drowned queen—her long white hair floating as if submerged, her skin pale as death, eyes glowing blue like the deep sea.

She raised her arms, and the fog obeyed, blinding Ari and Alek. Cleo felt the air turn cold and wet. Her breath came in plumes.

Ari loosed an arrow into the mist—it vanished with a hollow splash.

"She's masking them!" Ari shouted. "I can't see!"

Alek blasted apart another wave of the fog with divine force, trying to get to Cleo. He caught a glimpse of her through the swirling grey—her blade glowing, her stance defiant.

"Cleo, hold on!" he called, pushing forward.

She slashed at the creatures closing in. Her enchanted dagger burned bright, cutting through flesh that smelled of rot and sulfur. Then, in a desperate move, she reached for the pendant Alek had given her. Her fingers closed around the necklace, and she whispered his name. A shockwave of radiant gold light burst outward, blasting the nearest beasts backward and reducing two of them to ash. The rest recoiled, screeching in pain, the glow of divine energy repelling them momentarily. But they pressed in from every angle. Something clawed her back, another yanked her ankle.

Alek surged forward, ripping a shadow-beast from her side and hurling it into a boulder with a crack like thunder.

"We're not losing her!" he snarled.

But then the drowned queen surged forward, water trailing in her wake. With a gesture, vines and brambles curled around Cleo's feet, forcing her to stumble. Two shadow-creatures pinned her arms as she struck out wildly, dagger flashing blue fire.

"No!" Ari shouted, sprinting to help—but too late.

A final surge of mist burst outward—and Cleo vanished in the blast, dragged into the shadows by hands that felt like ice.

"CLEO!" Alek screamed, lunging after her.

His hand closed on air.

The ground cracked beneath his feet. Trees bent and broke. Mountains in the distance trembled, ancient stones falling like dust from Olympus itself.

Ari caught up, breathless, her eyes wide with horror. "She's gone," she whispered.

Alek dropped to his knees, fists slamming the ground. "I failed her," he whispered. "Again."

But the grief didn't stay quiet.

It erupted.

He screamed, the sound raw and ancient, and the sky above them split open with thunder. Lightning danced across the ridge, wild and uncontrolled. Cracks raced through the earth like veins of fury, opening fissures that spat smoke and light. Wind tore through the forest, snapping trees like kindling, and boulders dislodged from the mountainside above them, tumbling down in a thunderous cascade.

Ari stepped back, shielding her face as dust and debris swirled.

"Alek, stop!" she cried over the rising storm. "You'll bring down the mountain!"

But he couldn't. Or wouldn't.

Power poured off him in waves, his divine essence radiating unchecked. It wasn't just pain. It was rage—cosmic, relentless, grieving rage. The kind that had once sunk cities and scorched skies.

And beneath it all—shame. Shame for not being fast enough. For not being strong enough. For letting her slip through his fingers a second time.

When the energy finally subsided, Alek collapsed forward, hands digging into the dirt, chest heaving.

His voice was hoarse when he spoke. "I swore I would protect her. I can't lose her, Ari. Not again."

Ari knelt beside him, her voice fierce and low. "Then we get her back. Whatever it takes. And we make Pol pay."

The earth beneath them stilled, but the sky still trembled.

Chapter 62

The walls were carved from obsidian, veined with molten gold that pulsed like a heartbeat. The chamber was cold despite the glowing light, a kind of unnatural chill that sank into Cleo's bones—a cold that wasn't about temperature, but absence. Absence of hope. Absence of time. Absence of mercy.

She was bound—not with rope or chain, but with bands of magic, threads of shadow woven through iron and grief. They pulsed faintly, as if alive, responding to her thoughts and fears. The more she struggled, the tighter they drew, caressing her skin with a predator's patience, each thread a whisper of something ancient and cruel.

Her head ached. Her limbs were heavy. Every breath felt filtered through dust and centuries.

And still—she did not scream.

Pol watched her from a dais of stone, his form wreathed in dim amber light. He looked like a statue carved by grief itself, unmoved by time, untouched by compassion. His eyes, pale and unreadable, held the glint of someone who had waited too long and would wait no more.

"You held out longer than I expected," he said softly. "Even after they dragged you through the veil like a prize." He circled her slowly, his footsteps making no sound. "But he always breaks, doesn't he? That's the beautiful flaw. He loves."

Cleo lifted her head, defiant. Her voice came low but steady. "You're afraid of him."

Pol stopped. His smile didn't falter, but it froze—like the light before a storm.

"I fear nothing," he said. "I understand him. That's why I'll win."

He knelt beside her, cloak pooling like oil at his feet. "You are not a prisoner, Cleo. You're a mirror. And when he looks at you, he sees what he's not supposed to have. What we were never meant to possess."

"You mean love," she said. "Hope."

"I mean weakness."

Cleo shut her eyes again, but not in surrender. She focused inward—on her breathing, on the steady beat of her heart, on the quiet fire buried deep beneath her ribs. She found the warmth Alek had placed there, the echo of his essence in the necklace pressed against her skin. She remembered the weight of his gaze, the brush of his fingers across her cheek, the steadiness in his voice when the world threatened to fall apart.

Pol's words were weapons, but she had armor of her own.

She thought of the archives, of the scent of parchment and dust, of hours spent with texts that refused to give up their secrets easily. She had come into this world a scholar, not a warrior—but knowledge was its own kind of sword. Myth had shaped the world once. It still could.

"I'm not your mirror," she said. "I'm your reckoning."

Pol's eyes flickered. A muscle in his jaw tightened, the smallest fracture in his façade.

She met his stare, unflinching. "You think this will break me? I've already been broken. What's left is only what I chose to keep."

He stood again, straightening like a king returning to his throne. "You'll be the reason he falls. The moment he comes for you, I'll destroy what's left of the veil. And when the heavens open—when the gods are thrown into the light—they'll beg for the order we used to give them."

He stepped back into the shadows, vanishing between columns of flickering flame. His parting words clung to the air like ash.

"Rest now, Cleo. The end has already begun."

She watched him vanish.

And in the silence that followed, she whispered into the dark.

"Alek will come."

Chapter 63

The skies over Ari's villa had yet to recover. The mountain had settled, but the trees still leaned in strange directions, and thunder cracked along a horizon that no longer obeyed the wind.

Alek stood alone in the grove, his hands clenched, a silent tempest barely contained. Ari watched from the archway, her bow unstrung but close.

"She's alive," Ari said at last.

Alek didn't turn. "I felt it. But I don't know how long she'll stay that way."

"Then we stop waiting," Ari said. "We go to the Council. Rally the others. You know we can't do this alone anymore."

He exhaled slowly, grounding himself.

"I know who we'll need."

***

The Great Hall trembled when Alek and Ari entered it.

This time, they did not bow. This time, they came with fire.

Helena met them at the dais, Theo close behind. They saw the change in Alek immediately—less restraint, more storm.

"We're not asking," Ari said before anyone could speak. "We're assembling a strike. A force capable of reaching into Pol's strongholds."

"We warned you what that would mean," Hera began.

"And you've had your warnings," Alek interrupted. "Now give us allies—or stay out of the way."

Thor crossed his arms. "Who do you want?"

Ari stepped forward. "Ares. Athena. Any who remember the cost of war—and are willing to pay it again."

A low murmur ran through the gathered gods.

"What happened?" asked Dionysus, eyes narrowed. "Why now?"

Ari answered, voice cold. "We were scouting a breach in the veil. Searching for Pol's path. He sent an ambush. His creatures—beasts not seen since the burning of the first cities. They came for us in numbers."

Alek's voice turned to steel. "They weren't after us. They were after her."

"The girl," murmured Hera, tone heavy with implication. "The mortal. The one you've shielded from our eyes, the one who walks too closely beside you. This isn't just protection anymore, Alek. If there's love in it—true, divine love—you've broken a law older than this Council. You've risked exposing all of us for one soul."

Several of the gods turned sharply.

"There is more going on here than just protection," Helios said. "The bond is too strong. That's not allowed."

"Alek," said Demeter carefully, "have you broken the law of the Veil?"

Cracks of lightning snapped overhead. The Great Hall flickered in the flash.

Alek stepped forward, power radiating from every inch of his being. The air around him warped, shimmering with heat and divine force. Light burst from beneath his skin, and with it, a suit of liquid armor forged from raw divine power coalesced over his form—shifting, alive, echoing with forgotten languages.

He raised his voice, and it became a command that tore through the Hall like a divine decree.

"SILENCE."

The word rang out like a thunderclap. Every voice died. Even the air held its breath.

The gathered gods recoiled—not in fear, but in remembrance. Of who he had been. Of what he still was. The god of gods. The bringer of storms. The one they had once followed not because they chose to, but because the sky itself bowed before him.

"This is not the time for your judgments. Not when Pol is tearing the veil apart. Not when he's using our past to unravel our future. We stop him—or we lose everything."

The Hall fell into stunned silence.

Then a voice broke it.

Hermes stepped forward, eyes sharp with disbelief. "You would threaten us? In this sacred place? Over a mortal?"

Before the final word had left his lips, Alek's hand lifted.

The ground trembled. A streak of raw power—pure, incandescent—lashed through the air and struck the floor inches from Hermes' feet. The marble cracked, splintering outward like spiderwebs of lightning. Hermes froze, his breath caught in his throat.

Alek didn't shout. He didn't need to.

He turned his gaze on Hermes, his eyes alight with power and rage, demanding respect. The air between them thickened, as if the Hall itself bowed to the authority behind Alek's stare. The younger god staggered back under the weight of it.

"I do not threaten," Alek said, his voice low and terrible. "I warn. And you would be wise to heed it."

The light from his armor intensified, casting the Hall in shifting patterns of gold and shadow. "I am not your equal. I never was. The only reason you speak now is because I once chose silence."

The gods around them shifted, no longer merely cautious but uneasy. Remembering. Respecting.

Even Hermes said nothing more.

Alek straightened, voice carrying through the chamber.

"We face the end of all things. You can stand beside me—or behind me. But do not stand in my way."

It was Hera who spoke next. "Then let us help you. But understand—if this continues to escalate, the consequences will come."

"Then let them," Alek said. "I'll face them when she's safe."

He turned in a slow circle, meeting the eyes of every god and goddess in the Hall. Power pulsed from him in rhythmic waves, his voice dropping into something more ancient, more terrible.

"Remember who I am. What I have been. And what I still am capable of becoming."

His armor shimmered brighter, runes flaring along its surface, each one a memory of conquest, of storms unleashed and kingdoms bowed.

"Challenge me if you must—but know that doing so now would be unwise. I have no more patience to spare. Not for doubt. Not for delay."

Another crack of thunder split the rafters. Silence reigned once more.

Alek stood at the center of it all—unchallenged, unyielding. A god remembered.

∎∎

A stillness followed, fragile and weighty. Then, one by one, the gods began to speak.

"We cannot storm his sanctum blindly," Athena said, voice level. "He's had time to prepare. We need to understand where he draws his strength."

"He's using the ley lines," Ari cut in. "Sites where worship once ran thick. He's choosing them for their connection to our past—for their weakness in the Veil."

Ares leaned forward, resting an armored fist on the war table that shimmered into existence before them. "Then we hit the nearest stronghold. Test his defenses. Take out his supply lines."

"And draw him out," Thor added. "Make him move before he's ready."

"Too risky," said Demeter. "If we push too hard, he'll retaliate through the Veil. Mortals will suffer."

"They already are," Alek said, voice like distant thunder. "We hold back, he grows stronger. We act, we have a chance."

Athena nodded. "We'll need coordinated teams. One strike force. One containment. One for defense."

"I'll lead the strike," Alek said. "I'll find her. I'll bring her home."

Ari set her hands on the table. "I'll command the defenses. We'll need to protect the temples that remain intact."

Ares grinned, fire in his eyes. "I'll lead the charge."

"Then it's begun," Hera said solemnly. "We prepare for war."

***

The gods dispersed into action, each preparing in their own ancient way.

Ares stalked the edges of the divine barracks, flame dancing from his gauntlets as he called forth the forgotten war-kin—gods and spirits who had slumbered beneath the roots of ruined battlefields. Spears forged in the heart of volcanoes were raised. Shields etched with blood oaths shimmered back into existence.

Athena stood atop the eastern parapet, conferring with her spirits of strategy—ephemeral figures with eyes like mirrors and voices like wind through marble. She whispered plans not even time could unravel, drawing battle lines through the ley lines of the world, her every movement guided by visions only she could see.

Thor knelt beneath a lightning-struck pine, raising his hammer skyward. Storms answered him in great, swirling coils, thunder like war drums that echoed across dimensions. His presence alone rallied hundreds—beasts, lesser gods, and sky-born avatars.

Demeter and Artemis, rarely seen on the battlefield, gathered in the shadow of the sacred grove. They summoned beasts of fang and claw, guardians of old temples who would now taste war again. Even nature would fight if the Veil fell.

Alek stood in the heart of it all, watching the forces take shape. For a moment, he said nothing.

Then he raised his hand, and the sky cracked—not in rage, but in command.

"War is coming," he said, voice resonant and clear. "Let the heavens remember what it means to follow gods."

***

By twilight, they stood at the edge of the high pass, beneath a sky marred with black clouds.

Ares arrived first, flame trailing from his armor. Athena followed, silent and sharp-eyed, flanked by two of her forgotten spirits.

Alek's power crackled around him. But Ari stepped forward, placing a hand on his chest.

"You need to stop holding back," she said. "You weren't just Alek. You were Marduk. Zeus. Ra. The god of gods. You carried the names of empires, and they bowed because they had no choice."

He opened his mouth to argue, but she didn't let him.

"You held the sky together with your voice. You broke the earth open with your fury. You shaped the laws of reality

because no one else could. And now you're standing here—
chained by doubt."

His fists trembled, energy pulsing through his skin.

"I swore I wouldn't become that again," he said, voice
tight. "I swore I wouldn't burn the world just to stop one
man."

Ari stepped closer, voice soft but resolute. "Then
don't. But don't pretend that the power isn't still there. Don't
pretend that the world doesn't need him now."

Alek's jaw clenched, breath ragged.

"I don't want to lose myself."

"You won't," she said. "Because Cleo's your anchor.
And Pol is counting on you holding back. Let that be his last
mistake."

He looked past her, toward the line of gods
assembling under storm-colored skies.

Then he nodded once, slowly, a spark lighting behind
his eyes.

"Then let's remind them why they feared me."

Ari lingered beside him as the others moved off to
begin preparations. Her eyes didn't leave his face.

"What if she's not there?" Alek asked quietly. "What if
we're too late? What if he's moved her again?"

"Then we adapt," Ari said. "We get answers. We tear
the truth out of the ones we capture. Someone will know
where she is—and they will tell us."

Alek nodded, jaw tight.

"We will find her," Ari said. "And when we do, there
will be no sanctuary left for Pol. Not in this world. Not in any
realm."

Chapter 64

The gods moved like thunder through the night. No horns. No banners. Only power—raw and blinding—cleaving a path through the mountains as the strike force advanced on the stronghold.

The temple had once belonged to forgotten fire gods. Now it was a scorched ruin twisted by shadow—Pol's corruption wound through the stones like vines of ash and bone. The air stank of brimstone and old blood. Shrieks echoed from blackened windows—wails that didn't sound mortal.

Ares led the charge. His war cry split the sky as he barreled through the outer ward, his flaming sword cleaving through twisted beasts with molten fangs and glassy eyes. Their shrieks were drowned by the roar of flame. Behind him came Thor, wielding storm and hammer with blinding force, thunder booming through the valley as lightning reduced corrupted watchtowers to smoldering rubble.

Athena moved like a specter through smoke, blades spinning with mathematical precision. Her warriors struck in eerie synchronicity, their every movement dictated by divine logic. Their strikes were surgical—finding joints, tendons, and hidden weaknesses in Pol's abominations.

Ari loosed arrows that sang with divine light, pinning shadow-creatures to the earth. Each shot erupted in a searing burst, disintegrating her targets into howling ash. "They're bound to the wards!" she shouted to Alek.

But breaching the stronghold's layered defenses took more than brute force. The wards were old and knotted with shadow—residue of Pol's twisted magic. Athena's warriors moved ahead, dismantling arcane traps, while Ari's arrows shattered sentinel glyphs carved into the stone.

Ares and Thor pushed through outer barricades, smashing corrupted gates and battering cursed thresholds until the walls cracked. Golden light surged through the fractures—divine power breaking the ancient seals. With each breach, the gods pressed deeper into the stronghold's heart.

More creatures spilled forth—grotesque constructs of flesh and stone, dripping bile and screaming curses in forgotten tongues. One hurled a pillar like a spear, only to be shattered midair by a bolt from Thor's hammer.

And at the center of the storm walked Alek.

He didn't shout. He didn't run. He moved with calm fury, his divine armor glowing hotter with every step. Pol's minions broke against him like waves against obsidian. A six-armed abomination stitched from the dead leapt toward him. Alek caught it midair, hand blazing with celestial fire, and incinerated it with a glare.

He raised one hand—and the temple's gates exploded inward with a deafening roar.

"POL!" he bellowed, his voice a celestial quake. "Bring her to me—or I will tear this place apart, stone by cursed stone."

Silence fell.

Then the defenders came.

Twisted demigods. Broken followers. Warped things dragged from old nightmares. They surged from the sanctum, hurling magic and steel. Bolts of corrupted energy flew across the battlefield, tearing through rock and divine shield alike.

Alek met them head-on. Fire rippled from his fists. The ground cracked where he walked. He roared—pure divine fury—and a wall of enemies disintegrated. He turned a summoned beast to salt with a breath. Snapped his fingers, and a wave of annihilation swept through a phalanx of corrupted sentries.

But Pol did not come.

Not even his shadow.

Alek entered the inner sanctum and found it empty.

And Cleo was not there.

He stood at the center of the desecrated altar, chest heaving, energy coiled around him like a living storm.

"He's not here," Ari said behind him.

"Neither is she," Helena added, stepping through the fractured doorway.

Alek's scream split the heavens.

He raised his hands, and the temple trembled. Runes ignited across his armor. The sky turned black as thunder rolled from his voice. Pillars buckled. The floor shattered. Flames leapt high into the air as Alek unleashed everything.

Walls melted. Statues cracked and toppled. The foundation split open, and a plume of radiant energy surged skyward like a dying god's cry. When it was over, only a crater remained where the stronghold had stood.

Ash rained from the sky.

Ari and Helena approached slowly, stepping through dust and ruin.

"We managed to bind several of Pol's supporters," Helena said, her voice steady despite the devastation. "Some are old enough to know his plans. They will talk."

"We'll get her back," Ari said, placing a hand on Alek's shoulder. "And we'll make him pay for this."

Chapter 65

The cavern deep beneath the earth pulsed with a dim, infernal glow. Its walls shimmered with veins of molten gold and obsidian, the air thick with heat and silence.

Skae stumbled to his knees before Pol's dark throne, armor cracked, ichor bleeding from his side. His breathing was ragged, eyes wide with the shock of survival.

"They came," he gasped. "The gods... Alek. They leveled the stronghold."

Pol did not rise. He stared into the fire before him, its strange black flame reflecting in his eyes. For a long moment, he said nothing.

Then—

"I know."

The air twisted. The fire flared.

"You let them get that close?" Pol's voice cracked like thunder. His hands trembled at his sides, clenched tight. "You failed. They walked through our defenses as if they were nothing."

"I didn't—" Skae choked, trying to lift his head. "We weren't prepared. The wards fell faster than we expected.

Alek burned through the gate wards like paper. Ares and Thor shattered the guard lines. We barely had time to mobilize. I—I only escaped because one of the shadow corridors hadn't collapsed yet. I watched them tear through the sanctum. It wasn't a battle. It was a massacre."

"Silence!"

Skae collapsed under the force of the word, his body crushed by invisible pressure. The air around Pol surged with volatile energy, his fury a storm barely contained.

Pol rose, his silhouette framed by the infernal blaze. The fire shifted from violet to blood-red, licking the stone walls with seething heat.

"They destroyed everything. Everything I built with precision and intent. My stronghold. My sanctum. My vision, torn to ash before it even began."

He stepped down from the dais, and the ground trembled.

"That place was never meant to fall. Not now. Not like this. And they dare to think they can touch what's mine."

He turned sharply, eyes locking on Cleo.

She stirred against her bindings, defiant despite the burn in her throat. "You're unraveling," she said, her voice ragged. "All your plans, undone by the very people you thought beneath you."

Pol stalked toward her, his rage dark and unchecked.

"You think this is unraveling? No, girl. This is acceleration." He crouched before her, the heat of his presence scalding. "You've forced my hand. All of you. I will not wait for the perfect moment—I will create it."

"You're rushing into chaos," Cleo said. "And you'll fall before he ever breaks."

Pol's laugh was low, bitter. "Fall? You still don't understand. This was never just about victory. This was about showing the world the gods still exist. Even by destroying the stronghold, they're playing into my hands. You don't think mortals will notice that? That they won't start asking questions? The world is watching, Cleo. They just don't know it yet."

She glared back. "You're afraid of him. Of what he'll do. Of what he's become."

Pol's expression twisted. "I'm afraid of what he could become. And that's why I'll rip the choice from him. I'll make him into the very thing he fears. And when he breaks—when you scream and he can't save you—it will be me who decides how this world ends."

He turned to Skae, who writhed, still unable to rise.

"Reinforce this sanctuary. Fortify every entrance. Double the guards. Activate the deep wards and bleed the old sigils into the stone. If they come again, we will meet them with fire."

He paused, glaring at Cleo.

"And let them think we're running. Let Alek believe he's gaining ground."

He stood tall, voice booming.

"Let him rage. Let him burn. And then—let him fall."

Chapter 66

The storm had passed, but the air still trembled with the echo of divine rage.

The gods regrouped at the shattered ruins of the stronghold, its scorched bones barely standing under a bleeding sky. The crater Alek had carved into the earth still hissed with the remnants of his fury. But now, beneath the broken spires, they had prisoners—half-shadowed things bound by divine sigils, snarling and whispering secrets in broken tongues.

Alek stood at the edge of the circle, arms crossed, expression unreadable. His armor no longer glowed, but the power still pulsed beneath it, restrained only by will.

"They won't talk willingly," Ari said, eyes narrowed. "But they will talk."

One of the prisoners—a warped demigod with silver eyes and cracked skin—was dragged forward. As the divine restraints activated, they lashed out like glowing chains, slamming him down. The ground cracked beneath him as he was forced to his knees by an unseen weight, his limbs

twitching in protest. Runes flared along his restraints as
Athena stepped forward.

"Name," she said coldly.

The creature smiled through bloodied teeth.

Athena didn't flinch. She nodded once to Ari, who
loosed a small arrow of light into his chest. The creature
screamed, a sound that warped the air around them.

"Try again," Ari said calmly.

He panted, then muttered, "Khoras."

"What is Pol building?" Alek asked. His voice was
quieter than the others—but far more dangerous.

Khoras licked his lips, tasted blood, and grinned. "You
think you've won something. That crater was a distraction."

Alek stepped forward. The prisoner trembled.

"You've destroyed a front," Khoras continued, "but
not the heart. He doesn't need that stronghold anymore.
You've helped him."

"How?" Athena demanded.

Khoras looked up, eyes gleaming like mercury.
"You've stirred the world. The veil trembles. Mortals have
begun to feel it. They will ask questions. And when the Veil
falls, they will not turn to you. They will kneel to the one who
revealed the truth."

Silence fell.

"He's trying to tear the barrier down," Ari said, voice
low. "Just like we feared."

"Not just that," Helena said, stepping forward, brows
furrowed. "He's trying to merge the realms. Let the divine
bleed into the mortal. Not a return to worship—a reckoning."

Alek turned back to Khoras. "Where is Cleo?"

Khoras only smiled again. "You'll see her soon. When the world burns."

Alek raised his hand.

Lightning gathered at his palm. "You misunderstand. I'm not asking as a courtesy."

He extended two fingers, and the restraints pulsed. Khoras screamed again as light flared through the runes—searing, celestial, surgical.

"WHERE?"

Khoras writhed, muscles spasming. "He'll kill me!"

"If you don't answer," Athena said coolly, "you'll wish we had."

Another surge of divine energy coursed through the sigils. Khoras shrieked, smoke rising from his skin. Ari stepped forward, pressing her palm to his forehead.

"You think pain makes you strong?" she whispered. "Then let's see how strong you are."

The air shimmered as ancient light surged into Khoras's mind. His thoughts were not just read—they were ripped open.

He buckled.

"Mountains—" he gasped. "The red cliffs... west of the old river cities. A temple beneath the stone."

"Coordinates," Alek growled.

Khoras nodded frantically, eyes wide, tears of fire running down his cheeks. "Hidden entrance. Sealed in the cliffs. The sanctuary—it's already being fortified. He's preparing for the end."

Alek released the energy, and the demigod slumped forward, panting.

Ari turned to the others. "We have a location."

Khoras stirred again, barely able to lift his head. "You still can't defeat him," he rasped. "He will change the world. He'll make the mortals bend the knee."

Alek stepped closer. His voice was iron. "We'll see about that."

He raised his hand once more—and with a final surge of divine fire, reduced Khoras to nothing but ash.

Silence.

Alek said nothing. He only stared toward the western horizon.

There was no more time.

The war had truly begun.

He would stop Pol. And he would save her.

Behind him, the gods gathered in a tight circle. Athena's voice was firm. "He's not just positioning forces— he's preparing to strike across the realm."

"Then we act first," Thor said. "Divide our forces. Strike at his outposts before he can gather momentum."

"We'll need to move quickly," Ari added. "Coordinate our assaults. Keep him off balance."

"Let Alek lead the strike on the red cliffs," Helena said. "That sanctuary is the key. Let the rest of us pressure him from all sides. Give them cover."

No one objected.

The gods nodded in grim unity.

The war for the realms had begun—and now, they would answer.

Chapter 67

The sanctuary walls breathed with old power—thick stone laced with veins of forgotten divinity, pulsing faintly in the shadows like a heartbeat. Pol stood at its center, surrounded by swirling maps of fire and ash suspended midair, each one marked with sigils older than memory.

"They move," he said. "Just as I knew they would."

He waved a hand, and the projections shimmered, revealing the positions of divine outposts hidden across the globe. Some flickered, weakening. Others sparked red—already fallen.

"They think they can corner me," Pol muttered. "They think war is enough."

Skae knelt nearby, newly healed but still bearing the scars of his failure. He did not speak.

Pol lifted his hand and conjured a new thread of fire—a glowing tether between the mortal and celestial realms. It pulsed unnaturally.

"Send them," he said.

At once, shadowed creatures stirred from the alcoves of the sanctuary. Hulking beasts clad in armor of bone and volcanic stone. Winged horrors with mouths that whispered madness. One by one, they slithered into the light.

"To the temples of the old gods. To their vaults. To the last places where they still think themselves safe."

He stepped down into the ritual circle.

"Their unity is a lie," he said. "Their power, scattered. And now... we sever the ties they cling to."

The air behind him shimmered as one of his generals stepped forward, cloaked in robes stitched from the night sky. "What of Alek?" the voice rasped.

Pol didn't look back.

"Let him come. I want him to watch the world unravel."

He extended his arms, and the air fractured.

In cities hidden beneath sand and in forests lost to time, ancient gates shattered. Wards flickered and died. Monsters poured into holy sanctums and forgotten altars.

And above it all, Pol smiled.

"Send word to the remaining strongholds," he said quietly, yet with command that shook the walls. "Tell their commanders it's time. Begin tearing down the Veil. All of them. We strike together. Only with simultaneous collapse will there be enough power to bring it down."

Skae bowed his head, vanishing into shadow.

Pol closed his eyes, feeling the tremble in the distance, the crackling of resistance. It was starting.

"We will bring the war to them," he whispered. "The Veil will fall. And the world will bow."

Chapter 68

The wind screamed over the high cliffs of Anatolia, tearing through jagged peaks and ancient stone. Below, the shattered remnants of a temple clung to the mountainside, half-buried in thorn-choked rubble and brambles fed by forgotten blood. Once a sanctuary to the twin gods of harvest and fire, it now pulsed with corrupted energy—wards twisted like broken bones, the air thick with the scent of ash and rot.

A thunderclap split the silence.

Lightning tore open the sky as Thor descended in a bolt of stormlight, Mjölnir crashing into the stone with a deafening impact. The outer ward fractured beneath him, divine sigils unraveling in a shower of sparks.

"Clear the entrance!" he bellowed, his voice a booming force that echoed across the cliffs.

Beside him, Athena moved like a blade of wind and will. Her bronze-clad warriors spilled through a rippling gate of golden light, each step synchronized with god-forged precision. They met the first wave of defenders—shadow-beasts lunging with serrated fangs and seething flame. Spear met flesh, steel met shriek.

From the opposite ridge, Ares arrived in a roar of crimson fire. The God of War descended like a falling star, his armor flaring with rage, his greatsword an arc of destruction. He tore through corrupted guardians—once-priests twisted into monstrous husks—leaving ruin in his wake.

"We hold the outer ring!" Athena commanded. "Push inward—now!"

The assault surged forward. Thunder rolled. Runes flared. Divine power collided with darkness. The temple groaned under the force of old gods reclaiming sacred ground.

The inner sanctum loomed—pillars cracked and bleeding golden ichor, air trembling with the pressure of magic being unraveled. At its center knelt a figure, hands pressed against the blood-streaked floor, runes glowing beneath his palms. Veins of shadow spiraled outward from his body like spider cracks in glass, reaching toward the edges of the chamber.

The remnants of the Veil hissed and writhed above him, caught in the tug-of-war between realms.

Athena's eyes narrowed. "He's not just channeling power," she said. "He's tearing at the Veil itself."

Ares stepped forward, fury igniting in his gaze. "Then we end this. Now."

"Destroy it," Thor said grimly, stepping toward the heart.

Athena lifted her hand. "Wait. There's something else—"

But it was too late.

The gate exploded in a roar of unfiltered power.

A shockwave rippled outward, hurling even Ares back. Lightning danced across the air like living snakes. One of Athena's warriors cried out as shadow engulfed him, dissolving into a burst of screaming light.

Thor raised his hammer and hurled it.

The blow struck true. Mjölnir crushed the gate, and with it, the surge faltered. Light and shadow howled. The temple shook, its stone keening as the last pulse of Pol's influence cracked and bled away.

Smoke and silence settled.

Athena rose slowly, brushing soot from her cheek. "He nearly succeeded. One moment later—"

"We'd be standing in ruin," Thor finished.

Ares stepped cautiously toward the dais where the gate had been. His hand hovered over a scorched depression etched into the stone. He scowled.

"What is it?" Athena asked.

"Divine residue," Ares growled. "Not Pol's. Another god was here."

Athena knelt beside the traces of power, her eyes narrowing. "A minor one. Shrouded by layered illusions. But this wasn't just sabotage. They were amplifying the breach."

A plume of smoke coiled behind the dais.

A figure emerged, his robe shifting between hues of dust, night, and sand. Golden eyes glinted beneath a hood woven of threshold-thread and forgotten vows.

"Thalos," Athena hissed. "You dare show your face?"

The minor god of passage and forgotten thresholds smiled without regret. "You never noticed the cracks. I simply widened what was already crumbling."

Ares brandished his sword, flame licking its edge. "Traitor."

Thalos raised his arms, summoning glyphs into the air—wards blooming along the sanctums walls in pulses of twilight. "Pol was right. The Veil cages us. Mortals. Gods. I've only helped bring clarity."

Athena struck first.

Her spear clashed against Thalos's conjured blade, the impact flaring like sunfire against smoke. Ares charged, his blade carving arcs of molten fury. Thalos twisted, a ghost between worlds, slipping through shadows and striking back with blades of bent space.

"You never mattered," he snarled, parrying. "You clung to fading worship. I became something more."

"You betrayed the balance," Athena growled, spinning behind him and slicing a shallow cut across his ribs.

"I reset it."

Ares roared and brought his blade down. Sparks flew. Thalos faltered, his wards flickering. Athena drove her spear into his shoulder, pinning him to the sanctum wall.

Thalos collapsed to one knee, flickering like a faulty star. "You still think you're the future."

"We're the ones left standing," Ares said.

Athena raised a hand. Chains of radiant gold and anchored shadow erupted from the air, wrapping around Thalos's limbs and dragging him to the base of the altar.

"He'll be imprisoned in the sanctum's vault," she said coldly. "Let the Council judge his treason."

The temple groaned once more as Thalos's influence was purged.

Thor stepped through the clearing smoke. "Too close. He nearly brought it down."

Athena's jaw tightened. "If Thalos was helping Pol from within... how many more are there?"

No one answered.

The gate flickered back to life, dim and humming.

More sanctuaries awaited. More betrayals waiting to be uncovered.

The war was only beginning.

Chapter 69

Far to the north, where the mountains of the old world scraped the sky and ice clung to the bones of the earth, a fortress of ruin pulsed with corrupted light.

Built into the cliffs of the Stormspire Range, the stronghold was no mere temple—it was one of Pol's fortified outposts, carved from forgotten stone and drenched in dark rites. Once a sanctuary to Halryn, god of northern winds and omens, it now pulsed with treachery. Halryn had turned. Where once he guarded the Veil, now he worked to unmake it.

Hermes and Apollo had arrived with their divine legions—not to scout, but to strike. The Council had dispatched them to destroy the outpost before the Veil could be further damaged. They launched their assault at dawn, divine banners glinting in the frigid light.

Then the sky turned black.

The first sign came as silence. The sacred birds that nested in the cliffs vanished. The wind died. Then the howl— low, guttural, unnatural.

Monsters emerged from the mist. Twisted echoes of wind and flesh, fangs like glass, claws that tore through magic. And behind them, cloaked figures bearing bone-laced antlers chanted in a language older than time.

Hermes darted through falling rubble, a blur of divine motion and silver blades. Apollo's sunfire ignited the fog, burning with celestial heat—but the darkness held.

The horde surged forward.

The wards collapsed.

The gate fell.

The battle tore through the stronghold's heart. Hermes slashed and weaved with precision. Apollo summoned blazing constructs of golden flame. Their armies fought valiantly, divine weapons clashing against corrupted flesh.

Still, they were overwhelmed.

A shade wrapped in lightning and shadow slammed Apollo to the ground. Hermes was caught in a net of ethereal chains, pinned beneath falling stone. At the center of it all stood Halryn himself—no longer a protector, but a conduit. His hands rested on the altar, eyes alight with shadow, runes circling him like a storm.

"Halryn!" Apollo shouted, staggering to his feet, fire curling around his fists. "What are you doing, this is treason!?"

Halryn did not look away. "What the others call treason, I call truth. The Veil is a lie. A cage. Pol showed me what lies beyond."

Hermes growled, cutting himself free from the chains with a burst of speed. "You were one of us. We trusted you."

Halryn's eyes gleamed. "And you still cling to order while the world forgets us. I will not fade into myth."

Apollo raised his hand. "Then you'll fall into ruin."

The brothers charged.

Halryn lifted his arms, and wind screamed through the chamber. The altar cracked, divine power surging in chaotic bursts. Hermes struck first, his blades flashing in arcs of silver—but Halryn deflected them with a swirl of tempest. Apollo's flames roared toward the altar, but the shadows coalesced into a barrier that shattered his assault.

He channeled his divine essence into the fraying threads of the Veil, whispering words soaked in ancient betrayal. The air screamed. The sanctum walls bled light.

Above the outpost, the sky convulsed. Thunder spiraled in unnatural rings. Threads of reality tore loose like unraveling silk.

The Veil shimmered.

And cracked.

A burst of blinding light erupted from the altar, swallowing Halryn's form. When it faded, he was gone— vanished into the magic he had helped unleash.

Across the realms, the gods felt it.

In the Celestial Hall, voices rose in fear.

On the battlefield in the eastern range, Athena dropped to one knee, eyes wide.

In Ari's villa, Alek looked up from the war maps. His eyes narrowed as a tremor passed through the air—ancient and familiar.

In the sanctuary where Cleo was held, the walls shifted, the ceiling breathing with unseen life. Her hand clutched the amulet at her chest.

Something was unraveling.
And the Veil was no longer holding.

Chapter 70

The Great Hall trembled with restrained fury.

Gods from across the realms stood beneath its vaulted ceiling, where the constellations shifted and burned in consternation. The scent of ozone clung to the air—residual magic from the Veil's fracture still bleeding through every crack in the sky, like invisible wounds yet to scab.

Helena stood at the dais, her voice sharp as marble, slicing through the rising voices. "Halryn was no mere ally. He was a guardian of the Veil. A sentinel. He swore eternal watch over the boundary between worlds. And now he's gone—his power burned into the breach. Willingly. That kind of betrayal doesn't happen in a vacuum. It festers."

Theo's tone was more measured, but no less grim. "The strike at Stormspire proves Pol has more gods on his side than we ever realized. Not just beasts. Not mortals. Us. One of our own tore at the Veil. That changes everything. The sanctity of the pact is broken. What's left, if not trust among ourselves?"

Murmurs rippled through the gathered pantheon. Eyes turned to one another—measuring, questioning. Suspicion hung like a stormcloud, ready to erupt.

"Who else?" asked a grim-faced voice from the shadows—Miroth, god of forgotten laws. "Who among us still carries divided loyalties?" His eyes swept the chamber like a blade, daring anyone to meet his gaze.

"No names yet," Helena said. "But we suspect others are hiding their intentions. If Halryn fell, others may have followed. We must be prepared for betrayal from within."

A dry voice from the side: "Or are waiting for the right moment." It was Lysa, goddess of crossroads and choices. "He didn't act alone. He couldn't have. That kind of coordinated assault doesn't happen without inside knowledge."

Thor slammed his fist on the obsidian railing, the sound echoing like a war drum. "And while we argue, the Veil bleeds. What's next? Olympus? The Library of Stars? The Cradle itself?"

"We cannot panic," Helena replied. "But we must act. Now. Discussion must yield to decisions."

Ari's voice rose from across the chamber, calm but cutting. "Then let Alek lead."

All turned.

Alek stood just beyond the inner ring, shadowed but solid. His armor was half-summoned, divine power flickering like lightning at his shoulders. His face was calm—but his eyes were a storm. In their depths was a history none dared name—fire, sun, thunder, creation.

"If this council is too slow," he said, voice like distant thunder rolling over mountains, "then let those who still have the will to fight stand with me. We know Pol's target. We know his intent. He wants the Veil torn, the world reshaped in his image. We stop him now—or we lose everything. Mortals, gods—our very purpose."

Silence settled like a drawn breath. No one moved. Even the stars above seemed to pause.

Athena stepped forward, her gaze unwavering. "I stand with him. We were not made to cower in halls while the world burns. Action defines us. Not hesitation."

Ares followed, jaw set, hand resting on the hilt of his blade. "I'll fight with the god of gods, if it means we stop this madness. If we lose the world again, we won't get another chance to reclaim it."

Thor crossed his arms and nodded once. "Enough talk. The time for strategy is over. It's war. Let him lead. I'll bring the storm."

Helena raised a hand, her expression unreadable. "Then we divide our forces. Those loyal to preservation— try close the cracks in the veil. Those ready to strike—rally to Alek. But make no mistake—this is our last chance to turn the tide."

Theo's voice was quiet but steady. "We'll hold the center. Delay their next move. But we can't afford to lose another Veilpoint. If they crack the next, there may not be anything left to defend."

"We won't," Alek said. "Not if we act now. Not if we remember what we are."

The constellations above burned brighter, as if the sky itself bore witness to the vow.

And below, the gods moved—toward war, toward destiny, toward a reckoning long delayed Toward a world trembling beneath the weight of the divine, and the storm yet to come.

Chapter 71

The chamber was darker than shadow—lit only by the slow-burning coals of an ancient fire. The air vibrated with power, old and bitter, like smoke ground into bone.

Cleo sat against the far wall, bound by shimmering chains laced with divine sigils. Her body ached, but it was her mind that strained most—sensing something she couldn't explain, like the earth itself exhaling. A ripple through reality, subtle yet massive, brushed against her thoughts like a cold draft. The Veil was weakening. She could feel it fraying—like an ancient curtain tugged from both ends.

Pol stood near the center of the room, hands clasped behind his back, staring into the fire.

"You feel it, don't you," he said quietly. "It's coming down."

Cleo looked up, her voice raw. "The Veil."

Pol turned, the edges of his face catching the firelight. "Not all at once. But it's starting. The threads are unraveling. Every god that joins me, every ward that breaks, pulls another stitch loose."

She narrowed her eyes. "You think this makes you powerful? You're tearing the world apart."

He smiled. "No, Cleo. I'm pulling back the curtain. Letting the world remember what it once was. What it still can be."

"You mean what you want it to be," she snapped. "A monument to your ego."

He stepped closer, the heat of his presence thick in the air. "You still think this is about me. About revenge."

She met his gaze. "Isn't it?"

He didn't answer at first. Then: "You make him human. That makes you dangerous. But it also makes you valuable."

Cleo's chains pulsed with heat, but she didn't flinch. Her breath caught in her throat—not from fear, but from calculation.

She was still wearing the necklace Alek had given her.

Her fingers inched subtly toward it beneath her bound arms. The divine energy nestled in the metal was faint, dormant, but present. A promise wrapped in gold. She remembered his voice—If you're in danger, touch it. It will answer.

But would it answer here? In this place, so steeped in Pol's influence, surrounded by warded magic older than empires? She didn't know. Not yet.

Her mind raced. She couldn't strike too early. Not while Pol was this close. But she had one chance—one moment—if she could bait him, or if he dropped his guard.

"I will not be used," she said, keeping her voice steady.

Pol knelt, tilting his head. "You already are."

Then he stood slowly, turning away before pausing mid-step. His tone shifted—mocking now, almost pitying.

"You really have no idea who your boyfriend is, do you?"

Cleo frowned. "I know he's a god."

Pol chuckled, low and dark. "A god? Yes. But not always the peace-brooding pacifist you've come to adore. He wasn't always the gentle one hiding in shadows, playing at humanity."

He turned back toward her, voice rising with disdain. "People feared him, Cleo. Mortals bowed to him. Cities trembled at his approach. And gods—gods feared him."

Cleo held his gaze, her voice firm. "He changed."

Pol sneered. "No. He hid. And even then, I gave him chances. More than he deserved. I asked him to join me. To stand beside me when the world remembered our names."

She blinked, realization dawning.

Pol nodded. "Your captivity? That wasn't the plan. I didn't need this. But he made it necessary. He refused me—again and again. And so now, you're here. This is his fault, not mine."

Cleo's lip curled. "I would rather die than help you destroy the world."

Pol's smile vanished. "You think this is about destruction? If he had stood with me—if he had embraced what he truly is—we wouldn't need any of this. Alek is powerful enough that he could have dropped the Veil on his own."

Cleo's heart thundered. Not just because of what he'd said—but because she believed it. She'd seen the storm beneath Alek's calm. And yet... he had chosen her. Chosen restraint. Chosen love.

She tightened her grip around the hidden charm at her chest.

"You'll fail," she said.

Pol looked back into the fire. The flames shifted, casting shadows across the stone like cracks splitting a mirror.

Above them, deep in the crust of the world, the Veil gave another tremor. And in the far reaches of Pol's sanctum, bells forged of divine ore rang hollow and slow.

The old world was waking up.

And the new one was almost here.

Chapter 72

The sanctum was quiet.

Not silent—never truly silent—but hushed, like a beast holding its breath. A quiet threaded with tension, with a stillness that felt brittle, like glass stretched too thin. Somewhere in the distance, stone groaned softly as if the walls themselves were exhaling.

Cleo sat on the cold stone floor of her cell, her back pressed against the unyielding wall, chains still glowing faintly with divine sigils. The metal was too smooth, too cold, and the air was thick with power—old, oily, and unnatural. Her limbs ached from disuse. Her throat burned with thirst. Her thoughts, however, were sharper than ever.

But it was the silence that struck her most. Not complete—but different. The omnipresent hum that followed Pol wherever he went had vanished. His oppressive energy, the suffocating presence that shadowed her every breath, was gone.

She waited. Another minute. Then two. Listening. Watching the flickering shadows cast by the faint glow of enchanted sconces. Her pulse quickened. It was now or never.

Slowly, cautiously, she moved her hand to the amulet at her chest. Alek's gift. The one thing Pol hadn't noticed—or perhaps hadn't recognized for what it was. She closed her fingers around it and whispered, "Help me."

The sigils on her chains flickered.

Then the chain at her wrist pulsed once—then exploded outward in a surge of radiant energy.

A shockwave of divine light burst through the cell. The symbols etched into the stone hissed and cracked. Cleo shielded her eyes as the light poured from the amulet, coiling through the air like golden fire.

With a deep, resonant crack, her cell door flew open, slamming against the stone wall like thunder. The hinges buckled. Smoke hissed from the shattered glyphs, now dimming into oblivion. The ancient magic containing her had been sundered in a single flash.

For a heartbeat, there was only silence again.

Then Cleo was on her feet.

The corridor outside was dim and winding, lit by torches burning with blue flame that flickered unnaturally. Every surface was carved in old, curling runes—binding, concealing, confusing. Her bare feet touched the cold floor like whispers as she moved, ducking beneath archways, heart hammering against her ribs.

She didn't know where she was going. She had no map. No weapon. But she had something far more powerful.

Desperation. And resolve.

The stronghold was a labyrinth of ancient halls and subterranean vaults. She passed doorways sealed with golden glyphs, strange relics humming with dark resonance. Pillars carved in languages older than empire stretched to vaulted ceilings far above. And balconies opened into vast underground chambers—black voids with no end, their depths echoing with distant, inhuman whispers.

The walls seemed to pulse with a heartbeat not her own.

The further she ran, the heavier the air became. The Veil was above her. She could feel it—fractured and bleeding. The pressure built behind her eyes, like something pushing from within the bones of the world.

Her breaths came faster. Almost there.

She turned a corner, and at the end of a grand hallway framed in obsidian columns—she saw it. A stairwell. A passage leading upward. And at the top—moonlight.

Real moonlight.

A sliver of silver illumination cut through the darkness like a blade. Wind. Fresh, real wind kissed her skin.

Freedom.

She sprinted.

The echo of footsteps came too late.

"NO!"

A blast of force struck her from behind like a battering ram. She flew forward, crashing into the wall with a sickening crack. Her vision burst with stars. The stone was unforgiving, and her body screamed in protest.

Before she could move, chains slithered around her like serpents, coiling tightly—new ones, heavier, reinforced with ancient symbols that glowed red instead of gold.

Pol stepped from the shadows. His expression was unreadable, but his eyes burned like twin embers.

"Impressive," he said, his voice a low growl. "But foolish."

He raised one hand and snapped his fingers.

The stone around them moved. Shifted. Molded like clay.

A new cell took shape around her—seamless and brutal. It closed like a tomb. The floor shimmered. The walls vibrated with layered wards so dense she could feel them pressing into her bones.

Pol stepped forward and knelt. "No more games," he said softly. "You made your choice."

She glared at him, blood in her mouth. "You'll regret not letting me go."

"I don't regret anything," he replied. "But you might."

The cell sealed with a sound like the world swallowing its breath.

And the door vanished.

Leaving Cleo alone again. In darkness deeper than shadow. Silence returned, thick and absolute.

But not without hope.

She still had the amulet.

Its glow had faded, yes—but not gone.

She wasn't done yet.

Chapter 73

The Great Hall pulsed with tension.

The council had gathered in full—a rare sight, each divine seat occupied, each god shrouded in warlike stillness. The constellations above burned hot and erratic, their patterns unsettled, flickering like a storm trapped behind glass. Threads of divine power shimmered faintly in the air, warping the edges of light and space as anticipation thickened.

Alek stood at the center of the chamber, his hand clenched into a fist at his side. His eyes had gone distant, fixed on something only he could feel. A tremor passed through the marble floor beneath him, subtle but undeniable—a ripple of power traveling along the weave of reality itself.

He had felt it.

His power—echoing through the threads of the world.

Cleo was alive.

And she had used the amulet.

He closed his eyes briefly, seeing it—her courage, her desperation. The flare of divine light not his own, but born of him nonetheless. Not just a signal, but a cry. A declaration.

Ari stepped forward from the circle of gods, her eyes sharp with recognition. "What did you feel?"

"She tried to escape," Alek said, voice low and raw. "The power—the light—it was hers. She's still fighting."

Theo stepped down from his dais, war map unfurled and flickering with divine geography. "Is it the Red Cliffs?"

Alek nodded. "Yes. The signal came from there. She's being held in the stronghold buried beneath that canyon. Pol never abandoned it—he's been using it to hide her. To stage his next move."

Helena's eyes narrowed, the air around her shimmering faintly with restrained magic. "That place was sealed to keep it hidden—too dangerous, too steeped in forgotten magic. If he's reopened it, he's ready to reveal something the world was never meant to see."

"He already has," Alek said. "And she's there. Waiting."

The murmurs began—low, urgent, filled with dread and fury. Power shifted uneasily in the room. One by one, faces turned toward Alek—not with suspicion, but with expectancy. A storm was building behind their eyes.

Ari's voice cut through the unease like an arrow through silk. "Then we go. Now."

"Wait," came a voice from the far end—Miroth, the pale god of forgotten laws, ever cautious. "We go without council decree?"

"This isn't a vote," Alek replied, eyes glowing gold. "She called. I answer."

Silence fell. Even the constellations overhead seemed to pause in their eternal dance. The flames in the sconces dimmed, and the weight of his words settled like a blade drawn across a battlefield.

Then Athena stood. "I stand with him."

Ares followed without hesitation. "As do I."

Thor grunted and hefted his hammer, lightning coiling around his gauntlets. "Let's bring the storm."

Nemesis rose from her place among the shadows. "Justice waits for no council."

Within the hour, the skies over the world split with celestial fire.

Portals opened above the clouds like wounds in the firmament. Gods of war, judgment, vengeance, and retribution descended in streaks of gold and crimson—Athena, Thor, Ares, Nemesis, and others who had once stood atop mountains and empires. Each step they took cracked the sky with purpose.

The Red Cliffs loomed ahead—scarlet ridges twisted by time and scarred by old battles, their jagged spines silhouetted against a blood-colored sky. And beneath them, the stronghold pulsed with power like a dark heart beating in the depths of stone.

The very land trembled as the gods approached.

Winds howled through the ravines. Divine light glinted off summoned weapons and ancient armor. Thunder cracked above, echoing Alek's fury.

He stood at the front of the gathered host, divine energy rolling off him like wildfire—heat and lightning fused with will, his gaze burning with a singular vow.

"No speeches," he said. "No strategy debates."

Just purpose.

Just fury.

"We end this," Alek declared. "We break his hold. And we bring her home."

The heavens split in response.

And the gods moved as one, toward war.

Chapter 74

The sky above the Red Cliffs was on fire.

Lightning tore through clouds that churned with divine fury. Thunder boomed not from nature—but from gods descending in war. The heavens split open with streaks of light so bright they burned the eye. The air shimmered with divine tension, thick with power old enough to shake mountains.

Ares struck the ground first, his blade cleaving a jagged crack into the red stone. Lava hissed from the wound in the earth, a warning to all who stood against them. Flames erupted around his feet, curling in reverence and rage. Beside him, Thor roared, summoning a pillar of storm that surged through the cliffs, shattering the outer wards like glass beneath a hammer. Lightning coiled down his arms like chains of judgment, striking the sky and ground in violent rhythm.

The cliffs screamed.

Ancient defenses flickered to life across the rock face—glyphs of old power, etched in blood and bound by forgotten oaths. Crimson and gold sigils burned across the stone, weaving through every fault line and cave mouth. But they were already weakening. The divine force tearing at them from the outside was too great. Thunder echoed through the ravines like war drums, a primal sound older than civilization.

Athena moved like lightning incarnate, her warriors flanking her in perfect synchronicity. Shields clashed. Spears flared. They fought with no hesitation, executing plans formed in the quiet before the storm. Each blow landed with tactical precision. Nemesis's dark gaze scanned the battlefield, finding the cracks in the enemy's lines. Where she looked, death followed—clean, efficient, and inevitable.

Creatures born of shadow and divine corruption poured from the stronghold—misshapen, many-eyed, shrieking with voices twisted by Pol's influence. Some bore wings of fire and rot, others crawled on too many limbs, dragging chains of molten iron behind them. The cliffs became a maelstrom of divine war.

This was not a battle.

This was divine reckoning.

And from the heart of the storm, Alek descended.

His landing cracked the mountain.

The force of his arrival sent ripples through the stone, a seismic echo of power so dense it bent the air around him. Divine armor shimmered across his frame—raw power made solid, pulsing like a second heartbeat. Fire licked at the ground beneath his feet, drawn to him like a god returning to his throne.

He said nothing.

He didn't need to.

The gods around him moved with shared purpose. They followed his momentum. His fury became theirs. And the cliffs trembled underfoot.

Together, they pressed forward. Winged beasts—twisted by Pol's influence—erupted from the canyons. Constructs of bone, stone, and stolen divine essence surged from the stronghold, shrieking in voices that had never been mortal. The ground shook beneath stampedes of monstrous guardians—horned giants of obsidian and ash, their bodies stitched with soulfire.

The first wave fell in moments—Ares cutting through them like wildfire, Athena's troops moving in concert to bring down towering horrors. Thor's hammer shattered enemy formations, sending shockwaves that splintered stone and sent corrupted beasts tumbling into the chasm.

The second wave fought harder, but they could not stand.

Alek led the charge. He carved a path through the chaos, divine light bursting from every strike. Where he walked, the earth fractured. Where he swung, enemies turned to ash. His power was relentless—a storm unbound, ancient and terrible.

He passed through wards like mist. Magical barriers faltered under the pressure of his will. Every step brought him closer. He could feel her—like a note in a song only he could hear.

Alek raised his hand and tore open the stone with a command, ripping away a wall of the outer sanctuary. Flames and wind exploded inward. Behind him, the gods surged, overwhelming every defense that dared stand.

And still, his steps led him deeper—toward her.

***

Far below the chaos, Cleo stirred.

The air had changed.

She felt it—not through sound, but through the stone. Through the vibrations in her bones. The air in her chamber vibrated, resonating with energy so vast it seemed to press in from every direction. Something ancient was breaking. Power surged beyond the walls of her prison, crashing like waves against the cliffs.

And she knew.

Alek was here.

The thought struck her like lightning—not imagined, not hoped, but known.

The heat in her chest bloomed again. The necklace around her neck pulsed faintly, as though it recognized its creator's presence. The divine signature buried within it stirred like a coiled sun.

She crawled toward the wall of her cell, chains dragging behind her with metallic groans. Her body was sore. Her lip was cracked. But her spirit had never burned brighter. She pressed her hands against the stone, straining to feel more.

Thunder.

Not distant—but close. Not random—but rhythmic.

She felt it in her ribs.

The storm had come for her.

And with it, hope.

She closed her eyes and breathed deeply, centering herself in the storm's rhythm. Every second mattered now. The wards were weakening. The barriers above cracking. Her prison was no longer invulnerable—it was trembling.

A crack appeared in the far wall—small, jagged, but real.

She smiled then—bloodied and bruised, but unbroken. Her fingers brushed the charm.

"He's coming," she whispered. "And gods help anyone who stands in his way."

Chapter 75

The walls of the inner sanctum shook.

Dust rained from the arched ceiling like ash from a dying star. Veins of red light pulsed through the stone—warning signals woven into the bones of the stronghold, ancient alarms built by long-forgotten gods. Magic cracked and hissed in the air like a wounded serpent, coiling along the arches and sputtering against the strained wards.

Pol's footsteps echoed through the war chamber, uneven and sharp. His cloak billowed behind him like black smoke, his jaw clenched, eyes wide with fury and something rarer—fear.

"They're breaching the outer gates," Skae said, stumbling in from a side corridor. His armor was scorched, streaked with soot and ichor. One side of his face was bleeding. "Ares leads the vanguard. Athena and Thor are with him. Alek is at the front."

Pol's expression twisted. He slammed his fist against the obsidian war table, sending a violent shockwave through the chamber that rattled armor, cracked stone, and dimmed nearby flames.

"Hold the gates. Hold everything!"

He spun toward the line of commanders stationed along the edge of the room—twisted demigods cloaked in corrupted radiance, dark conjurers whose robes still bled shadow, and two titans, bound in iron and loyal only through threats of annihilation.

"Mobilize the last of the guardians," Pol barked. "Unleash the cyclops. Wake the hydras. Seal the eastern wing. Collapse the lesser halls if you must—but keep them out. Do you hear me?"

The air pulsed with dread.

One of the commanders stepped forward, hesitation in their voice. "Lord Pol... the Veil—what of the final breach?"

Pol's eyes flared. "Forget the Veil!" he roared. "This is no longer about plans or prophecy. This is survival."

Another blast tore through the structure. The ground beneath their feet quaked, sending cracks across the obsidian tile. A statue toppled in the corner, one Pol had carved himself, depicting a chained god bowing to a rising sun. It shattered on the floor, its fragments skittering like bones across the stone.

"They came faster than we expected," Skae muttered. "We didn't have time to finish the siphons or reroute the warding channels—"

"We had time," Pol hissed, whirling on him. "You failed to use it."

A moment passed in silence, heavy as stone.

Then Pol turned toward the far wall, where a shimmering disc of scrying light hovered over a dais. Scenes flickered within—blinding flashes of fire and lightning, the roar of divine forces colliding. Winged beasts fell like comets. Shadows burned. Gods pushed forward.

And at the center of it all, Alek.

His silhouette carved through the chaos like a blade of living dawn.

Pol stared, unmoving, his breath shallow.

"He's coming for her," he whispered, voice thick with dread.

He whirled again, cloak snapping behind him. "Double the guard on the lower sanctum. Layer it with every ward we have left. Bind the soulforged sentinels and position them at the heart."

Another commander stepped forward. "Should we evacuate? Prepare the lower tunnels—"

"No," Pol snapped. "We stand. We bleed if we must, but we do not run. Not while I still breathe."

He moved to a smaller alcove in the chamber, fingers dancing across a control panel etched in celestial glyphs. The walls around them began to hum, pulsing with energy.

"I built this place for a final stand," he muttered. "Let it be remembered as such."

Then, quieter—almost to himself—his voice cracked at the edges. "I'm not losing. Not now. Not to him."

As the stone screamed above them and the heavens thundered with divine wrath, Pol turned back to his commanders, eyes alight with wild determination.

"Make them pay for every step."

Chapter 76

The storm of gods tore through the upper cliffs like a wrathful tide.

Alek's light surged ahead of the vanguard, parting stone and shadow. Around him, divine fury raged—Athena's blades cut clean lines through summoned constructs, Ares' war cry shattered the air, and Thor's hammer split the very sky. Fires burned blue and gold, casting flickering shadows across crumbling battlements. The air reeked of scorched stone and magic turned bitter with desperation.

The stronghold of the Red Cliffs groaned as the gods forced their way inward. Wards collapsed like broken glass. Sentinels forged from forgotten rituals shattered under celestial might. Divine thunder echoed through the mountain's veins. Every explosion, every scream, rang through the heart of the stronghold like a funeral toll.

The cliffs themselves bled light. Runes seared into the walls ages ago flared and vanished, unable to withstand the divine pressure. Towers collapsed into dust. Shadows broke and fled.

And still, they pushed forward.

Alek moved like a storm incarnate. Lightning cracked in his wake. Walls bowed to his fury. Each swing of his hand tore through enemies and barriers alike. His thoughts were fixed—singular. Beneath all this ruin, Cleo waited.

Behind him, Ari danced through falling debris, loosing arrow after arrow, each one a star of pure light. "We're breaking through!" she cried. "They can't hold us!"

Nemesis followed close, blades dripping with voidlight, her expression cold and resolute. "Push harder," she said. "We're almost at the core."

But Alek was already gone—into the heart of the stronghold, alone.

Far below, in the inner sanctum, Pol stood frozen, watching his plan collapse.

The ground trembled—flames and shadow twisting as the divine assault intensified. Wards blinked and failed. Guardians fell. He could see the light of Alek's power drawing nearer, like a second sun bursting through the dark. The walls of the chamber vibrated with every impact.

The entire fortress groaned around him.

Skae stumbled into the chamber, one arm limp, blood trailing behind him. His armor was cracked and glowing where divine fire had burned through.

"They're in the lower halls," he gasped. "Your inner lines are collapsing. The cyclops are failing."

Pol's mouth curled into a snarl. "Then bind them to the core and blow the passage behind them. If they will not hold, they will become the wall."

A commander nearby hesitated. "There's no more time, my lord. Alek will reach the sanctum within moments. The gods are tearing through our last defenses like paper."

Pol turned, rage writ across his face, his eyes glowing with fractured fire.

"Then make every heartbeat count," he snapped. "Delay him. Bleed him. Break his allies. Collapse every corridor. Poison the stones if you must! I want the ground itself to resist him."

The ground shook again, more violently this time. Red dust filtered from the high arches. The chandeliers swayed on chains that groaned with age and pressure. Sacred tapestries caught flame from stray sparks and crumbled into cinders.

Pol's cloak flared as he strode toward the center dais. He raised one hand, and a new ward ignited around the sanctum's core—black and seething, pulsing with stolen essence. Sigils flared to life beneath his feet, etched into the floor with magic not meant to be used.

"They think they can take her," he muttered. "They think they can take me."

His voice rose to a snarl. "I have torn empires from their peaks. I have unmade kings and gods alike. I am the shadow they forgot, the storm they buried."

He drew a dagger of obsidian and carved fresh sigils into the floor. The air burned with the scent of sulfur and old blood. A low hum rose from the chamber—something ancient, alive, and furious.

"I will not let her go."

Then the ceiling boomed.

Dust fell like rain. Cracks snaked down the central pillar. A divine voice thundered through the stone—not words, but force. A command. A promise.

Pol looked up, eyes blazing.

Outside the door, the footsteps of gods drew near.
And the final defense of the Red Cliffs braced to fall.

Chapter 77

The sanctum doors shattered inward with the force of a cataclysm.

Alek stepped through the smoke and falling stone, haloed in blinding light. His armor burned with divine fire, every plate etched with glowing sigils from a dozen pantheons. Each step he took cracked the obsidian floor, sending fractures racing outward like lightning. The air around him warped with raw, ancient power. Behind him came only silence—the silence before annihilation, before judgment.

Across the vast chamber, Pol stood waiting.

His silhouette was jagged, cloaked in a corona of seething magic. The circle of sigils beneath him pulsed with volatile energy—runes older than memory, fed by stolen divine essence. The chamber stank of ozone and blood, of power not meant to be touched by mortal or god. Shadows slithered through the air like snakes made of smoke and hate.

"Alek," Pol said, voice low and sharp, echoing with the resonance of too many names. "Finally."

Alek's eyes blazed like twin suns. His voice was calm. Cold. "This ends now."

Pol laughed—a jagged, broken sound, devoid of mirth. "You brought an army to tear down my walls. And now here you are... alone."

"I only need me."

Pol struck first.

Dark fire roared from his outstretched hands, jagged and feral, a living torrent of malice. Alek raised his arm, and a shield of golden light flared into being, catching the blast and scattering it across the sanctum in molten sparks. The chamber shuddered. Columns buckled. The mountain groaned.

Alek countered with a wave of divine force. The blast caught Pol in the chest and hurled him across the dais. He hit hard, rolled, and rose with a snarl, blood gleaming at the corner of his mouth.

"You think you've changed," Pol spat, "but you haven't. I remember what you are. What you were. The God of Judgment. The World-Ender. The First Wrath."

"I remember too," Alek replied, stepping forward, divine energy pooling at his feet like molten gold. "And I chose to become more."

They collided.

Light and shadow tore the chamber apart. Each strike resounded like a thunderclap. Walls shattered. Wards exploded. The sanctum's ceiling cracked, raining stone and flame. Pol moved with desperation, hurling bolts of chaos, conjuring blades of screaming void. Alek met them all with the calm rage of a god who had held creation in his hands and chosen to spare it.

Stone cracked. Sigils flared and sputtered. The very air bled magic. Each blow was a hymn of destruction. Each movement a symphony of ruin. Their powers danced—gold and black, fire and silence—until even time seemed to falter.

Pol screamed, fury and fear twisting his voice. He gathered the last of his strength, every ounce of stolen might, and forged it into one final strike—a spear of dark matter, humming with uncreation.

He threw it.

Alek caught it.

The weapon shattered in his grasp, exploding into harmless sparks.

Before Pol could react, Alek was on him.

He seized Pol by the throat, lifting him from the ground. Power surged through Alek's hand, burning away illusions, draining every stolen secret from Pol's form. Eyes wide, Pol thrashed, but Alek held firm.

"You will not touch her again," Alek said, voice a blade of thunder.

The sigils beneath Pol's feet shattered like glass. The circle collapsed inward, consuming its own power. A shockwave tore through the chamber, dimming every light.

Alek let go.

Pol fell, choking, gasping for air. His magic fled him like water through broken fingers.

But it was already too late.

The mountain had begun to die.

Overhead, the ceiling cracked in long, agonizing lines. Fire raced through the fractures of the sanctum. Wards failed with a shriek, and the walls wept molten stone. The fortress that had stood for millennia was breaking apart.

And through it all, Alek stood.

He turned slowly, already sensing her—Cleo's presence flickering like a candle in a storm. Weak, but alive. Near.

The chamber burned behind him. Pol lay in ruin.

Alek walked into the smoke.

Each step felt like a lifetime. The corridor narrowed, charred and crumbling. Divine senses reached through the stone, following the tether that bound him to her. He turned a corner, flames licking the ceiling, and found the door to her prison hanging askew.

She was inside.

Her eyes widened at the sight of him—burning bright through the smoke and ruin. "Alek!" she cried, voice hoarse but alive, filled with disbelief and desperate hope.

Alek moved forward, hand outstretched—

—and was struck from behind.

The force blasted him into the wall. Stone cracked. His armor splintered. He fell hard, the world spinning.

Pol stood at the threshold, eyes wild, hand still raised with the last dredge of his power. His body shook with exertion, but madness burned bright in his gaze.

"You don't get to take her," he hissed.

He moved fast—too fast.

Before Alek could rise, Pol crossed the chamber, seized Cleo in his arms. She cried out, struggled, but her strength was gone.

"No!" Alek roared, rising in a surge of power.

But Pol vanished.

Not in a flash, not in a shimmer. Just gone. Ripped from the world like a name unspoken.

The chamber trembled.

Ari burst in moments later, followed by Athena and Thor.

They found Alek on his knees, staring at the empty space where Cleo had been.

"She was here," he said. "I had her."

Then his voice broke.

Chapter 78

Wind howled through the ruined arches of a distant temple, its spires long collapsed, its stones scorched black from forgotten wars. The sky above churned with unnatural clouds, thick as ink, bleeding red lightning. The air was heavy with the stench of ozone and decay. High atop a crumbling altar of obsidian and bone, Pol stood with Cleo imprisoned, her body suspended within a cage of shadow forged from raw magic and hate. The storm of his rage radiated outward, warping the very atmosphere, turning the wind into knives and the air to ash.

The ruins groaned beneath his fury.

He paced before her like a predator kept from the final kill, hands clenching and unclenching at his sides. His cloak of smoke snapped in the wind, its edges hissing with stolen power.

"You cost me everything," he snarled, voice edged with venom and exhaustion. "Everything I built, everything I prepared. Years of work—centuries of planning— undone. Again."

Cleo's wrists bled where the restraints bit into her flesh, her arms trembling, but her eyes never wavered. "You brought this on yourself," she said, her voice cracked but strong.

Pol barked a bitter laugh, sharp and humorless, echoing like a blade drawn too quickly. "You sound just like him. All righteousness and restraint. All hope and mercy. You have no idea who your precious Alek really is, do you?"

"I know he came for me," she said, teeth clenched against the pain.

Pol stepped closer, his face twisted in something between amusement and loathing. "He always does. That's the problem. He always thinks he can save everyone."

He turned from her and strode toward the edge of the broken altar, gazing out at the jagged horizon. In the distance, the remnants of shattered cities glittered like bones under moonlight. "This was supposed to be it. The final act. A new order. The gods returned to their rightful thrones. Mortals kneeling once more in reverence. The Veil undone and the world remade."

He turned back sharply, voice rising. "And twice now, he's stopped me. Twice."

The wind howled around them, pulling his words into the storm.

"Do you know what that does to a man? To be denied—not by fate, but by him? The one god who should've stood beside me?"

He stepped closer again, eyes burning.

"So now I don't care about balance. Or power. Or worship. I don't want a throne. I don't want temples."

He pressed his face to the bars of her cage. "I just want him to break."

His hand reached through the shadows and touched her cheek, mockingly gentle, fingers ice-cold against her burning skin. "And I finally understand how to do that."

Cleo jerked away, hatred flaring in her eyes. "You're insane."

Pol smiled. It didn't reach his eyes. "No. I'm enlightened."

He stepped back, arms spread as the storm above cracked open.

"He's going to watch you die. Helpless. Powerless. Just like I was—watching everything I built fall apart."

He turned in a slow circle, shouting now—not to her, but to the sky, to the gods above, to whatever remained beyond the veil.

"And there will be nothing he can do to stop it."

Thunder answered him.

And Cleo, bruised but unbowed, whispered into the chaos, "He'll come. He always comes."

Pol lowered his arms and extended one bloodstained hand toward the altar's heart. Ancient runes carved into the stone began to glow with a sickly red hue. With a guttural incantation, he poured his remaining strength into the glyphs. A flare of energy erupted upward—a beacon, blazing against the dark sky like a wound torn into reality.

A signal. A challenge.

A promise.

He turned back to Cleo, eyes gleaming with hatred.

"Let him come."

Chapter 79

Smoke clung to the ruins like a second skin.

The shattered remnants of the sanctum still burned, cracks glowing beneath the blackened floor. The air was thick with the bitter tang of charred stone and lingering divine power. Shards of broken columns jutted out like the bones of something ancient, and the faint flicker of failing wards still shimmered faintly in the corners of the room.

Alek stood at the center of the devastation, motionless, fists clenched at his sides. His armor was scorched and cracked, glowing faintly at the seams where divine fire still smoldered beneath the surface. Power bled from him in waves, invisible to the eye but palpable in the air—an oppressive force like the weight of a storm held back by sheer will.

Beside him, Ari stared into the smoke, her bow slung across her shoulder, hair damp with sweat and ash. Her expression was unreadable—tight around the eyes, drawn at the mouth. She didn't speak, not at first. They stood in silence for what felt like hours, the weight of Pol's escape pressing down on them.

Then, Ari straightened.

Her head tilted slightly, eyes narrowing toward the distance. Something shimmered faintly in the east—a flare, like a red pulse across the clouds.

"I found him," she said quietly, her voice cutting through the stillness.

Alek's head turned slowly, his expression unchanged. "Where?"

She pointed east, toward the dark horizon beyond the fractured walls. The sky there churned with sickly crimson, clouds spiraling unnaturally.

"He lit up the sky like a beacon," she said. "Power that raw—it can only be Pol. He's not hiding anymore. He's daring you to come. He's made sure you'll follow."

Alek's jaw tightened, but he didn't speak.

Ari stepped closer, urgency creeping into her tone. "We should regroup. Get the others. We're not ready for this. Not again. You don't have to do it alone."

Alek looked away, his gaze settling on the scorched altar where Cleo had stood moments before. The space was empty now, but it echoed in his mind like a scream.

"There's no time," he said softly. "Every second we wait is another moment she's in his hands."

Ari caught his arm. Her grip was firm, grounding. "If you go alone, and something happens-"

"I have to go alone," he said, cutting her off. He turned to face her fully now, golden light flaring faintly in his eyes, the energy beneath his skin rising again.

"I won't risk anyone else. Not for this. And I won't let him hurt her again. Not while I still breathe."

Ari's hand dropped. She saw it then—the storm behind his calm. His focus was absolute. His mind already far ahead of them, already at the heart of the nightmare he meant to end.

Ari drew in a breath. "Then go. If you insist on going ahead, I'll rally the others and meet you there. Just hold the line until we get to you."

Alek nodded once. "I will."

"He's waiting," he said, his voice low and filled with certainty. "Then let's not disappoint him."

He stepped into the open, the swirling smoke parting around him. Energy gathered at his feet, pulling from the ground and sky in equal measure. The heat of his resolve bent the air. A flash of blinding gold ignited around him.

And then he was gone.

Leaving only silence—and the faint tremble of the earth beneath their feet.

Chapter 80

The sky above the shattered ruins was torn in half.

Ancient stones jutted from the earth like the ribs of a fallen titan, their surfaces scorched by time and magic. The remnants of a once-great temple lay strewn across a craggy plateau, surrounded by twisted columns and fractured arches, their carvings long faded. The wind howled through the skeletal remains, carrying with it the scent of dust, ozone, and ruin. Scattered throughout the ruins, flickering glyphs and charred runes still pulsed faintly, remnants of old wards and forgotten oaths.

Divine power surged through the heavens, splitting clouds with raw light. Thunder cracked through the mountain air, rolling like cannon fire. The ground trembled beneath Alek's feet as he arrived—materializing from a column of flame and thunder. His eyes burned gold, his armor rebuilt anew, radiant and heavy with purpose, forged from wrath and righteousness. Each step he took turned shattered stone molten beneath his boots.

Across the broken court, Pol waited.

Cleo hung suspended in a lattice of shadow and rune-fire, her limbs bound, her body bruised, her voice hoarse as she screamed, "Alek!"

Pol sneered. "How poetic. The god of restraint, come to lose everything again."

Alek took a step forward, power coiling at his back like a tide on the edge of breaking. "Let her go."

Pol raised a hand, and Cleo's cage constricted. Dark magic snarled around her like a living net. She cried out in pain, her voice echoing off the broken stone.

"I gave you chances, Alek. I offered you a place beside me—twice. But now?" Pol's voice twisted with venom. "Now I'll make sure you break. I'll do what the mortals never could. I'll end you."

"Try," Alek said—and unleashed his wrath.

He struck first. The world cracked.

Waves of divine fire slammed into Pol. The impact blew apart the nearest columns, disintegrating rubble and shadow alike. Pol met the blast with a screech of magic, dark tendrils and fractured spells hissing through the air. They collided midair, fists and will crashing like galaxies in collapse.

The sky turned to storm. Mountains in the distance cracked and split. The ground beneath the ruined temple ruptured in gaping wounds, sending tremors across the plateau. Fire and lightning spilled across the battlefield.

Cleo's cage was flung violently into the air by a stray shockwave. She screamed. Ari, Athena, and Thor appeared in flashes of divine light, shields raised against the chaos. Ari launched a flare of radiant arrows that cut through Pol's summoned beasts. Athena's blades whirled in arcs of steel and flame, while Thor bellowed and brought down a hammer-blow that cracked the ridge in two.

Pol howled and drove Alek backward with a shriek of ruin. A cascade of darkness poured from his hands, consuming air and light. But Alek did not fall.

He roared—pure and elemental—and surged forward. His armor glowed white-hot, veins of power shining through its seams. With each strike he pressed Pol back, carving a path of scorched earth. Magic clashed in great arcs. The sky burned.

The gods fought alongside him, the air churning with light and fury, the ruins crumbling under the weight of their wrath. Divine echoes rippled across the realms, as if the world itself held its breath.

Then—

In a final, desperate move, Pol vanished in a blink of shadow and reappeared behind Cleo. His arm wrapped around her throat, pulling her close, a blade of black magic pressed to her heart.

"Back off!" he roared, eyes wild. "Or she dies."

Alek froze mid-step, chest heaving, every inch of him alight with the tension of restraint.

The other gods stilled, eyes fixed on Pol.

Cleo's eyes met Alek's. Her lips trembled, but her voice was steady. "Don't stop," she whispered. "Don't let him win."

As she spoke, her fingers moved slowly toward the necklace at her throat—the one Alek had given her, warm with his power. Her fingertips brushed the pendant, her will coiling around it—

Pol's gaze shifted just in time to see her fingers close around the charm.

A blinding pulse of light erupted from Cleo's chest.

The force blasted Pol backward, tearing him away from her with a scream. The shadow cage shattered into fragments of black glass, flung into the wind. Cleo dropped to her knees, gasping, smoke rising from her skin but alive.

Alek surged forward, golden fury reignited.

And the storm finally roared.

But Pol was not finished.

Blinded by pain and fury, he snarled and raised both hands. From the air, he conjured a spear of crackling obsidian magic—dark energy wrapped in red lightning, sharpened by hate.

With a furious roar, he hurled it toward Cleo.

The spear struck her in the stomach.

Cleo gasped, the sound small and broken. Her body jolted, eyes wide with shock as the spear's dark power sank deep. Time seemed to stop.

"Alek..." she whispered, collapsing to the ground.

"No!" Alek screamed, his voice shattering the air.

The storm above exploded into chaos.

Something inside Alek broke.

There were no thoughts. No plans. Only fury.

He had just watched the woman he loved fall. And that—that—was the last tether to restraint.

He raised his hands to the heavens, and the ground answered. Power surged up from the core of the world—older than gods, deeper than time. His armor flared blindingly bright, then split apart as his divine form emerged in full. The air around him screamed. Reality bent.

He summoned power he had not used since the birth of the stars, since the forging of oceans and flame.

Alek hurled it at Pol.

The blast struck like judgment itself.

Pol raised a shield of shadow and screamed, pouring every stolen ounce of power into deflection. It wasn't enough.

Light devoured shadow.

A final scream tore from Pol's throat—rage, fear, disbelief—and then he was gone. Obliterated in an eruption of energy.

The explosion rolled outward like a divine shockwave. It struck with the force of a hundred suns. The ruins, the plateau, the very earth shattered. Mountains split and skies ignited.

When the light faded and the ash settled, nothing remained of Pol.

Only Cleo, still and bloodied. And the gods, silent in the aftermath.

The storm was gone.

Alek dropped to his knees beside her.

And the world held its breath.

Chapter 81

Ash rained from the sky like snow.

The gods stood at the edge of the crater in stunned silence, their forms silhouetted against a sky still fractured by the aftermath of divine fury. Lightning flickered distantly, thunder murmuring like a forgotten threat. The wind carried heat and ash across the blackened plain, lifting it in spirals that danced around scorched stone and broken columns.

No one spoke.

Where once there had been rage, now there was only awe and disbelief. Thor's hammer hung limp at his side, crackling weakly. Athena's blades had vanished, reabsorbed into her bracers, her gaze locked on the epicenter of the devastation. Ari stood slightly apart, her bow at her back, eyes wide and haunted, her mouth parted in wordless shock.

They had seen many wars. They had quelled rebellions, silenced storms. They had ended empires with a thought.

But this—

This was something altogether different.

Pol had been a god. Cunning. Dangerous. Eternal.

And now... he was ash.

Vaporized by Alek's fury—by a force none of them had thought possible. No god had ever truly died. Wounded, imprisoned, exiled—but never erased. Not like this.

The crater still glowed at its edges. The ruins had collapsed into themselves, scorched earth folding in layers where divine power had cracked the mantle. Trees miles away had been flattened. The wind carried a deep, unsettling quiet.

No one had believed it could be done. Not truly. Gods did not die. Their essence resisted annihilation. They endured.

But Alek had undone that certainty.

The one who had once been called the first—Marduk, Zeus, Ra—the god who forged stars from smoke, who wove order from chaos. The old one. The destroyer of worlds. The god of gods.

And in the stillness of what he had wrought, the others remembered why they had once feared him.

Alek was kneeling now, surrounded by the devastation he had unleashed. At the heart of the ruin, beside the crater's core, he cradled Cleo.

His hands shook as he gathered her into his arms. Her blood stained his skin. Her breath was shallow—too shallow. The spear wound was deep, glowing faintly with lingering corruption.

"Stay with me," he whispered, voice raw and jagged. "Please, Cleo. Just... stay with me."

His power bled into her, wrapping her in golden light. It flickered across her wounds, trying to seal what the spear had undone. But he was no healer. He was force and fury, fire and sky.

Ari stepped forward cautiously. Her eyes flicked to the others, then back to Alek. "We need to get her back," she said quietly. "There might still be time."

Alek didn't respond. He pressed his forehead to Cleo's, golden light spilling from his fingers, pouring what remained of his strength into her body. Her skin shimmered faintly, but her eyes remained closed. Each breath she took was a shallow thread.

He had destroyed a god.

He could not save her.

Helena moved closer, her voice steady but carrying urgency. "We will take her back to the city of the gods. We will try to heal her—but we must go now. Before it's too late., before she is beyond healing."

Her words broke through the haze. Alek looked up. His eyes were twin suns—burning and empty, filled with sorrow and rage.

"Then lets go," he said. "Before it's too late."

The gods exchanged glances. Not as rulers. Not as divine figures towering above the world. But as witnesses. As kin. As comrades.

Together, they gathered around Alek.

And in a shimmer of divine light, they vanished.

Leaving behind only silence.

And the scorched, sacred ground where the impossible had happened.

Chapter 82

The sky above the Celestial Realm shimmered as the gods reappeared in a burst of divine light.

The Eternal City rose before them, a breathtaking sprawl of silver towers, golden bridges, and domes carved from crystal and light. Its walls gleamed with runes that pulsed in time with the rhythm of the divine. The streets, lined with trees that bore leaves of flame and starlight, seemed to hold their breath as Alek stepped forward, Cleo cradled in his arms.

The gods around him made way.

No one spoke.

Even the city, alive with divine energy, seemed to fall silent.

From the Temple of Vitalis, a pulse of healing energy bloomed, reverberating through the golden stone pathways like the heartbeat of the realm itself. Ari broke from the group and ran up the marble steps, her boots ringing like bells across the polished floor as her voice echoed through the temple's inner sanctum.

"Aesculapius! Come quickly!"

The hall stirred. A moment later, the god of healing emerged, robed in white that glowed with a soft, steady light. His golden eyes swept over them, instantly locking on Alek and the motionless form in his arms. The expression on his face turned grim, the divine serenity dimming.

"Bring her inside," Aesculapius said. "Now."

The gods followed as Alek moved, steps heavy but swift. The Temple of Vitalis opened before them like a living heart—walls of alabaster etched with sacred texts, lanterns burning with celestial fire, and pools of sacred water rippling along intricate mosaic channels. The high dome overhead reflected the faces of the gods with shimmering distortion, a kaleidoscope of uncertainty.

The air was thick with incense and old magic, alive with the whisper of blessings layered across time. Ancient herbs and glowing petals floated in the air, and every stone vibrated with the echo of healing prayers spoken over millennia.

Outside the sanctum, near the outer colonnade, a quiet conversation sparked among a cluster of gods.

Ares stood with arms crossed, his expression hard as stone. Beside him lingered Dionysus, Nemesis, and Moros, each cloaked in varying shades of unease. Their gazes flitted between the temple entrance and one another, careful not to speak too loudly.

"She's mortal," Ares muttered, voice edged like a blade. "No matter what she's survived. You all know what her survival meant for him. For us."

Dionysus frowned, his fingers drumming restlessly against his goblet. "You want to be the one to tell him we should have let her die?"

"No," Ares snapped. "I'm saying this spares us that decision. The laws remain intact. Alek will grieve—but perhaps now he'll remember who he is. What he's meant to be."

Moros's voice slithered like smoke. "That solves the problem. Cleanly."

Nemesis narrowed her eyes. "Did you see what he did to Pol? That wasn't just power—it was finality. We believed it couldn't be done, and he did it."

They all fell silent again, the weight of that truth thick in the air.

Ares exhaled slowly, staring toward the temple's glowing entrance. "If he did that for her while she still lived..."

Dionysus shook his head. "Then what will he become if she dies?"

The question lingered unanswered.

Inside the temple, Alek laid Cleo on the central dais, her blood staining the polished marble surface like a wound on the temple itself. Aesculapius knelt beside her, hands hovering above the wound. His brow furrowed as he began to murmur words older than any mortal language. Divine light spread from his fingertips, weaving threads of warmth and life into her fading pulse.

"I need silence," he said. "And space."

The gods stepped back without hesitation, shadows flickering across their solemn expressions.

All except Alek.

He remained where he was, rooted to the spot, his fists clenched, his eyes burning with helplessness. He had wielded enough power to level mountains and unmake a god—but now he could only watch.

As the light of the healing rites began to build, Helena placed a hand on his shoulder.

"We brought her here," she said gently, her voice touched with empathy. "Now we let him do what we cannot."

Still, Alek did not take his eyes off Cleo. His aura flickered like a restrained tempest, rippling across the chamber walls. The air around him crackled with dormant rage, grief, and love interwoven into something barely containable.

The chamber filled with golden radiance. For a moment, it felt like hope.

And then it faded.

Aesculapius lowered his hands slowly. His expression was solemn, carved in grief. "I'm sorry," he said, voice barely above a whisper. "Her wounds were too great. I was too late."

The words struck Alek like lightning.

His breath caught. The light left his eyes. He fell to his knees beside her, a great silence crashing down in his chest. Her hand lay limp. Her skin was cooling.

"No," he whispered. "No, no, no..."

He bent over her, his golden armor trembling with each shallow breath. The flickers of his power flicked across her brow, trying to coax something—anything—back into being. But the light was gone.

Ari turned away, unable to bear the sight. Thor's fists clenched. Helena whispered a prayer, her voice cracking.

Inside, Alek bowed over Cleo's still form.

And the light in the temple dimmed.

Then, in silence so complete it pressed against the walls, Alek gathered her body in his arms.

He stood slowly, his gaze meeting no one's. The divine around him shimmered—violent, unstable. The gods who remained watched, uncertain if he would erupt or vanish. No one dared to stop him.

In a flash of gold and grief, Alek disappeared.

Chapter 83

The sky above Ari's estate was clear and still, painted in soft hues of lavender and gold. The olive trees whispered gently in the breeze, their silver-green leaves brushing against one another like murmured prayers from the earth itself. Birds that usually flitted through the branches were silent, as if the world itself was holding its breath.

Alek appeared in a blinding flash of golden light, sudden and searing, like the rupture of a new star. His armor was cracked and darkened, remnants of divine battle and the grief that clung to him like a second skin. In his arms, Cleo lay limp, her skin pale as moonlight, her presence too still, too quiet.

He moved without a word, a god carved from anguish, walking the familiar path past marble columns veined with ivy and sacred fountains that wept crystalline streams. Every step echoed memories—of laughter, of whispered confessions, of stolen kisses beneath starlight.

He reached the olive tree. Their tree.

It stood like a sentinel, its ancient limbs arching protectively over the patch of soft earth where they had once lain together, where he had dared to love her openly, vulnerably, irrevocably. The ground was sacred now, not because the gods had blessed it, but because they had.

He knelt and laid her gently in the grass. Her hair spilled like silk across the roots, a crown of shadow and gold. Her features were peaceful, but the weight of her silence was unbearable.

Ari appeared behind him, stepping from the villa, her face etched with sorrow. Her bow was slung uselessly at her back. She said nothing at first. The scene before her stole the breath from her chest.

"Alek…" she finally murmured, voice cracking with unspoken grief.

He didn't turn. His hand trembled as he brushed a strand of hair from Cleo's face.

"I unmade a god," he said, voice raw and low. "I will not lose her. I cannot lose her. Not now. Not ever."

Ari took a cautious step forward. "You don't know what will happen. The cost—"

"There is no cost I would not pay."

"You know this breaks our laws," Ari said firmly. "We do not make gods out of mortals. It was forbidden for a reason. You cannot just decide—"

"Fuck the laws," Alek growled, his voice thunder and flame. "I am divine. I am power. I was the first. I do not answer to the rules written by those who came after me."

Ari's eyes narrowed, her voice sharp with warning. "You're starting to sound like Pol."

That struck him. His jaw clenched, nostrils flaring. But he didn't deny it.

"I'm nothing like him," Alek said darkly. "He wanted power to control, to punish. I want it to save her."

"Alek," Ari pleaded, her voice cracking, "if you do this and it goes wrong, she could be lost. Her soul might not find shape. It's not just dangerous—it's irreversible."

He knelt by Cleo again, eyes locked on hers as if willing her to open them. He pressed a kiss to her forehead, reverent, desperate.

"Then I won't fail."

He closed his eyes.

Power surged.

The sky darkened as clouds gathered unnaturally above. The olive tree's leaves stilled. The very earth beneath them seemed to inhale.

A blinding light exploded from Alek's chest, flooding the grove with brilliance. It poured into Cleo's body in shimmering waves—raw, untamed power drawn from the veins of creation itself. The wind screamed through the branches. The ground cracked in glowing fault lines. The air shimmered with divine heat.

Light spiraled around them, wrapping Cleo in a cocoon of gold and silver, a tapestry of stars and storm.

Ari stumbled back, eyes wide, shielding her face with one arm.

The olive tree glowed, its bark pulsing like a heart, its roots illuminated in ancient fire.

And then—

A breath.

A sound so soft it was almost missed, but Alek felt it like thunder.

Cleo gasped.

Her chest arched upward as light surged through her veins. Her skin glowed faintly, her hair lifted in a breeze only she could feel. Her eyes flew open—no longer green, but radiant gold, threaded with the glint of galaxies.

She was alive.

And she was divine.

Alek collapsed beside her, his strength spent, the last reserves of power leaving him like smoke. He fell to the earth, breathless, weeping.

Ari dropped to her knees, overwhelmed. "By the stars," she whispered. "He did it."

Cleo sat up slowly, disoriented. Her fingers flexed. Energy rippled from her skin in gentle waves. She blinked, dazed. "What... happened?"

Alek looked at her with tear-filled eyes. "You came back to me."

She looked at her hands—glowing faintly, humming with power—and back at him. "What am I?"

"You're mine," he said, voice soft, awed. "And you're a goddess now."

The grove was silent once more.

Only this time, it was reverent.

Chapter 84

The air at Ari's estate was thick with the lingering hum of divinity. The olive grove glowed faintly with residual energy from Alek's impossible act. The tree under which Cleo had lain—where she had died, and where she had been reborn—stood tall and ancient, its roots still pulsing faintly with light, as if echoing the miracle it had just witnessed.

Cleo sat on a carved stone bench beside Alek, wrapped in a soft cloak woven from starlight and warmth. Her movements were slow, thoughtful, reverent, as if she were relearning how to inhabit a body remade by divine fire. Her eyes, now golden and threaded with celestial shimmer, moved slowly over the grove. She could feel every heartbeat in the soil, every breath in the wind, every shift in the cosmos. The world no longer simply surrounded her—it sang to her.

Alek sat beside her in silence, watching her with a gaze that held wonder, sorrow, and deep, consuming love. He had done the unthinkable. Not out of pride, not out of rebellion—but out of devotion. Out of desperation. And now he waited.

After a long moment, Cleo broke the silence.

"What am I now?" she asked, her voice quiet but steady. "I feel... everything. The earth. The wind. I can hear the stars, Alek. They whisper things I don't understand. What does this mean—for me, for us, for everyone?"

Alek turned to her, his expression solemn. "It means you've crossed a threshold few ever reach. You're no longer mortal. You're one of us now. A goddess—born not from lineage or war, but from love and sacrifice."

Cleo drew her knees to her chest. "But I didn't choose this." Her voice trembled. "It's like waking up in someone else's skin. I don't know who I am anymore. Will the others accept me? Will they see me as one of them—or just a mortal who was given too much?"

"You are more than they will understand," Alek said gently, taking her hand. "You always were. If they cannot see that, then they are the ones who are blind."

Cleo looked down at their joined hands, the glow of her skin matching his. "I feel connected to everything, but more alone than I ever have."

"I know," he said. "Divinity is a heavy weight. Even for those who have borne it for eons."

She looked up, eyes sharp now. "Will they come for me?"

"They might," he admitted. "Some of them won't be able to accept what I've done. But if they do, they'll have to go through me first."

Before she could respond, the stillness was broken by the distant shimmer of divine arrival—two flashes of radiant light descending just beyond the tree line. The olive branches bent in deference as Theo and Helena stepped into the grove, their expressions heavy with grief and purpose. They had come to mourn.

But what they found stopped them in their tracks.

Cleo stood slowly as they approached, her golden eyes locking on theirs. The soft glow of her aura illuminated her skin, casting her in a light that was no longer mortal.

Helena's lips parted in stunned disbelief. Theo's mouth tightened, his brows furrowed in confusion and alarm. He turned slowly to Alek.

"Alek…" Helena's voice was a whisper, ragged with shock. "What have you done?"

Alek rose to his full height, stepping beside Cleo. His stance was calm, but immovable.

"I brought her back," he said, his voice ringing with unrepentant power. "She died because of us. Because of all of this. I would not let her be lost to our mistakes."

Theo stepped forward, incredulous. "You made her divine. Alone. Without consent. Without the Council."

"I don't need consent to save the woman I love," Alek replied. "And I won't ask forgiveness for it."

Helena's gaze lingered on Cleo, then shifted to Alek. "You know what this means. The consequences this will bring. The Council—"

"They've said enough," Alek interrupted. "Let them say more if they wish. I'm done listening."

Cleo stepped forward, her expression steady despite the whirlwind behind her eyes. "I didn't ask for this," she said. "But I won't apologize for being alive. Or for loving him. If my existence is a problem for the gods, then perhaps the problem is with them."

The silence that followed was thick, not with anger, but with uncertainty. The world had changed again—and the gods knew it.

Theo's shoulders sagged as he exchanged a glance with Helena.

"You've crossed a line," Helena said softly. "And so have we. What comes next will not be easy."

Alek nodded. "It never is."

He looked at Cleo again, his hand still in hers. "But we face it together."

Cleo turned to him quietly. "What do we do now?"

Alek held her gaze for a long moment, then smiled faintly. "For now, we live."

And under the olive tree where life had ended and begun again, nothing else mattered.

Chapter 85

The Grand Hall blazed with celestial light as the gods convened beneath the watchful heavens. The chamber, carved from the bones of constellations and ancient time, pulsed with energy. The dome above them swirled with constellations, each star flickering in time with the pulse of divine thought. Runes floated midair, alive with ancestral voices. Marble columns, etched with the earliest vows of the gods, stretched into infinity. This was not merely a hall—it was the axis of judgment, of destiny.

Around its circumference, thrones of crystal, obsidian, flame, and living wood stood occupied by the pantheon's most powerful: Helena, Thor, Hermes, Hera, Ares, Dionysus, Moros, Nemesis, and dozens more. Each figure was radiant in their own truth, cloaked in shadow, authority, and long memory.

At the center, silence fell like a blade.

Helena stood first, her golden robes brushing the marble floor. Her voice, crystalline and unwavering, echoed across the vast chamber. "You've all heard. Cleo Tenner, a

mortal, has been transformed into a goddess—by Alek.
Without Council. Without consent. Without precedent."

Murmurs rippled like thunder across the circle.

"He broke our law," Hera said, her tone ice. "He acted
alone. He is not above the order we swore to uphold."

"And yet," Thor countered, his voice rough as a
mountain storm, "he destroyed Pol. He ended the war. He
protected the veil when we could not. We all saw it. He did
what had to be done."

Hermes leaned forward, his eyes shadowed. "Which
is exactly why we should be afraid. He did what none of us
thought was even possible. What's next? What if he decides
the Council itself no longer matters?"

"There are laws for a reason," Moros said, his voice
like falling ash. "We cannot let love blind us to danger.
Passion leads to destruction. We've seen it before."

"Have we?" Helena challenged. "Or have we simply
used fear as a shield? Eros and Antithesia were a tragedy,
yes—but maybe they were an anomaly. Maybe this is
something else entirely."

Ares scoffed, voice a blade's edge. "You want to bet
the fate of the world on a maybe? He's unstable. The oldest
among us. He held the sky in his hands before we had names.
If he loses control again—if grief breaks him—we
lose everything."

"But he hasn't," Dionysus said, soft but firm. "He
could have destroyed us all and didn't. He could have defied
us long before this and didn't. He broke the law not to
conquer, but to save. And the world still stands because of
him."

Nemesis stood slowly, arms crossed. "If we do nothing, we send a message that even the oldest among us can circumvent our order at will. The Council's voice will mean nothing."

"And if we punish him," Helena said, "we send a message that compassion has no place among us. That we are relics clinging to a law that no longer fits the world we live in. Hasn't he earned more than that?"

"Then what's the answer?" Hera snapped. "Do we bow to him now? Do we pretend he didn't just upend everything we stand for?"

"No," Helena said. "We evolve. Or we fracture."

More voices rose—some calling for immediate censure, others pleading for understanding. The Council teetered on the edge of rupture, not in war, but in ideology. In fear. In awe.

Then, Theo rose.

His presence did not demand silence. It commanded it.

He stepped into the center of the circle, his gaze sweeping the chamber. "We are at a crossroads," he said. "We've seen the edge of oblivion. We've watched cities fall, creatures rise, the veil tremble. And we were not saved by the rule of law, or by strength in numbers. We were saved by a single act of love—reckless, yes. Unprecedented, yes. But undeniable."

He paused.

"We don't have to decide tonight. But we will decide. Because this isn't just about Alek or Cleo. This is about who we are now. What we choose to become. The old ways are no longer enough. The world has changed. So must we."

The chamber stilled. Even the stars above seemed to pause in their orbit.

And for the first time in an age, the gods, eternal and uncertain, sat in judgment of one of their own.

Epilogue

The sky above Alek's estate stretched wide and unmarred, a canvas of silver-blue and dawn-gold, the veil intact—but no longer silent. Its pulse—once invisible, ethereal—was now faintly perceptible to those who had touched the edge of eternity and returned changed. The air shimmered with something ancient, as if reality itself was adjusting to accommodate what had happened.

In the olive grove that crowned the hillside above the villa, where gods once walked in secret and love had triumphed over law, grief, and death, a new dawn bloomed. The trees stood sentinel, their gnarled trunks bathed in morning light, their leaves whispering softly to one another like old souls remembering.

Cleo stood barefoot in the dew-soaked grass, golden eyes turned skyward. Her skin glowed with the faint luminescence of divinity, her hair catching the light like molten bronze. Though her feet were on the earth, she stood apart from it now—something more, something newly made. She was no longer tethered by mortality, but she remained deeply connected to everything living and sacred. The grove around her thrummed with quiet reverence, as if it recognized her.

She breathed in the cool morning air, scented with cypress, olive, and memory. The breeze curled around her like a benediction, and for the first time in what felt like lifetimes, she felt grounded. Whole. Belonging not just to one world, but to many.

Alek appeared behind her, emerging from the veranda with the quiet grace of someone who had faced the abyss and chosen love over fear. No armor now. No divine fury. Just the quiet presence of a god who had once created stars and shattered empires—and now stood humbled by the miracle he had wrought.

His steps were soft on the ancient stone path, winding through the garden as sunlight poured through the branches above.

He reached for her hand, his thumb brushing across her knuckles. "Do you regret it?"

Cleo turned toward him, studying his face as if seeing it anew. "Dying?" she asked. "No. Being brought back like this? I don't think I can regret something that feels so much like fate."

She paused, the golden light glinting in her eyes. "But I'm not who I was. I feel... vast. Infinite. And I don't know what that means yet."

"You'll learn," he said. "We'll learn together."

The sun crested the eastern ridge, painting the estate in hues of gold and rose. Light spilled over the hills, warming marble and earth alike. The grove shimmered, alive with something holy.

Cleo exhaled, then laughed under her breath. "What am I going to tell Jasper?"

Alek blinked, then chuckled. "That depends. Do you think he's ready for the goddess of resurrection and sarcasm?"

Before she could reply, the air changed.

A ripple of energy rolled through the grove, subtle but unmistakable. Cleo turned, her brows knitting. Alek's hand went still in hers.

Two figures stepped from the tree line—solid, divine, unmistakable. Ares, clad in muted bronze, eyes like war-forged steel. And Apollo, radiant and calm, golden light haloing his form.

They said nothing at first.

Ares looked at Alek.

Apollo looked at Cleo.

And the silence that followed was heavy with meaning.

www.ingramcontent.com/pod-product-compliance
Lightning Source LLC
Chambersburg PA
CBHW031741180726
48283CB00005B/1614